CRAZY

HAN NOLAN

HARCOURT

HOUGHTON MIFFLIN HARCOURT

BOSTON | NEW YORK | 2010

Harcourt is an imprint of Houghton Mifflin Harcourt Publishing Company.
www.hmhbooks.com

Text set in 12-point Abrams Venetian
Book design by Christine Kettner

LIBRARY OF CONGRESS CATALOGING-IN-PUBLICATION DATA
Nolan, Han.
Crazy / Han Nolan.   p. cm.
Summary: Fifteen-year-old loner Jason struggles to hide his father's
declining mental condition after his mother's death, but when his father
disappears he must confide in the other members of a therapy group he
has been forced to join at school.
ISBN 978-0-15-205109-9 (hardcover : alk. paper)
[1. Friendship—Fiction.
2. Family problems—Fiction. 3. Fathers and sons—Fiction. 4. Mental
illness—Fiction. 5. Missing persons—Fiction. 6. Grief—Fiction. 7. High
schools—Fiction. 8. Schools—Fiction.] I. Title.   PZ7.N6783Cqr 2010
[Fic]—dc22   2009049969

Ten lines from The Oresteian Trilogy: Agamemnon, The Choephori, The Eumenides
by Aeschylus translated by Philip Vellacott (Penguin Classics, 1956).
Copyright © Philip Vellacott, 1956. Reproduced by permission of Penguin Books Ltd.

ACKNOWLEDGMENT
Many thanks and much admiration to the following people
for their generous help and advice:

For professional advice concerning legal matters, child protection and social
services, and psychological issues in this novel:
Lee Doty, Caroline Kahler, Ann Martyn, Ellen Groff, and Jane Hundley.

For professional advice and criticism of the novel in its many, many, many stages:
Karen Grove, Barbara Kouts, Jen Haller, and Kathy Dawson.

For extra readings again and again, and for much support:
Brian Nolan, Adrienne Nolan, Rachael Potter, and Barbara Kouts.

Manufactured in the United States of America
DOC 10 9 8 7 6 5 4 3 2 1
4500247741

To the three people most involved in the creation

of all my novels but most especially this one:

Brian Nolan, Barbara Kouts, and Karen Grove

CHAPTER ONE

EVER SINCE the fifth grade, I've had this imaginary audience in my head who follow me around and watch me like I'm the star in a movie. I talk to them, and yeah, they talk to me, but I know they aren't really there. I'm very clear about that. Anyway, I don't think I'm the only fifteen-year-old who does this. It's our culture. It seems everybody is famous now. You can get yourself on TV for doing almost anything, the stupider the better. Everyone thinks his or her life is movie worthy.

So now *you're* here. This is my honors English class we're in right now. Don't ask me how I got into honors. Okay, I know this classroom is pretty drab. There aren't nearly enough windows, but it's an old school. They're building a new one over on Clement.

I haven't named you yet. I'll just call you You for now. Maybe you'll just be part of my laugh track, a body filling one of the seats in my theater but having no singular voice. We'll see. If you are part of the laugh track, you get to do more than laugh. You get to say, "Uh-oh," and whisper loudly, "Isn't that a shame." You can even cry. But maybe you'll become one of the outspoken ones, the ones with a personality, like the fat bald guy with a mustache who sits in the back of the theater writing movie reviews. I call him FBG with a mustache, for short. There's also Sexy Lady, who's supposed to just tell me I'm hot all the time. She usually has on a low-cut red dress. Then there's Aunt Bee—yep, *the* Aunt Bee from the old *Andy Griffith Show*. You always wondered what happened to her. Well, here she is, in my head! She's very sympathetic. And finally, there's the kid who Krazy Glued the fingers of his left hand together. I just call him Crazy Glue.

CRAZY GLUE: *Boring! His life is boring. Get out now while you can.*

SEXY LADY: *Oh, but lately it's been heating up again. He was just in a lull.*

Yeah, a nice, safe four-year lull. I don't like this new exposure I've been getting. I liked being invisible.

AUNT BEE: *That's most understandable, poor boy. You've had it very rough in the past. I remember the time your father woke you up in the middle of the night. He had on that horrible mask.*

FBG WITH A MUSTACHE: *It wasn't a mask, my dear. It was a helmet, a Spartan helmet. It was a replica, not the real thing, made of steel with a mane running over the top and down the back of it. Quite authentic-looking, though. It had real horse hair.*

AUNT BEE: *Well, it covered most of his face, and he was frightening coming into Jason's room like that, then scooping him up and taking him outside to bury him. He dropped him right down into that hole he'd dug and started shoveling the dirt on top of him. Oh dear, that was so horrifying.*

2

CRAZY GLUE (ACTING AS JASON): *"Daddy, stop it! I'm scared. I don't like it down here. It's cold. I want Mommy. I want Mommy!"*

FBG WITH A MUSTACHE (ACTING AS DAD): *"It's okay. Just stay there, Jason. I'm covering you over so they'll never find you."*

CRAZY GLUE: *You should have given my lines to Sexy Lady or Aunt Bee. Why should I always get stuck being you?*

You're the closest to my age and I was going for a little realism.

AUNT BEE: *It's too real. I wish you'd stop reliving that night over and over. It can't be good for you.*

I was only six. I screamed and screamed. I was scared out of my wits. Dad thought the Furies were after us. Mom said he was just trying to protect me. That's all.

CRAZY GLUE: *It figures I missed all the good stuff. And what are Furies, anyway?*

FBG WITH A MUSTACHE: *They're part of Greek and Roman mythology. They're the goddesses of the underworld. You'd love them. They have a mass of snakes for hair and blood running from their eyes. They come up through the ground, seeking revenge for people's crimes. They'll hunt you down until you're driven mad with their chase.*

CRAZY GLUE: *Awesome!*

I didn't think so. The Furies always scared me. They still do. Anyway, my mom heard my screams and she saved me before I was buried alive, but Dad was taken away. He stayed away a long time. That was my fault. I've always felt it was my fault.

3

AUNT BEE: *Well, dear boy, you couldn't let him bury you alive, could you?*

SEXY LADY: *I think you'd look hot in that helmet.*

I hate that helmet. Any time I see Dad wearing it, I know he's sick again—like now.

CRAZY GLUE: *I would have loved to have seen you scratching and scrambling and clawing your way out of that grave. Cool beans!*

Shows what you know.

AUNT BEE: *It's no wonder, then, what happened in fifth grade. I mean, how you reacted.*

LAUGH TRACK: *Uh-oh! Here it comes.*

My best friend turned on me! Just because I got the ball away from him and scored the only points in the soccer game, he got all jealous and got the gang to help him flush my head in the toilet.

LAUGH TRACK: *(Laughter).*

CRAZY GLUE: *A swirlie! Jason got a swirlie! Cried like a baby, too. Called for his mommy. Made a total fool of himself.*

AUNT BEE: *Of course he cried, and you would, too. It was his father burying him all over again.*

CRAZY GLUE: *No friends after that—just us. Four and a half years now, and still not a single friend.*

I don't need friends. Friends are dangerous.

FBG WITH A MUSTACHE: *What was it you and your soccer buddies called yourselves?*

Fili Mou. It's Greek for "my friends."

FBG WITH A MUSTACHE: *That's right, but you spelled it "F-E-E-L-Y M-O-O." You were the Feely Moos.*

4

Don't remind me. The whole school picked on me after that swirlie. I'm sorry my grandma died back then, but I sure was glad she left my parents her house and we moved to Virginia at the end of the year. I got to start all over.

CRAZY GLUE: *Start all over? You went into hiding! Bor-ring!*

SEXY LADY: *But now, after all these years of trying to make yourself invisible, you've been caught. You're beginning to come out into the open again. I see how the girls are starting to take notice of you with your dark curly locks and those blue, blue eyes. Tall, dark, and handsome, that's how we like 'em. You're like a young Greek god.*

I'm not coming out in the open—not on purpose, anyway. It was just a slip-up, just a few things getting out of control, but I'll fix it. I'll straighten everything out.

CRAZY GLUE: *Fat chance. Anyway, you're more interesting this way.*

SEXY LADY: *You've got that innocent, wouldn't-hurt-a-fly look about you. Girls feel safe around you. You're way too thin, but with a little meat on your bones . . . Oh, to be a sophomore in high school again.*

Okay, be quiet, everyone. Mrs. Silky's talking to me.

"Jason, would you stay a minute after the bell, please."

"Woo-ooh, Ja-son!"

Great, the whole class thinks I'm a dweeb now.

CRAZY GLUE: *Yeah, like they didn't already.*

LAUGH TRACK: *Uh-oh! (A twitter of laughter).*

You, you might as well sit down and watch the show. Later you can decide what kind of audience member you'd like to be.

AUNT BEE: *I hate when you get yourself in trouble.*

CRAZY GLUE: *Old Silky's going to give it to you now.*

SEXY LADY: *Come on over here, You, and sit next to me. Make yourself comfortable. Don't worry if you're a little confused. Jason will explain everything. He narrates his life as he goes along.*

CRAZY GLUE: *Yeah, he does it for the visually impaired in the audience.*

FBG WITH A MUSTACHE: *That's not it at all. Jason likes to keep his mind busy because he's afraid of mental silences. Disturbing thoughts lurk just beneath the surface and he knows it. Keep up the mental chatter, my boy.*

Everyone has disturbing thoughts. It's normal. It's perfectly normal.

CRAZY GLUE: *Sure it is, pal.*

CHAPTER TWO

THE BELL RINGS. I sit at my desk and wait for the rest of the class to leave. I hear some of the kids snicker behind me. I hear my name. I remember that swirlie I got in fifth grade and I feel sick to my stomach.

After more than four years of keeping to myself and flying under the radar at school, I've blown my cover. Not that I didn't have some help. Somehow, maybe through the newspapers, the school found out my mom died a few months ago. That's what started it.

And now I've been having these strange impulses . . .

SEXY LADY: *Mmm, impulses! Very hot!*

Not like that. It's like in this honors English class. We're reading *Moby Dick*. We had to write these weekly essays on the book and every time I wrote about Captain Ahab, I wrote "Cap'n," which is driving Old Silky nuts. She's written on each essay, "*Captain* Ahab, please!" She took two points off my last paper for every "Cap'n." Now I know she's making me stay after class to talk about it. That's a first. Staying after class is a definite attention

7

getter. What was I thinking? I mean, I don't know what I'm doing lately.

SEXY LADY: *It's those impulses.*

I'm just tired, that's all—tired and grouchy.

Everyone's gone, so I stand up and make my way to Silky's desk. I do this thing now when I get really embarrassed so that my face doesn't turn red—I press my tongue really hard against the roof of my mouth. So that's what I do, but my bird heart is flapping like crazy. It wants out of its cage!

AUNT BEE: *You haven't explained to You about the bird heart.*

CRAZY GLUE: *I'll do it! I'll do it! Jason, raised by his parents on the myths of Greek gods and heroes, thinks his heart is really a bird, a cardinal, flapping around in his rib cage. He came up with this dopey idea when he was just a kid, but even now at fifteen he half believes it. What a goob!*

FBG WITH A MUSTACHE: *Buck up, son. Here it comes.*

"Jason, what is this 'Cap'n' you keep writing? I told you on your other two essays that I didn't want Captain Ahab's name abbreviated. He's not a box of cereal."

LAUGH TRACK: *Ha. Ha.*

Mrs. Silky is short and plump but with tiny bird bones, so her wrists and ankles look too skinny for her body, and she has lots of loose cheek skin, so when she talks, all that skin wobbles. Her head kind of shakes, too. Maybe she has the beginnings of Parkinson's disease.

I watch her cheeks wobble, and I nod in response because, with my tongue still pressed to the roof of my mouth, I can't talk.

Mrs. Silky continues. "I know you understand what I'm saying. I'm beginning to think this is just sheer belligerence. I don't know what's gotten into you."

She looks at me. She seems plenty angry. Her cheeks and head are really shaking; her eyes look hard. I think she wants me to explain what's gotten into me, but I don't know, so I just stand with my arms straight down, crossed in front of me like a shield, hands in fists, head bowed, and I wait for her to dismiss me.

She doesn't.

LAUGH TRACK: *Uh-oh!*

"And why are you dating all your papers with the wrong dates? Other teachers are complaining, too. Mr. O'Hagan, Mrs. Eugene, all your teachers." Silky picks up my essay and shakes it at me, but I keep my head down, just seeing her out of the corner of my eye. "July fifteenth, you wrote here, and this other one"—she picks up my other essay—"you wrote October twelfth. It's January. I know you know that." Silky sets the papers down and reaches a hand out to me, almost touching my arm, and I lift my head.

"Is this about your mother? Hmm? She died last October, didn't she? You know we're all very sorry for your loss."

"Thank you."

LAUGH TRACK: *Isn't that a shame.*

CRAZY GLUE: *Jason hates when people mention his mother. He doesn't like to think about her.*

AUNT BEE: *If I weren't just a figment of his imagination, I'd fix him a nice apple pie. That would help him feel better.*

I ought to tell her to lay off. I hate that people are talking about me.

CRAZY GLUE: *Go ahead, dumb-dumb. Explain about the dates while you're at it.*

FBG WITH A MUSTACHE: *Don't listen to him.*

Old Silky gives me this pitying look. Her baggy eyes sag a little lower. "Life is unfair, but that doesn't give anyone a free ride. I expect excellence from you, Jason, as always. I don't know what you're doing writing these silly dates down but . . ."

CRAZY GLUE: *Tell her! Go ahead. Just do it! Say what you're thinking, for once!*

"It's—it's just that dates and times are really so arbitrary—I think."

Silky lets go of my paper and it lands on her desk. "Arbitrary? If everyone felt that way, where would we be?" Silky shakes her jowls side to side and stares up at me. I hate that I'm taller than she is. It feels wrong, somehow.

"Well, it's like—we've all supposedly agreed to start counting from the year of Jesus' birth, like the world didn't exist until then. It's just a way of counting that we all are supposed to go along with, but I don't remember getting a vote. I mean, I don't agree."

CRAZY GLUE: *That's telling her.*

AUNT BEE: *Be careful, Jason. I don't have a good feeling about this.*

CRAZY GLUE: *Go on. Tell her what you're thinking. You're already into it now; a little deeper won't hurt anything.*

"It's just, well, no offense to Jesus, but why not use the Jewish calendar or the Greek lunar calendar? Why don't we have a vote every four years, like with the presidents, and give everybody's calendar a chance?"

Silky's got her cheeks and jowls all puffed out now, like a blowfish.

LAUGH TRACK: *(Laughter).*

She lets it blow. Her breath hits my face. It smells like mothballs. " 'No offense to Jesus'? Jason Papado-poulos, I'm surprised at you! I really am."

CRAZY GLUE: *Way to go, buddy!*

"I—I—I, well, I just can't bring myself to write January. I mean, what's January? It's nothing. It means nothing. It's just a word—blah—a dumb word."

FBG WITH A MUSTACHE: *I hate to mention it, but maybe the present dates don't mean anything to you because your mother's no longer in them. You've been dating your papers with the date your mother came out of her coma, and the date she came home from the hospital, and the day before she went back into the hospital and died. Am I the only one who's noticed this?*

LAUGH TRACK: *No! (Laughter).*

11

Silky shakes her wobbly head one more time. "'Nothing'? 'A dumb word'? Jason, I just don't know what's gotten into you."

CRAZY GLUE: *She said that already.*

I don't know what's gotten into me, either. Maybe I'm just tired of being invisible.

LAUGH TRACK: *Uh-oh!*

AUNT BEE: *You want a friend, dear.*

Old Silky clears her throat, and I bite down on my lower lip and wait for her to blast me some more, but her voice is suddenly quiet, kind of tender.

CRAZY GLUE: *Oh puke!*

"I'm just going to warn you, on tomorrow's exam I want to see you write 'Captain,' not 'Cap'n.' One 'Cap'n' and you just might flunk the test. Do you understand?"

I nod. "Yes."

"Good." She straightens her shoulders. "And I want the proper date, as well." She hesitates, and then, with her index finger on her chin she adds, "I think it might help you to see Dr. Gomez. Hmm?"

LAUGH TRACK: *Uh-oh!*

"Now, here's your pass. You'd better get on to your next class."

Dr. Gomez! The school shrink? No way, lady.

CRAZY GLUE: *Better not write 'Cap'n' anymore.*

I take the pass and leave. Behind me I hear her mutter, "No offense to Jesus, indeed."

CHAPTER THREE

FOUR DAYS LATER I've decided I'm in a Greek tragedy. My mom's dead, my dad's crazy, and now it's lunchtime and I'm on my way to Dr. Gomez's office. What could be worse?

CRAZY GLUE: *You could be dead, for starters.*

You all are like my Greek chorus. Yeah, I'm a real live, walking Greek tragedy.

FBG WITH A MUSTACHE: *To be accurate, since you're living in America, it would be an American tragedy, and we're your American chorus.*

Anyway! The point is I can't go see a shrink.

AUNT BEE: *What are you so afraid of, dear?*

I'm not afraid. Who says I'm afraid? It's just that there will be other kids there. I'm going to be wasting my whole lunch hour talking with a shrink and a bunch of psycho kids.

CRAZY GLUE: *Better than eating alone like you usually do.*

I don't need to see a shrink. Is writing "Cap'n" on my test really a reason for therapy? I don't think so. Oh, and I've got to lug this tray of hot food from the cafeteria with me because I'm on the free lunch program. I know nobody else in the group will have a tray. They'll know I'm on the program. They'll know we don't have any money. I mean look, people in the hallway are staring at me. Man, this is the pits. And we have to sit on the floor in there. That's what I heard. What are we, five years old?

CRAZY GLUE: *You had to do it. You had to write "Cap'n" on that exam.*

LAUGH TRACK: *(Laughter).*

FBG WITH A MUSTACHE: *Not once but three times. She took off thirty points, plus five for the answer you actually got wrong and five points off for writing the wrong date, for a final grade of sixty. You failed, my boy.*

I couldn't help it. I don't know why, but I had to do it. I had to write "Cap'n."

SEXY LADY: *It's those impulses again.*

It was an easy test, too. Now I have to see a shrink because Old Silky feels I'm not coping well with Mom's death. What does she know about it? How am I supposed to cope? I'm doin' great!

SEXY LADY: *I think people who see shrinks are hot.*

CRAZY GLUE: *Don't do it. Don't go. Ditch it. You've got too many secrets. What about your dad? Your mom always warned you not to draw attention to yourself. Now look at you—you're doing it left and right. You want everyone to find out about him? They'll haul him away and then where will you be? Homeless, that's where.*

AUNT BEE: *Oh dear, Jason, I told you to be careful.*

14

FBG WITH A MUSTACHE: *Are we all forgetting the letters? Jason, a young boy of fifteen, who pictures himself in some kind of Greek tragedy, can't navigate his own life to, well, save his life, and yet he's giving advice to other kids in the school newspaper.*

CRAZY GLUE: *He's a Dear Abby! How ironic is that? Man, if anybody ever finds out, they'll hang him by his nostrils.*

FBG WITH A MUSTACHE: *He'll give himself away talking to a shrink. They're very good at prying secrets out of unsuspecting young people. They're sneaky. Whatever possessed you, son?*

The letters. Crap! I almost forgot about them. How was I to know that my letter to the editor would get other kids writing to me asking for advice?

SEXY LADY: *I think letter writers are hot!*

AUNT BEE: *It was a very good letter, Jason. Let's see—how did it go?*

Dear Editor:

I just wanted to get a few things off my chest. For instance, J.C. and T.F., get a room! I mean, every day you're in front of the lockers, rolling all over them and swallowing each other's tongues. Nobody can get to his locker without having to unhitch the two of you. Give it a rest for five seconds, why don't you? Try having a conversation for once. And M.V., what are you thinking? P.R. isn't going to ever, ever, ask you out. I know this for a fact. Give up already and find somebody worthy of you. You're beautiful and talented, and you have a really pretty laugh. If P.R. can't see that, then he's a jerk. He's a jerk, anyway. Besides, look to your left in English. Somebody over there likes you, and no, it's not me. I'm not even in your class; I just hear things. Also, a certain teacher says "well" a million times per class. If you don't know who you are, you do now. Find something else to say, or just be silent for a second and gather your thoughts. You're driving your students crazy. They can't concentrate on anything besides counting how many "well"s you say. Finally, S.S., you're cool no matter what anybody thinks. Your parents are totally wrong about you; you'll make something of yourself. You just need to build up your confidence a little. I bet you'd be a good swimmer. You're built like a swimmer. You ought to try out for the swim team or get into karate if you have the money. Anyway, you're smarter than anybody gives you credit for. I know; I've been listening to you.

Okay, that's it for now.

A. Nonny Mous

CRAZY GLUE: *I always liked that signature. Very funny. A. Nonny Mous, ha, ha!*

LAUGH TRACK: *(Laughter).*

CRAZY GLUE: *And now the kids just call you Mouse in their letters. How appropriate is that. You are such a total mouse!*

FBG WITH A MUSTACHE: *Not anymore, he isn't. This mouse is starting to have an edge.*

AUNT BEE: *You're the mouse that roared. Isn't there a book by that name?*

I wish I hadn't done that. But I felt I just had to e-mail that letter to the editor before I went nuts. People are so thick sometimes. Since I'm invisible around here, people don't even notice what they say around me. I know practically everything that goes on in this school. Anyway, I think I'm getting grouchy in my old age.

FBG WITH A MUSTACHE: *Something's got hold of you lately. And that's what's going to get you in trouble in this group. You can't shut up anymore. Years of holding it in and now—look out, world, Jason is on the rampage.*

Oh, I'll keep my mouth shut in there. Only reason I'm going to this thing is because I have to or Old Silky will get the school to call Dad. I had to fake his signature on the permission slip.

AUNT BEE: *You write just like him. No one would ever guess.*

I swear, I'm just going to sit there, and if I have to answer any questions, I'll just lie. That's all. I'll just lie through my teeth.

SEXY LADY: *I think your teeth are hot. Very straight and white. If only you could get your father to brush his teeth and groom himself, he wouldn't look half so crazy.*

CRAZY GLUE: *You're so going to screw up. (Laughter).*

LAUGH TRACK: *(Laughter).*

Okay, I'm here. Everybody be quiet.

CRAZY GLUE: *(Whispers) Enter the goob, wearing jeans that are way too short, a dark plaid shirt taken from his father's drawer, holes in his dingy white socks, and for that extra goob effect, his dad's old leather boat shoes—a perfect fit on the feet of his growing, and growing, son. How's the weather up there, goob?*

LAUGH TRACK: *(Laughter).*

SEXY LADY: *I think tall men are hot.*

AUNT BEE: *Leave the boy be, now. Can't you see he's nervous enough? I just wish you had some better food. I think it's malnourishment making you so cranky.*

Come on, everybody—be quiet. If I blow this, I'm out on the streets and my dad gets locked up in a loony bin. I've got to focus.

CRAZY GLUE: *Focus, everybody. Let's focus!*

LAUGH TRACK: *Uh-oh. (Nervous laughter).*

CHAPTER FOUR

I STEP INSIDE Dr. Gomez's office and I'm hit by bright colors everywhere: reds, greens, yellows, oranges, a kaleidoscope of colors. The place is a mess. The desk is covered with papers and books and little gadgets, painted rocks with words on them like peace, and love, blah blah blah, and there's this one wall with a painting of birds and trees and mountains and sunshine, and painted in black is the line, "Somewhere over the Rainbow." The mural is by a girl in my class, Shelby Majors.

CRAZY GLUE: *What a showoff. She can never paint just a painting. It's always something huge. She's got that huge canvas hanging in the sophomore wing, too.*

FBG WITH A MUSTACHE: *It's a collage.*

AUNT BEE: *It's a mess. I have to agree with Crazy Glue; she is a bit of a showoff.*

Hey, haven't any of you noticed, there aren't any windows in here? I don't think I can breathe in a room without windows. I'm starting to panic.

LAUGH TRACK: *Uh-oh! (Nervous laughter).*

"It's pretty busy in here, isn't it."

I whip around to find Shelby Majors standing in

19

the doorway behind me. The food on my tray slides to the right and I quickly straighten the tray, but my cling peaches dish soars. It lands upside down at Shelby's feet.

LAUGH TRACK: *(Laughter)*.

I squat and, with one hand steadying my tray, try to reach the peaches to pick them up with the other. "Oh jeez! I can't believe I did that."

CRAZY GLUE: *Good one, goob.*

"Oh, sorry, my fault for sneaking up on you like that. Let me help." Shelby kneels beside me and helps me scoop up the mess. If she weren't there, I'd put it all back in the dish and eat the peaches anyway. I'm that hungry. But now I drop them in the black plastic waste-basket I find beside Dr. Gomez's metal desk.

Shelby grabs my napkin and dabs at the peach juice on the rug. She finishes with a big wipe, then wads the napkin and pitches it into the basket. "Oh well, at least it wasn't your spaghetti, right?"

SEXY LADY: *She's being nice, but she's still a showoff, remember.*

"What? Oh yeah." I check my spaghetti to make sure it's still on the plate. "Right." Focus, everybody.

We both stand up and I notice I tower over her. She has to be just barely over five feet tall, maybe five two, and I'm five eight, at least last time I measured I was, which was a while ago, back when my pants actually fit me. She has a head of thick, rusty-colored hair, and she's got on a Yankees baseball cap that just kind of floats on top. I don't know how she's keeping it on her head. She's wearing some shapely flowery shirt thing, shorts or pants that come to her knees, and those clog-type shoes with no socks. It's January, people! It's fifteen degrees out, people!

LAUGH TRACK: *(Laughter).*

"Anyway," Shelby says, "I was just saying, it's kind of noisy in here with all the stuff—all the colored walls and the shelves with the games and books and these flags"—she points to the red, green, orange, and purple flags hanging from the ceiling—"and the pillows on the floor. Even my mural's noisy, but I like it." She flops herself down on one of the pillows, sits cross-legged, and sets her bag lunch in her lap. "Notice there aren't any windows in here? I'm sure it's intentional. Like a cocoon, or a womb, right?"

I press my tongue to the roof of my mouth when she says "womb." I check the door. I want to bolt.

CRAZY GLUE: *I told you you should have ditched.*

AUNT BEE: *Sit down, Jason. She won't bite.*

SEXY LADY: *I don't think she's pretty. All those freckles all over her face and arms and legs. Does anybody else think she's attractive?*

LAUGH TRACK: *Yes!*

SEXY LADY: *Okay, she's got big boobs, but boobs aren't everything.*

CRAZY GLUE: *Yes, they are.*

FBG WITH A MUSTACHE: *I have to agree with C.G. on that one.*

"So sit down. The others will be along in a minute."

Shelby pats the floor. "Dr. Gomez is usually a little late 'cause she's driving over from one of the other schools she works at."

"Oh yeah? Well, okay," I say. I sit down on a large red pillow across from her, set my tray on the floor so it covers up the peach juice stain, and since I don't know what else to do, I twirl some spaghetti on my fork and take a bite. Then I notice Shelby unwrapping a roast beef sandwich. She pulls it out and mashes it between her hands.

CRAZY GLUE: *I know what you're thinking. Go ahead, say it.*

AUNT BEE: *Shh. Don't say a word.*

CRAZY GLUE: *Say it, goob!*

"So, uh—what are you doing there to that sandwich, 'cause like the cow's already dead."

LAUGH TRACK: *(Laughter).*

Shelby laughs, too, only her laugh doesn't reach her eyes. Her eyes look tired, sad. "What, this?" She holds out her sandwich with the bread now pounded flat. "I like to flatten the bread so I get more of the roast-beef flavor and less bread flavor."

"Why don't you just take the meat out of the bread and eat it plain, then?"

"Oh, I like the bread, just not too much." She takes a bite and smiles.

CRAZY GLUE: *Okay, now we know why she's in therapy.*

LAUGH TRACK: *(Laughter).*

CRAZY GLUE: *She's even weirder than you are. That's what this group*

22

therapy is, a group for weirdos. You'll get labeled a weirdo and then what will happen to you? More swirlies?

Shh!

We sit across from each other saying nothing for about a minute, eating our lunches, and I keep catching myself staring at her—uh—legs.

CRAZY GLUE: *Right, her legs.*

SEXY LADY: *She's not that hot.*

Shelby opens her mouth to speak, and since I figure it's probably something like "Knock it off, you perv," I stare down at my food and press my tongue against the roof of my mouth. Then the door opens and two guys walk in. They're laughing, and behind them I see Dr. Gomez.

FBG WITH A MUSTACHE: *Notice they all have sack lunches.*

They say hi to Shelby and me, really casual-like, as if I've been in this group all along.

I move my tray up off the floor, uncovering the peach juice stain, and set it in my lap before one of the guys steps on it.

AUNT BEE: *I know you're embarrassed about the tray of food, but remember, you need this meal. It's the most food you get to eat all day.*

LAUGH TRACK: *Isn't that a shame?*

Dr. Gomez folds herself into a giant beanbag, spreads out a napkin on her lap, and sets a sandwich, pear, and carrot sticks on it. She flips her long thick braid behind her. Then she takes a bite of one of the carrot sticks and nods at me. "Does everyone here know Jason Papadopoulos?"

Dr. Gomez smiles and I press my tongue against the roof of my mouth. I glance at the three of them staring at me and give a quick nod. There's Shelby, of course, and then there's Haze Horton, a junior. He's this lanky guy who always looks like he slept in his clothes all week and just woke up. He's got smudgy eye makeup with three white teardrops outlined in black that run from his left eye down his cheek. He also has a scraggly black beard and a voice that's about two octaves lower than mine. He's in my phys ed class because it was the only time he could fit the class into his schedule, so I know he can't play ball to save his life.

CRAZY GLUE: *He runs like a dork.*

Finally, there's Pete Funkel, also a junior. I feel a bit better seeing that he's in this therapy thing, too. Pete's an activist for animal rights and peace and stuff. He speaks up for what he believes. I really admire him for that. He's got a shaved head, which has something to do with his being a Zen Buddhist, but I don't know what.

The three of them nod at me and Haze says, "Sure, we know Pope-a-Dope. How ya doin', man?"

"All right," I say, then press my tongue to the roof of my mouth.

AUNT BEE: *Pope-a-Dope. The phys ed teacher calls you that, or the Popester. I wish he wouldn't. Now everyone's calling you that.*

FBG WITH A MUSTACHE: *He's just trying to make him feel included—one of the guys.*

AUNT BEE: *Well, I wish he wouldn't try so hard.*

Pete puts his hands together like he's about to pray, bows his head toward me, and says, "Welcome."

I mumble, "Thanks."

CRAZY GLUE: *Get out now! That Zen stuff is too weird.*

Dr. Gomez smiles this big smile so that her eyes squint up really small and friendly. She's got big dangling earrings on and this rainbow-colored skirt. She's just like her office, kaleidoscopic.

FBG WITH A MUSTACHE: *Great word—kaleidoscopic.*

"Jason," she says, turning her smile on me, "we always start these sessions by telling the group something that we're grateful for."

CRAZY GLUE: *Gulp!*

"Okay—uh-huh." I smile.

CRAZY GLUE: *Nice fake smile, there, goob. Are they going to force you to talk? Or will they just sit and wait for you until you say something?*

Shelby wrinkles up her nose. "It's one of Pete's Buddhist ideas. You'll get used to it."

"And it's a good one," Dr. Gomez says, glancing at Pete. "It reminds us there's always something we can be grateful for, no matter what our situation." She turns to Haze. "Haze, why don't you start and we'll go around the room counterclockwise."

I look from Haze to Pete.

FBG WITH A MUSTACHE: *That's right, Pope-a-Dope. You're third.*
What are you going to say?

CRAZY GLUE: *Make something up. Lie!*

I glance at the exit across the room. I want out.
The bird in my chest is crashing up against its cage. I
can feel the heavy *thump, thump, thump* of its feverish
body inside, and I open my mouth, not to speak, but to
let the bird out so I can breathe.

Haze says, "Yeah, okay, I'm grateful for . . ." He
pauses and looks up at the ceiling, his big Adams apple
poking out of his neck from beneath his beard. "Yeah,
all right, I'm ready." He looks at us. "I'm sooo grateful
that Mr. Moon didn't ask us to turn in our homework
today, because I didn't do it." He glances at Dr. Gomez.
"Our house was a complete madhouse yesterday; I mean
berserko."

Pete says, "I'm grateful that my dad spent last
night safe in a shelter." He bows his head at me, indicating it's my turn.

"Who, me?"

CRAZY GLUE: *Way to buy some more time, jacko.*

AUNT BEE: *Tell them how grateful you are to have that tray of food
you're gripping so hard, and that you're happy to be in this nice
warm room, and you're grateful you didn't have rain dripping
through the cracks in your ceiling last night, and that your dear
father is still safely at home, we hope.*

CRAZY GLUE: *Do not listen to her. Lie!*

"I'm—uh—I—I pass," I finally say.

2 6

Shelby slams down the last bit of her sandwich and yells at me. "What? No way, Pope-a-Dope. You can't come in here and listen in on our lives and just sit there. We're not a peepshow, you know. No passes! No passes!"

While she's saying this, Dr. Gomez is trying to shush her, and Shelby turns her fiery gaze on her. "What? It's no fair. He can't just come here and spy on us."

"Hey man, lighten up. He's not spying. He's just nervous and wants to check us out some more. Right, Dr. G?" Haze nods at her.

Before Dr. Gomez can speak, Shelby jumps back in. "If he can't even come up with something to be grateful for, I mean, give me a break. It's not like he's telling us how many times a day he jerks off."

"All right!" Dr. Gomez raises both her hands. She looks at me with this smile that I think is supposed to be friendly, but I can tell she's irked.

CRAZY GLUE: *Irked? She's pissed.*

SEXY LADY: *Does anyone think this Gomez lady's hot?*

LAUGH TRACK: *Yes!*

SEXY LADY: *But I'm hotter, right?*

LAUGH TRACK: *Yes!*

SEXY LADY: *Okay, then.*

"Jason, you don't have to speak if you don't want to."

Shelby huffs and leans against the wall, crossing her arms.

Dr. Gomez, both hands still in the air, directs one at Shelby, using her hand as a stop sign. "You don't

27

have to speak, but please know you're safe in here. Despite Shelby's outburst, we're all pulling for one another in this group. Now"—she lowers her arms and settles her hands back in her lap—"I'm sure you have many things to say that would be helpful to the rest of the group."

CRAZY GLUE: *I'm sure he doesn't.*

I nod. "Yeah, okay." I think of my dad and the can of soup I left on the counter for his lunch. I hope he's eating it. "I'm—uh, I'm grateful for soup."

Pete and Haze laugh, but Shelby makes this teeth-sucking noise and lets out another big sigh.

CRAZY GLUE: *Soup! Way to go, bozo.*

LAUGH TRACK: *(Laughter).*

"Care to elaborate on that?" Dr. Gomez smiles at me, and this time it's her friendly, squinty-eyed smile.

CRAZY GLUE: *No.*

"Um, it's nourishing?"

Haze and Pete chuckle again, and Shelby shakes her head and rolls her eyes.

Dr. Gomez tilts her head as though trying to figure out whether I'm really this stupid.

LAUGH TRACK: *Yes!*

Then Gomez nods slowly as if she's understanding something very deep and, after another couple of seconds, changes direction. "Shelby, it's your turn."

Shelby raises her arms, then lets them flop in her lap. "Well, crap. I was going to say I'm grateful that Jason has joined our group, but now I don't know what to say."

"Well, I'm grateful," Pete says, and then Haze nods.

"Me too. Glad you're here, dude."

"Shelby," Dr. Gomez says, "why don't you tell Jason why you particularly wanted him to join us."

LAUGH TRACK: *(Everyone's mouth hangs open in disbelief).*

FBG WITH A MUSTACHE: *Didn't Old Silky send you here?*

CRAZY GLUE: *Yeah, to deal.*

Have they all been talking about me?

CRAZY GLUE: *And you thought you were invisible.*

Shelby sits up and inches her butt away from the wall a little.

CRAZY GLUE: *She's blushing.*

SEXY LADY: *She thinks you're a hottie.*

I press my tongue extra hard against the roof of my mouth.

FBG WITH A MUSTACHE: *Why don't you keep it there and save yourself some time.*

CRAZY GLUE: *You're sweating something fierce. You've got wet rings under your arms. Really attractive there, buddy.*

Haze and Pete are staring at me as if my last forkful of spaghetti is sitting in a pile on top of my head.

"Well," Shelby says, "I thought you could tell us about your mother and, like, what happened to her and all, and how you dealt with her dying and how you got over it. I—I'm just glad to have someone here who's kind of in the same boat. I mean, my mom's dying. She'll be gone by the end of the school year. I just want to know what it's like." She shrugs and blinks her eyes several times. She turns toward Haze. "Haze, your parents are getting a divorce and that's really hard to go through, I know, but your parents are still alive, right? And Pete"—she glances at him—"your dad's doin' drugs again and it's bad, and it's taking a lot out of your family to care for him, and I know it's terrible, okay, but, like, I need to talk to someone who's been through just what I'm about to go through, someone who's lost his mom." She fixes her eyes on me. "I want to know that there's the other side of all this pain. I want to know that someday I'll make it to the other side and it won't hurt so much. I just want Jason to tell me this."

Now everyone's staring at me, waiting for me to say something, and I don't know what to say 'cause I'm so blown away.

CRAZY GLUE: *I'll tell you what to say. Nothing! What pain? You're doing great. You didn't even cry when your mother died, and you loved your mother.*

AUNT BEE: *But aren't we supposed to cry when someone dies?*

FBG WITH A MUSTACHE: *Don't go there.*

CRAZY GLUE: *Say nothing. You're doing fine. Your dad's doing fine. Everything's fine. There's no pain. What the hell is she even talking about?*

FBG WITH A MUSTACHE: *The dad's not so fine.*

CRAZY GLUE: *Okay, so he stopped taking his meds after the mom died, but goob's dealing with it. The dad'll turn back around.*

30

He always does. Just give him time. It just takes time. They don't have any money; that's the real problem.

FBG WITH A MUSTACHE: *That's because his dad hasn't worked since the stroke—since before that, even.*

CRAZY GLUE: *Big deal. We've been here before, when his mom was alive, and we managed. It's fine. It's great, Jason; you're doing great.*

SEXY LADY: *I'm with Crazy Glue. You're handling things just fine.*

I really need some windows in here. I need fresh air. I don't feel well at all. I feel like something's splitting inside of me, ripping right down the center of my brain. I've got to do something to stop this feeling. My throat is so dry. I need air!

CRAZY GLUE: *Didn't mean to stir things up, buddy. Come on—keep it together. You're fine, remember?*

LAUGH TRACK: *Isn't it a shame? He's falling apart.*

FBG WITH A MUSTACHE: *Just hold on, kiddo.*

AUNT BEE: *It's all right, Jason. It's going to be all right.*

Everyone is waiting for me to say something. I put my fork down and I notice my hand is shaking. I look at Dr. Gomez. She nods.

"Well," I finally say, "I don't know." My voice is hoarse. I take a gulp of milk.

"*What* don't you know?" Shelby asks, leaning toward me.

"Patience, Shelb," Pete says.

I move my tray to the floor and stare down at the few green beans left in the dish. "I don't know what happened to my mother. I mean, one minute we're hiking up Mount Washington in New Hampshire and the next minute she's fallen on the rocks. But she didn't really fall; she had a stroke." I pick up a bean and squeeze it between my fingers.

CRAZY GLUE: *You don't want to go there.*

"Whoa! That's intense, man," Haze says. He leans forward, puts his hand on my shoulder, and kind of shakes me.

AUNT BEE: *He's odd-looking and runs like a dork, but he's a nice young man.*

"So what did you do?" Shelby asks. "I mean how do you cope? I think when my mom goes, I don't know. I think I'm going to want to go with her. I'm already in mourning. I cry all the time. I just can't see my life without her. I don't know how you can sit here like nothing's happened. I mean, your mom's dead!" Shelby shouts the word "dead" and it rings in my ears.

Everybody in the room says, "Shelby!"

Shelby turns and shakes her head at them. "What? I'm just being honest. Sorry, Jason. I need to know how you get over something like—"

I don't let her finish. I pitch the green bean onto my tray. "I don't know how *you'll* deal with getting over losing your mother. I mean, you just—you just kind of have to keep going, okay? What else can you do? Jeez!"

CRAZY GLUE: *Your arms are flapping. Rein it in, buddy.*

I drop my arms, then fall against the wall and draw my knees up in front of me.

CRAZY GLUE: *Shut up! Just shut up! Shut up!*

SEXY LADY: *You knew better than to go there.*

"Yeah, man," Haze says, nodding. He pulls a container of applesauce out of his lunch sack, pulls the foil off the top, and takes a lick. I see a big blob of sauce on his tongue before he pulls it in and swallows. "Yeah, like my dad, whoa! He drove his car straight into our garage last night—with the door closed! The garage door was *closed*, man. He *sooo* did it on purpose." He looks at all of us. "Wild, right? My mom's getting the main house in the divorce and he's totally freakin' over it. I swear." He shakes his head and tosses a potato chip into his mouth. "I mean, by the time they're through playing dueling banjos, man, one of them's gonna be dead in the bed, you know?" He chuckles and wags his head again, but he doesn't look too happy about it. Then he jerks his head back and pops his eyes wide open and says, "But, what the hell, like Jason says, what ya gonna do? You just gotta keep going. Right? Right?" He looks at all of us.

"Your parents are nuts," Pete says. He sits with his legs crossed and his back straight. He looks as if he's meditating. He runs his hand over his bald head. "Who cares about a house? He's got his life. That should be enough. Why isn't that enough?"

I stare at my knees and think about the leaks in our roof and the chunks of plaster that keep falling from the ceilings upstairs.

"You're right," Haze says. "Americans have too much stuff these days, man. My parents are doin' a tug of war over fur coats and the Lexus and who gets which house, and it's absotively, posolutely crap. It's all crap. Who cares? You know?"

"But do you really think that's what they're fighting over?" Dr. Gomez asks him.

Haze and Pete and Dr. Gomez spend the rest of the lunch period discussing power battles and control issues—that's what they call them—and I sit there just listening and staring at my knees.

I look up when Haze says, "My dad's acting like a complete lunatic," and I see Shelby staring right at me.

I look back down at my tray, and then after a minute or so I steal another glance at her. She's still staring at me with her Yankees cap tilted back so her brown eyes, her big, sad, nonblinking brown eyes, bore right into me. What's her problem? She's making my skin crawl.

SEXY LADY: *It's love.*

CRAZY GLUE: *More like she's trying to figure out if the goob is really as dumb as he acts.*

Pete tells us about his family's plan to do an intervention on his father and we all clap.

"I've been lighting candles and meditating on it a long time, now, and I think an intervention is the only option we have left," Pete says. He lowers his head toward his clasped hands and adds, "He'll die if he doesn't get back into rehab."

Shelby reaches over and hugs Pete, and everybody nods and agrees that an intervention is a good idea. I just sit there.

When the bell rings, we all stand. Shelby, Dr. Gomez, and Haze wad their lunch sacks and toss them into the wastebasket on top of my cling peaches, but Pete, who hadn't taken a bite out of his lunch all period, sets his sack on my tray. He says, "Real glad you're in the group, Jason." Then he gives me another one of those weird bows with the prayerful hands, and before I can think through what just happened and decide whether to give the lunch back or take it gratefully and give it to my dad, he's gone, lost in the throng of students making their way to their next classes.

CHAPTER FIVE

AFTER SCHOOL, I walk along the Potomac River, crunching through the ice at the side of the road. I'm on my way home from the bus stop and I'm thinking about the letter I just answered for the school paper.

Dear Mouse:

My parents forgot my birthday again. My brother had a big game and me and my parents went to that. After the game, we went out to eat to celebrate his victory. It's all about football in our house. Nobody notices me at all.

Unloved in Potomac Crossing

Dear Unloved:

That totally sucks! I don't know what you should do. I mean, jeez! Well, okay—you didn't say, but I have a feeling you never reminded them that you had a birthday coming up. Yeah, it's wrong that they're so into football and their own stuff to notice you, but maybe you should make a louder noise. So, like a week or two before your birthday, start talking about it a lot. Mention the date a lot, too. Tell your mom you're thinking of having a birthday party this year. Hand your parents a list of things you want for your birthday and ask if they would pick something out from that list. I mean, make a big deal out of it. If that doesn't work, then you've got A-Hs for parents and you've got to just drop it and find a group of friends who will treat you right. I mean, don't pick friends who treat you just like your family all over again. Then throw your own party with them. Anyway, that's my advice, for what it's worth.

    Mouse

    P.S. Speaking of friends who treat you right, A.R., maybe F.C. wouldn't have to lie to you if you treated her better. You treat her like a fungus on your butt. F.C., dump the dude already. Why do you let that loser treat you that way?

    I write my letters on one of the library computers during study period. We don't have a hookup anymore at home. We don't even have a phone line anymore, or a cell phone, either, for that matter—it costs too much.

AUNT BEE: *Oh dear. You've had to spend so much money to pay the hospital bills for your mom's coma.*

LAUGH TRACK: *It's such a shame.*

CRAZY GLUE: *Five months she was in a coma. You'll be paying those bills the rest of your life, jacko.*

    Can we get back on topic, please? I was explaining to You about the Dear Mouse letters.

CRAZY GLUE: *So explain already. Who's stopping you?*

    Anyway, I don't send the letters from school;

otherwise someone might figure out that the letters always come in during fifth period on Thursdays and come looking for me in the library, so I wait and duck into the library near our house to send them to our school newspaper. I can't believe they actually publish what I write. Even the faculty advisor on the paper doesn't know who I am.

CRAZY GLUE: *A lot of kids think it's Pete Funkel.*

AUNT BEE: *And lots think it's a teacher pretending to be a student.*

FBG WITH A MUSTACHE: *When they find out it's you, you're going to have to move out of the country and go into the witness protection program.*

CRAZY GLUE: *Just think, if Pete ever gets beat up over what you've written, it will be your fault and you'll have to sit in that windowless room with him, staring at his broken nose for months. Then how will you feel?*

AUNT BEE: *Pshaw! I think it's wonderful. The whole school looks forward to the paper now. Dear Mouse is the first thing everybody reads. And these people who write to you need help.*

SEXY LADY: *If you ask me, I think the whole situation is hot!*

CRAZY GLUE: *And getting hotter. You stay in that group therapy and you'll get found out fast.*

FBG WITH A MUSTACHE: *Shelby's dangerous. She's making you talk.*

CRAZY GLUE: *Yeah, ditch it now, while you still can.*

AUNT BEE: *I should think it felt good to yell at Shelby and get a thing or two off your chest, and Pete and Haze aren't too bad. They're glad you're in the group, for some reason. And you do need a friend. You've been so lonely.*

38

FBG WITH A MUSTACHE: *I liked that Pete told Haze his parents were nuts and Haze didn't care.*

CRAZY GLUE: *Don't listen to Aunt Bee. You can't afford to have friends. Are we all forgetting about Dad?*

I stop and look across the street at my house. It's a three-story, 1820s brick townhouse, the last house in a row of four. My grandfather painted the bricks on the house white and the trim a deep blue, the colors of the Greek flag. Now a lot of the white on the house has worn away on the top and the blue is peeling, too, as if the flag is waving at half-mast. These four townhouses are the final holdouts from the city's restoration of the downtown riverfront. On either side of us are old warehouses. One is now a gallery and arts studio, and the other is a bunch of shops and restaurants. Across the river is Washington, D.C.

FBG WITH A MUSTACHE: *I think you're stalling. You don't want our new audience member to meet your father.*

SEXY LADY: *Just remember, you're a chip off the old block, and you're hot!*

I just want to say in my dad's defense that when he's in his right mind, he's the best dad in the world. He taught me to paddle a canoe and to ride a bike and how to write Jason Apollo Papadopoulos when I was five so my teacher wouldn't keep making me stand in the corner. He told me the stories of the ancient gods and heroes of Greece. We read *The Iliad* and *The Odyssey* together when I was nine and ten years old.

FBG WITH A MUSTACHE: *Ah, the stories.*

AUNT BEE: *You treasure that the most. Sitting together under those bushes in the backyard of your old house, eating Oreos, drinking Cokes, and telling stories.*

CRAZY GLUE: *A totally cool, secret hideout—all those bushes, that wide-open space underneath, and a nice, flat dirt floor.*

FBG WITH A MUSTACHE: *Stalling.*

If only I could get those days back. If only he'd get better already.

CRAZY GLUE: *I don't know, buddy. It doesn't look like he's getting any better. He's back on the meds and it ain't happening. And you're getting low on those pills. What will you do when you run out? You can't afford to buy more.*

Just—just leave me alone. I'm handling it.

AUNT BEE: *What are you so afraid of, dear?*

Nothing! I'm not afraid. Everybody stop saying I'm afraid. I'm not. He's fine. I'm fine. It's all fine. And he's not going away again. Not on my watch. Not to some state mental institute where they'll tie him down again, or lock him in a room by himself. No way! No way! I put him there once; I won't do it again.

AUNT BEE: *Now look what you've done. He's very upset, poor boy. You were just six years old. He was going to bury you alive! Oh dear, everything is very, very upsetting.*

LAUGH TRACK: *Isn't it a shame.*

SEXY LADY: *You're still hot.*

FBG WITH A MUSTACHE: *Buck up, kiddo, and get in there. Go on. Go take care of your dad. We're here. We're always here for you.*

40

I cross the street. I taste tears and I didn't even know I was crying. I wipe the stupid mess off my face, walk up the steps, and open the front door.

There's no warmth in the house as I step into the hallway, no smell of dinner cooking, no sound of my mom's voice singing from the kitchen, or my dad's shouting "Hi-ya!" from his study. It's almost as cold inside as it is out. We heat with oil, and oil costs an arm and a leg, so we keep the thermostat set really low. There's a smell of mildew in the house, and wet plaster, and dad's B.O. It's quiet, too quiet.

CRAZY GLUE: *Jeez, now what's your dad up to? Hope he didn't yank another tooth out of his mouth with that rusty set of pliers again.*

SEXY LADY: *Blood everywhere. And what a time you had on the bus getting him to the clinic. It was a mess.*

FBG WITH A MUSTACHE: *It wasn't so bad. Jason took care of it. He handled it.*

"Dad?" I step from the hallway into the living room. "Dad? Where are you?" I head back to the kitchen, passing through the dining room on my way. He's not there. I check his study off the dining room and go around to the front of his desk to make sure he's not hiding under it the way he does sometimes. The room is small and square and jammed with books and stacks of folders filled with writing projects my dad has yet to complete. He's written two books. Both are about Greece. They don't make him much money and he hasn't completed anything new

41

in more than a year. We lived off the money my mom got photographing weddings and occasionally birds. The birds were for a bird watching magazine.

"Dad?" I call again. No answer.

LAUGH TRACK: *Uh-oh! (Nervous laughter).*

I run upstairs and I hear voices coming from the bathroom at the other end of the hallway.

"Dad?"

AUNT BEE: *He's all right. Take it easy, Jason.*

I hurry down the narrow hallway to the bathroom and push open the door.

CRAZY GLUE: *Oh shit!*

My dad's sitting up fully dressed with his helmet on in a tub full of water. His radio is plugged into the outlet above our sink, and it's resting on the edge of a plank he's laid across the top of the tub, ready to fall into the water and electrocute him.

CRAZY GLUE: *Shit to hell!*

"Dad, what are you doing?" I yank the plug out of the wall. "Huh? What are you doing? Are you crazy?" I grab the radio and set it on the toilet lid.

LAUGH TRACK: *Uh-oh!*

CRAZY GLUE: *Time to go to the nut house.*

AUNT BEE: *He's going to kill himself one day.*

Dad looks up at me, blinking. I shake my head. "Dad, you can't put the radio near the water. You could kill yourself! Jeez! What were you thinking?"

"I got cold. It's warm in here," he says, unconcerned.

He looks me over. "So you're back from the wars, are you, Apollo? What news have you from the front? Any Furies lurking about?" He presses the sides of his helmet as if to make sure no Furies can get in. "And Athena? Have you brought her with you this time?"

FBG WITH A MUSTACHE: *Tell him Athena's dead. Your mom's dead. That's who he means, isn't it?*

AUNT BEE: *Tell him no such thing. Tell him you brought him some food.*

CRAZY GLUE: *Man, your bird heart is flapping like a hundred flaps a second. Sure it's not a hummingbird you've got in your chest?*

"Did you hear me, Dad? You can't have a radio on in here."

"But I need the music. I need the violins. It's the only sound that blocks the Furies' voices. They're singing. They're wanting to eat away my brain. Can you hear them?"

Dad presses his hands against his helmet and tries to squeeze it tighter about his head. His round gray eyes stare out at me from behind the masklike pieces of metal that hide his nose and cheeks. "Their song is ear piercing. They're tuned too high. Chalk on a chalkboard, metal scraping stone. You know it. You know their song. You know they're after me." He begins to chant:

"Now by the altar,
Over the victim,
Ripe for the ritual,

Sing this enchantment:
A song without music,
A sword in the senses,
A storm in the heart,
And a fire in the brain;
A clamour of Furies
To paralyse reason,
A tune full of terror,
A drought in the soul!"

Dad hugs himself and rocks back and forth, repeating this, faster, and again, faster. A wave of water sloshes onto the floor.

CRAZY GLUE: *Here we go! He's revved up now! You'll have to slap him to get him to stop.*

FBG WITH A MUSTACHE: *Pull the plug! Pull the plug!*

AUNT BEE: *Shove some food in his mouth!*

I kneel down and pull the plug to drain the tub. I shake off my backpack and open it. I pull out Pete's sack lunch and yank it away just before another wave sloshes over the rim. "Dad, would you stop it already?"

"'A clamour of Furies to paralyse reason!' To paralyse reason! To paralyse reason!"

I shove Pete's sandwich toward him. "Here. Eat this."

Dad takes the sandwich and shoves it into his mouth, plastic wrap and all.

LAUGH TRACK: *(Laughter).*

*   *   *

Twenty minutes later Dad has eaten Pete's lunch. The good food calms him. I help him out of his wet clothes, and when I get to his undershirt and pull it off, I find a long red zigzag running the length of his chest. I touch it. It looks like my mom's nail polish.

"Dad? What is this?"

"A wound," he says. He puts his hand over his chest.

"What wound?"

"All wounds. The world's wounds. I'm all wound up in the wounds of the world. They told me to do it."

I ease the helmet off his head, and Dad draws in his breath as if he's in great pain.

"Don't listen to those Furies, Dad. Just because you hear them doesn't mean you have to obey."

He puts his hands over his ears. "They were on the radio. They're in the airwaves. They got through. I had to purify myself with water and a wound, for your mother's sake."

CRAZY GLUE: *At least he didn't use a knife. Be grateful for small miracles.*

"Mom doesn't need you to do anything for her sake."

"For my sake, I mean. For my sake, to cleanse my sins against your mother."

CRAZY GLUE: *Here we go again.*

"You didn't kill Mom. I keep telling you. Don't listen to the Furies. You didn't do it. She had a stroke. You weren't even there."

"I should have been there."

"Dad, let's just drop it."

AUNT BEE: *You need to talk about it sometime. I worry about you. A boy should cry for his mother.*

CRAZY GLUE: *Aunt Bee, I mean this in the nicest way—shut up!*

I refill the tub with hot water and Dad has the first bath he's had in about a month. He looks better when he's all scrubbed and in a set of clean clothes. He's lost about twenty pounds, though, so his chest is lean and pale, and I can count all his ribs.

CRAZY GLUE: *Have you taken a look at your own rib cage lately?*

My dad's cheeks and eyes are hollowed out, and his hair has grown up and out—a white flame consuming his fragile skull. He has the look of someone who is being hunted, a wide-eyed, wary, hungry look. He creeps, slightly hunched, along the hallway, stopping at each doorway and tensing as if he's expecting something to jump out at him.

I get him comfortable on the living room couch and cover him up in lots of blankets. Then I sit down in a chair nearby, wrapped in my own pile of blankets, and read to him. I'm reading him *The Odyssey*, the same book he read to me when I was nine.

After I've been reading for a while, Dad interrupts me. "Did you see what I wrote today?" he asks.

I look up from the book. He sits across from me wearing aluminum foil over his ears because I've hidden the helmet.

"No. Did you write something?"

AUNT BEE: *Thank goodness! Maybe the meds are starting to work. He's writing!*

CRAZY GLUE: *Hold your horses! We don't know what he's written yet.*

"It's on my desk in my study." Dad nods and one of his foil ears drops off. "Didn't you see it? It's the story of everything." He quickly wraps the foil back around his ear.

I get to my feet and head for the study. I hold my breath. Is he really writing again?

SEXY LADY: *I just know it's going to be good, whatever it is.*

I grab Dad's old work-in-progress folder off the top of his desk and take it out to the living room. I hold it up. "Is this it?"

Dad's eyes light up. "Yes! That's the story of what happened—how I had to finish writing my book and how I couldn't go to the mountain." He swats the air. "So you Furies had better read it and leave me alone." He gets onto his knees on the couch, tangling himself with the blankets. While he wrestles with them and shouts at the Furies, I open the folder and read the top page. It's written in pencil. It begins: *Word whaf fork mountain mouth rain fraibe frube.* I scan the page. It doesn't get any better. My heart sinks. I look at my dad. His eyes shine with hope.

"What do you think? Will it save me? Will they leave me alone now?"

I've never lied to my dad before, but I look him straight in the eyes and say, "It's perfect, Dad. It explains everything."

CHAPTER SIX

I KNOW WHAT you're thinking. Man, is that dude crazy or what? Jason's dad needs a doctor. He needs help.

CRAZY GLUE: *Good guess, Sherlock.*

He's really not that bad. He'll get better. He always does. It's just that he was off his meds too long. Now he's back on them, so he'll be fine. It's okay. I mean, what else can I do, right? If he doesn't get better, he has to stay in the hospital, permanently. That's what my mom told me. So I ask you, could you put your dad away like that? Yeah, I didn't think so. And I'm guessing you think I'm a little crazy, too.

CRAZY GLUE: *Because you talk to us.*

Right.

AUNT BEE: *But you know we're just a figment of your imagination, so it's okay.*

That's right.

SEXY LADY: *We're just voices in your head.*

Right again.

CRAZY GLUE: *Just like your dad's.*

No!

LAUGH TRACK: *Uh-oh!*

FBG WITH A MUSTACHE: *He doesn't actually hear us. That's the difference. We're not coming out of the radio or rising up out of the ground.*

Exactly!

CRAZY GLUE: *Glad we got that all straightened out—again.*

Yeah! Me too.

So, I'm supposed to go to those shrink-wrap lunch sessions twice a week, Mondays and Thursdays. I go two more times, and both times I don't say much of anything. Shelby's so irritated, she looks ready to choke me, and even Haze and Pete, I think, are getting frustrated. Dr. Gomez is harder to read. I don't know what she's thinking, but I refuse to talk. They can't make me, can they?

CRAZY GLUE: *I'm with you, buddy.*

AUNT BEE: *You can't get help if you won't speak up and ask for it.*

CRAZY GLUE: *Who says he needs help? He's fine. He's handling it.*

FBG WITH A MUSTACHE: *Oh, is he really? He's falling asleep in all his classes because of those suffocating nightmares he keeps having that scare the bejeezus out of him and keep him awake the rest of the night.*

CRAZY GLUE: *He wets the bed every time he has one of those dreams. That's what keeps him up—doing the laundry.*

FBG WITH A MUSTACHE: *Whatever. He's not sleeping, he's not getting all his homework done, and now he's gone and told Mr. O'Hagan in front of the entire class that an isosceles triangle is a private matter between his Greek cousin, Isosceles, and his wife and mistress.*

LAUGH TRACK: *Ha, ha.*

Crazy Glue pushed me! I never should have said that. O'Hagan looked like he wanted to kill me.

CRAZY GLUE: *It got a laugh, didn't it? The boy did it. He got a laugh!*

SEXY LADY: *Funny men are hot.*

If I weren't so tired and cranky these days, I wouldn't have said it. And what was that mathematical equation O'Hagan was doing on the board? Something about falling bodies? Falling bodies? I totally slept through that.

Now I'm pushing through the cafeteria line, hurrying to get my food because Shelby has called an emergency meeting. It's Wednesday. Dr. Gomez is at another school on Wednesdays, but Shelby says she lets us meet in her office if we want to. I have half a mind not to show up.

AUNT BEE: *Shelby, Pete, and Haze are the closest thing to friends you have, Jason. Don't blow it. Just try to say something in there besides "I agree with you on that." Smile, at least.*

CRAZY GLUE: *Jason's pissed because the paper came out today and he wants to stay in the cafeteria to hear what kids have to say about his Mouse column.*

AUNT BEE: *Just go on, Jason.*

I hustle down the long corridor toward Dr. Gomez's office. When I get there, I find I'm the last one to arrive. Pete and Haze are reading the school paper over Shelby's shoulders. Pete's in his usual white T-shirt and jeans, only the shirt has a large purple peace sign on it, and Haze is wearing a sombrero and a striped poncho that looks a hundred years old and like it's never been washed. I've discovered he loves costumes. Shelby's dressed all in green and looks like a pixie with boobs. All three look up when I enter.

"I was just saying I don't think it's Pete," Shelby says when she sees me.

I step inside. "Huh?" I lower myself onto a pillow, trying not to spill my tray of food. I've missed having dinner three nights in a row 'cause of dealing with Dad, and I'm starving.

"Mouse," Shelby says. "I no longer think Pete's Mouse. If he were Mouse, he would have told Mortified Guy to join this group. He would have told him to talk to his dad."

"Why? What's it say? I haven't picked up the paper yet."

CRAZY GLUE: *Very clever, Mouse. And you look so innocent, too.*

Haze laughs. "Oh man, you've got to hear this. It's so screwball." He notices his jeans are sliding off his butt and uses the wall to support his back while he pulls his pants up and tightens his belt.

"It's not screwball," Pete says. "It's just different."

"Guys, just let me read it, okay?" Shelby adjusts the paper, holding it higher and out from her face more. Then she squiggles her butt on the pillow the way she does when she's about to make an announcement or say something important about herself. She begins:

"Dear Mouse:

   I was coming back from somewhere (I won't say where or you'd maybe guess who I am), and I got home early. I headed upstairs to my room—I'm real quiet, not on purpose or anything, but our house is carpeted, so you can't hear anybody walking around—and when I pass my parents' room, I see my dad through the opening in the door. He's got women's clothes on. I don't know what to think. He doesn't know I saw him. Now I can't look him in the face. He disgusts me. I hate him. I don't want to live in the same house with him anymore.
   Mortified Guy."

Shelby stops and looks over the paper at me.
   "Oh wow," I say. I feel myself starting to blush, so I press my tongue against the roof of my mouth.
   "Yeah, and here's what Mouse wrote," Shelby continues.

"Dear Mort:

   I don't know why you're writing to me. I'm nobody. I'm just Mouse, but since you did write, I'll answer. Yeah, so that's messed up! I know I should probably tell you to talk to your dad about what you saw. If you want to do the right thing, I guess that's what you should do, but if someone told me to do that, I'd probably tell them to blow it out their—. If he was ready to talk about it, he'd come to you, right? But you do have to live in the same house. It's probably good if you could talk to him, you know, like at least say, "Pass the butter," that kind of thing, without wanting to strangle him for not being the guy you thought he was. Do you hate him because he dresses in women's clothes, or do you hate him just in a general sort of way because he stands for everything that you don't, or do you hate him because maybe you're afraid this could be you in another twenty years? Have you always hated him? Did you ever get along? When you were a little kid, did you love him? If you did, whatever reason you loved him is still there inside you and inside him. So I don't know. I'd just remember that. I'd just hold on to that memory if you can.

Mouse."

Shelby slaps the paper on her lap and Pete and Haze both startle. "What kind of stupid answer is that? Telling Mortified Guy his father's messed up!" She looks around at all of us. "He should talk to his father, no maybes about it. Mortified saw him, so the father doesn't get a choice about when he should 'come out.' It's not when the dad's ready to talk; it's 'Talk to me now, because I saw you. I saw you wearing Mom's clothes!'"

"Whoa!" Haze says. "Take it down a notch, would ya? You're way too intense."

CRAZY GLUE: *Yeah she is.*

Pete shrugs. "Sometimes there are no easy answers. I think that's what Mouse was trying to say."

"Aha! It *is* you! I knew it!" Shelby says, turning toward Pete and shoving him with both hands.

Pete falls sideways, laughing. Then he sits back up and his round face gets serious. He rubs his hand back and forth over his bald head. "It's not me. I'd tell you if it was."

"Promise?" Shelby kicks off her clogs and wiggles her bare toes.

Pete holds up his right hand. "Promise."

"Hey, why doesn't anyone ever think Mouse is me?" Haze asks. He nods at me. "Or Pope-a-Dope."

CRAZY GLUE: *Look real innocent now, Mouse.*

"Get serious," Shelby says. Then she stops smiling, brushes a wavy mass of hair out of her face, and wiggles her butt on the pillow again.

CRAZY GLUE: *Gotta love that wiggle.*

"So, anyway, speaking of no easy answers, I wanted to talk to you all about something, and I couldn't wait because it's bugging me and I can't sleep. Also, I wasn't sure I could say what I wanted to say in front of Gomez."

LAUGH TRACK: *Uh-oh!*

I set down the dry hamburger I had been gnawing on and struggle to my feet. "Look, I know I'm not really a part of you three. I shouldn't be here if you're

going to say private stuff. Dr. Gomez isn't here, so . . .
I think I'm gonna just . . ." I turn my head toward
the door.

Before I can say anything more, Shelby jumps to
her feet and blurts, "I'm really, really sorry. I know I
come on too strong. I know I've got strong opinions
and I scare people off, but I want you to stay. You're a
part of us now. And I need all the friends and support
I can get. So even if you don't say much—just stay."
Shelby's eyes look glassy and her mouth is turned down
like she's about to cry.

CRAZY GLUE: *Way to go, goob.*

AUNT BEE: *Bless my soul, she said you're one of them. You've got
friends, Jason. It's been so long.*

FBG WITH A MUSTACHE: *Calm down, calm down—let's not all get
too excited.*

CRAZY GLUE: *There goes that hummingbird heart of his again.*

Pete gets onto his knees and sits back on his heels.
"Jason, come on—sit back down. Socks just has a big
mouth sometimes." He shrugs. "But it's cool. We accept
people for who they are in here. That's the rule, and we
all say what we think, you know? It goes both ways.
You can tell us what you think, too."

CRAZY GLUE: *Socks? Her nickname's Socks?*

"Yeah, I guess so," I say.

Pete continues. "It can get kind of intense in this
room, but it all stays in here."

Haze takes off his sombrero and pitches it onto

Dr. Gomez's desk. "Yeah, what's said in here stays in here. What's said in here stays in here," he repeats, laughing at himself as if he invented the phrase.

"So come on, both of you—sit," Pete says. "Peace." He sits back on his pillow and crosses his legs.

I glance at the peace sign on his T-shirt.

AUNT BEE: *Sit, Jason.*

"Okay, maybe," I say. I sit back down.

FBG WITH A MUSTACHE: *See, that wasn't so hard.*

Shelby sits, too.

"So what's this about, man?" Haze says.

Shelby tosses a chunk of cheese in her mouth. "Just wait a second. I'm not—I can't bring myself to say it yet." She doesn't look at any of us and her face beneath all her millions of freckles burns red.

SEXY LADY: *She looks miserable. Look at her eyes. They're so bloodshot. She's not so attractive now, huh?*

CRAZY GLUE: *Yes, she is.*

I stuff a bunch of cold french fries in my mouth and wish I had remembered to grab some ketchup packets.

"What do you mean, you're not ready? You just said . . ." Haze begins, but Pete puts his hand on Haze's arm to stop him.

"Is it about your mother?" Pete asks.

Shelby nods. "What else?" She bites down on her lower lip.

Haze, Pete, and I exchange glances. Then Pete says, "Center of the room. Come on, everybody."

Pete scoots on his butt toward the center, and then Shelby and Haze do the same thing.

CRAZY GLUE: *Okay, now we're in for it. Touchy-feely New Age mood ring stuff, just great.*

I don't move. I don't know what to do.

Pete nods at me and says, "Jason, kill the lights, will ya?"

"Yeah, thanks, Pete," Shelby says.

I jump up.

CRAZY GLUE: *Yes! Something easy to do. Go ahead, goob.*

I flip the switch on the wall and the room becomes pitch black. I had forgotten that we have no windows in the room.

"Perfect," says Pete.

And Haze says, "Ah, darkness. I do my best business in the dark."

"Eew, gross," Shelby says, and Haze laughs.

I crawl on my hands and knees till I reach the circle and sit down between Shelby and Pete. We all sit cross-legged, knees touching. Then Pete leans forward and puts his arms around Haze's and my shoulders. The rest of us do the same so that we sit in a huddle with our heads almost touching, closing off the top of the circle.

CRAZY GLUE: *Very touchy-feely! Do we like this?*

SEXY LADY: *I know I do.*

We sit there for a couple of minutes, quiet, in the dark, with our arms around one another's shoulders, breathing in one another's lunch breath. It all smells mostly like smoked cheese.

Then Shelby sighs. "Okay, I guess I'm ready now." Her voice sounds shaky as she begins.

"My mom, she's really hurting, you know? I mean her brain is all there. She's as with it as ever, but her body is just wasted and her insides are like, well, I don't know. She's having trouble breathing now. She's got all this mucus she chokes on, and she can barely speak because her tongue doesn't have much muscle tone, and she can't hold her head up at all. The only thing she can move, really, is one finger on her right hand, and the doctors say—" Shelby sniffs and takes her hand off my shoulder to wipe her nose and sniff again. "The doctors say she's probably going to suffocate. That's how she'll die. And every night, she's choking, and the nurse has to come in and clear out her lungs, and when the nurse has a night off, since my dad's not usually there, I do it, and my mother, she doesn't want to live like this anymore. She—she doesn't want to live. She doesn't want the nurse or me to clear her lungs—and"—Shelby sighs again, only more deeply, and pauses to wipe her nose—"and, sometimes—sometimes I think maybe she'd be better off—you know—dead."

"Whoa!" Haze says.

Shelby sniffs. "I know, right? It's terrible, what I'm thinking. But I can't help it. Sometimes when I hear her choking in the next room, I—oh jeez, I think about just leaving her there, just plugging my ears and leaving her there till it's all over." She raises her voice a little. "But—but it's only for an instant. Just a flash of a thought, and then I shake it out and run into her room, and I'm so glad she's still alive. I still need her. But that thought, that terrible thought is there. I hate it. I hate myself when I think it. I just hate myself."

Shelby's voice is so close. We're all so close, we can hear one another breathing and feel one another's pulse through our arms placed across one another's backs. My own breathing is faint, shallow. I don't want to breathe at all. I want to just listen. It feels as if we're so far away from the rest of the world, caught up in the hush and darkness of this room.

Pete whispers, "Sometimes I've wished my dad were dead, too. Our lives would be so much better, and easier, you know? But then I'm sorry. I'm always sorry when I think that. He's an asshole, but I love him."

"Yeah, my parents can both be royal assholes, but you know, you love them anyway," Haze says. "So like, what's that all about?"

AUNT BEE: *All the months your mother was in a coma, you never thought that. You begged and begged God to let her live.*
CRAZY GLUE: *God had other plans.*
LAUGH TRACK: *Isn't that a shame.*

Shut up, everybody!

We sit huddled together for a few minutes, just being there with one another, and it feels dangerous to me that nobody is saying anything.

FBG WITH A MUSTACHE: *Ah, the dreaded silences.*

Then Shelby starts again. "My mother wants me to help her die now." Her voice is just a whisper, but it feels like it's coming from inside my own chest. "She wants me to leave her when she's choking and just let her suffocate, and I'm so afraid that one day I'm going to do it."

I feel Shelby's hand claw my back and grab my shirt as though she were looking for something to hold on to, to save her and keep her from falling into that terrible place where those kinds of thoughts live, but I know from my own experience, there is no holding on, not for any of us. We have become, through no fault of our own, these falling bodies. That's what it feels like, there in that windowless room. Just like we're one of O'Hagan's odd mathematical equations for falling bodies, and as scary as that is, sitting with Shelby, Pete, and Haze makes me feel for the first time that I'm not alone. At least we're all falling through space together.

CHAPTER SEVEN

SLEET PELTS ME on the walk home from my bus stop. Little chips of ice burn my cheeks and the tips of my ears. The sky and river are both a dreary gray, the water choppy where it hasn't yet frozen. I walk past the warehouse turned art studio, the collar of my coat turned up and my shoulders hunched against the wet wind. It's always windiest on that corner. My mind is on Shelby and the meeting. The street is slick with rain and black ice, so I watch my steps, careful to avoid the puddles since the sole of one of my shoes has a crack in it.

CRAZY GLUE: *You've got to put a piece of milk carton in your shoe. That'll fix it.*

FBG WITH A MUSTACHE: *He's not worrying about his shoes.*

CRAZY GLUE: *Yes, he is, or we wouldn't be talking about it.*

My mind drifts back to the meeting in Dr. Gomez's office. Right before we left the room, after we had turned the lights back on, Haze asked Shelby if she could ever do it—leave her mother helpless and choking—and Shelby lost it. She burst into tears and said she didn't know. Even if her mother wanted her to do it, how could she?

CRAZY GLUE: *You're starting to think about your own mom, goob. Careful.*

AUNT BEE: *He needs to think about her. It's not healthy pushing her memory away.*

I stop as usual just across the street from my house and as usual I stare up at it. The windows look dark and the house vacant. I shiver and remember when we first moved in and the house seemed gigantic to me. Back then, there were only small cracks in the ceilings and no holes in the roof. We could fill the cupboards with food.

CRAZY GLUE: *Yeah, yeah, and you had plenty of heat, and cable, and the phone worked—don't go there.*

I wait for a car to pass, then cross the street, climb the steps, and pause at the door.

LAUGH TRACK: *As usual. (Laughter).*

FBG WITH A MUSTACHE: *Now he will conjure up some sweet memory from the past that will remind him of his dad in the good old days.*

LAUGH TRACK: *As usual!*

AUNT BEE: *It's important for him to remember something nice about his father before he goes inside.*

Remember that Christmas when the chimney guys were fixing the flue in our chimney in the old house, and Dad got the idea on Christmas Eve to dress as Santa and climb into the chimney and have Mom call me outside to see him?

AUNT BEE: *He knew you were starting to doubt the whole Santa Claus myth. He just wanted you to believe. There you were* standing out in the cold staring up at your father all dressed up like Santa.

CRAZY GLUE (ACTING AS JASON): *"Look, Mom—it really is Santa!"*

FBG WITH A MUSTACHE (ACTING AS DAD): *"Ho! Ho! Ho! I'm Santa Claus. Jason, have you been a good boy this year?"*

CRAZY GLUE (AS JASON): *"I guess so. Sometimes, right, Mom?"*

FBG WITH A MUSTACHE (AS DAD): *"Well, since you've sometimes been a good boy, I've brought you lots of pr—pr—Lara? I think I'm stuck. Uh! Ah! I am. I'm stuck here! I—can't—get—out!"*

CRAZY GLUE: *Yeah, he got stuck in the chimney! He got so totally stuck! He had so many pillows stuffed in his costume, they were coming out through the neck hole.*

LAUGH TRACK: *(Laughter).*

All those police and firefighters and reporters came, and it took forever to get him out because they couldn't figure out what he was caught on.

FBG WITH A MUSTACHE: *It was his hiking boots. He was wearing those monster hiking boots—remember?*

CRAZY GLUE: *Yeah, and the whole time he was stuck, he was holding on to that big sack he'd filled with clothes and books. He was stuck for hours, but he still held that sack over his shoulder.*

LAUGH TRACK: *(Laughter).*

SEXY LADY: *That photo of Santa in the chimney went all over the country—Reader's Digest ran it, People magazine, even Time. Your dad was famous.*

I loved him for doing that—dressing like Santa and all.

MY SUBCONSCIOUS: *Ah-hem. I hate to interrupt this trip down memory lane, but doesn't anyone else smell fire?*

ALL: *Shit!*

I burst into the house and decide the smell is coming from the kitchen. "Dad!" I run through the living room and dining room and call again. "Dad!"

I arrive at the kitchen and see a pot on the stove glowing red at its base. I grab a potholder and sweep the pot into the sink and turn on the faucet. It sizzles and hisses, and steam rises, blinding me for a second. I jump away from the sink and turn off the stove.

"Dad!"

There's an empty can of soup on the counter and, stuck to the burner, bits of what must have been chicken and rice burned almost to ashes. I shut off the faucet, then turn around and notice a newspaper spread out on the kitchen table. "Jeez, you didn't steal the neighbor's paper again. Dad!" I grab the paper and wad it as best as I can, then shove it into the wastebasket under the sink.

CRAZY GLUE: *Way to hide the evidence, goob. That's the first place the police will check.*

FBG WITH A MUSTACHE: *No one calls the police over a stolen newspaper or two.*

CRAZY GLUE: *Or three, or five, or seven.*

AUNT BEE: *I'm worried. Why isn't your father answering you?*

LAUGH TRACK: *Uh-oh!*

I open the back door and check outside. "Dad!" I call. Our backyard isn't big—just a little lawn, a few dogwoods, a sycamore, and a garden bed where my mom used to grow all her varieties of onions.

CRAZY GLUE: *All her heart-healthy onions. How ironic. A fat lot of good they did her.*

I don't see my dad anywhere.

I slam the door and check down in the basement, where my mother kept her darkroom. Then I hurry upstairs and go through all the rooms. I check under the beds. Back when my grandmother died, members of the Greek Orthodox Church came calling. They brought casseroles and cakes, and my dad hid under his bed until everyone left. He hates crowds.

I see the helmet I hid from Dad still pushed under my bed, but nothing else. There's nothing under my parents' bed, either, but I notice a large box sitting on top. It's Dad's memories box from Greece. I glance inside as if I think he might be hiding in there; then I hurry out of the room. I keep calling him, but there's no answer.

My hands shake when I grip the banister on my way downstairs and my legs threaten to buckle beneath me. I don't know what to do. Where can he be? I go through the house again, calling everywhere.

AUNT BEE: *Everything will be all right. Calm down. Don't panic.*

FBG WITH A MUSTACHE: *But this is bad. He's left the house. He could be anywhere. Anything could have happened to him.*

CRAZY GLUE: *I don't have a good feeling about this.*

What should I do? If I call the police and they find him, they'll put him away, but if I don't call them and I don't find Dad, then what?

FBG WITH A MUSTACHE: *Go, son. Go look for him!*

I leave my backpack in the hall and run out into the street calling for my dad. I go into town, where the sidewalks are deserted because of the weather. The lights in the shops that line the streets look warm and inviting. Maybe Dad went looking for a warm place to spend the day and was drawn by these lights. I go into every store, down every aisle—no Dad. Nobody's seen him.

I stand at the top of the street facing the river. From here the sky and river look like one great big charcoal fog. My jeans are soaked from the thighs down, and I can feel the cold burn my legs. Ice water has seeped into the crack in my shoe and soaked my sock. I want to go home and change into dry clothes.

AUNT BEE: *Go on home. Maybe he's there now.*

CRAZY GLUE: *He could be anywhere. He might never be found.*

I head down toward the river and slip on a sheet of black ice. Landing on my back, I lie in the road with my arm over my face.

CRAZY GLUE: *This can't end well. Get up!*

FBG WITH A MUSTACHE: *You have to do something about your dad. Every day is some new disaster.*

Yeah? Like what?

SEXY LADY: *Is this your life for the rest of your life? This isn't hot, Jase.*

I love my dad. If you love someone, you stand by him, forever, no matter what.

FBG WITH A MUSTACHE: *Is it really love?*

Mom could always handle it. Why can't I? Was it always this hard?

AUNT BEE: *You're not your mother. You need help. You can't do this alone anymore.*

CRAZY GLUE: *If you don't get up, the rest of your life might only be a few seconds longer. A car's coming, goob. Get up!*

I scramble to my feet and a car horn honks at me. I wave and try to smile.

The guy in the car rolls down his window. "You okay?"

"Yeah, watch out for the ice there."

The guy nods. "Crappy weather, huh?" Then he rolls up his window, not waiting for my answer.

I give it to him anyway. "Yeah, and a crappy day, too—a crappy, crappy day."

CHAPTER EIGHT

I DECIDE to turn around and go back into town to the phone booth in the alley at the top of the hill. I check the change in my pocket.

FBG WITH A MUSTACHE: *If you had a working cell phone, you could keep track of your dad better and maybe this sort of thing wouldn't happen.*

Mind telling me something useful?

FBG WITH A MUSTACHE: *I'm just saying what's on your mind.*

I slip a coin in the slot and get the numbers for the local hospital and clinic, thinking that maybe Dad's mouth was giving him trouble again, so he rode the city bus out to one of them. I'm happy to hear there's no George Papadopoulos registered at either place. I hang up and stare at the phone for several minutes.

CRAZY GLUE: *If you're waiting for it to start talking to you on its own, you're in for a long wait.*

AUNT BEE: *Go ahead. Call him. Call Pete. That's who you want, isn't it? It's the right thing to do. He's okay. He's got a car. He can help.*

I grab the receiver, call Information, and get Pete's

number. Then I count out my change again. My hands are shaking and stiff with cold.

I hesitate. I don't know if I can do this. He'll know. I'll have to tell him about Dad.

FBG WITH A MUSTACHE: *Look at it this way. There might be a whole lot of people out there right now who are finding out about your dad. Better you find him and find him fast.*

CRAZY GLUE: *Yeah, come on already. Pete's father's a drug addict. Haze's folks are reenacting the Civil War, Shelby's thinking about assisted suicide, and you're worried what Pete's going to think about your crazy father? Get on with it, goob.*

I put another coin in the slot and dial Pete's number. He answers on the second ring.

I'm surprised for some reason to hear his voice. It sounds different on the phone, kind of thick. He says hello, and I just stand with my mouth hanging open.

CRAZY GLUE: *Say something already, goob. He's said hello twice already.*

"Uh, hello—uh—Pete? It's—it's Jason, uh—yeah, and I'm—I'm in trouble. I need your help."

"Pope-a-Dope? What's happened? Where are you?"

"It's my dad—he's missing. I can't find him anywhere." My voice cracks. It feels like a wadded sock is stuck in my throat. I squeeze my eyes shut. "And he—he's got mental problems. He's a little—mentally ill." There, I've said it. For the first time ever. I feel sick. I'm dizzy. I've betrayed my dad—and my mom.

FBG WITH A MUSTACHE: *She may have told you never to tell anyone, but these are extenuating circumstances.*

I hold on to the metal shelf below the phone.

AUNT BEE: *Steady. Steady. Everything's okay.*

"Oh man, have you called the hospital?"

"Yeah. Yeah, I've called around. He could be anywhere. I don't have a car and I thought that maybe . . ."

"You're in the old section by the warehouse galleries, right?"

"Right, number four-oh-nine River Road."

"Be there in about twenty minutes."

"Thanks, Pete." I try to swallow the sock in my throat. It hurts too much. "Be careful; the roads are really slick," I say, but he's already hung up.

I stand there a moment, stunned, but then I think of Dad and I hurry back home, stopping on my way at our neighbors' houses. Only one person has come home from work, so far, and she says it's been weeks since she's seen my dad—or her newspaper.

LAUGH TRACK: *Uh-oh!*

I run home and head upstairs to get into a dry pair of jeans and a dry flannel shirt and wool sweater. I notice Dad's coat missing on the rack at the bottom of our stairs. At least wherever he is, he's got his coat.

I wait in the living room by the windows so I can see Pete coming down the road. I want to meet him outside so he doesn't come in and find out how we've been living.

"My dad has mental problems." I say this out loud just the way I said it to Pete. I listen to the sound of it.

CRAZY GLUE: *You did that real good, goob. It sounds just as natural as saying your dad has a blue car or he's got a pocket watch.*

Pete's orange VW Beetle pulls up outside. I hustle out the door and wave before he has a chance to step out of his car. He leans over and unlocks the door for me on the passenger side, and I get in.

"Thanks for coming, Pete." I notice a crystal hanging from the rearview mirror. The car, an old seventies model, smells like a garage—heavy on the gasoline.

"No problem." He smiles. "I've just got to be back by seven. We're doing that intervention for my dad tonight."

I shake my head. "I shouldn't have called you out here. I'm sorry. I just didn't know who else to call."

"Really, it's no sweat. This will take my mind off my own family's mess for a while." He snickers. "Fathers, huh?"

CRAZY GLUE: *"Snickers"? Did you just say "snickers"?*

"Yeah." I nod. "Fathers."

He pulls out into the street. "So, where should we look first?"

I shake my head. "He could be almost anywhere. I've gone into all the shops, but I thought we could maybe ride down all the back roads along here and see if we can see him, and then go over to the park. He and my mom used to like to go walking there."

71

"Good, okay." Pete speeds up and shifts into third gear.

"So, what's your father been into lately? Maybe that would give us a clue."

CRAZY GLUE: *Being nuts!*

"Mythology, I guess. I mean, my dad and I are both into Greek mythology, only now he's—he's kind of living in it full-time." I grip the door handle. I can't believe I'm telling him this.

AUNT BEE: *Go ahead, dear. It's all right.*

Pete looks at me as if he doesn't understand, so I push myself to explain some more.

CRAZY GLUE: *Yeah, you don't want him to think you're nuts, do you?*

"So it's like every morning when I leave for school, he thinks I'm Jason, of *Jason and the Argonauts*, off to capture the Golden Fleece, but in the afternoon he thinks I'm Apollo—that's my middle name—and I'm just home from the war. He thinks the Furies, or uh, the goddesses of the underworld, blame him for my mom's death."

"Uh-huh. Wow. For real?" Pete nods to show he's listening to me and scowls as he studies the road ahead. The sleet has turned to rain and the cars in the streets are churning up dirty water and mist with their tires, making it hard to see. He drives with one hand on the steering wheel and one on the stick shift, and leans his shoulder against his door. I look left and right for my dad.

"So, has he always been ill? I mean, ever since you can remember, or—?"

"No! Oh no. He's been healthy lots of times— well, I mean, pretty healthy—I mean, he's mostly healthy—most of the time. It's no big deal."

CRAZY GLUE: *Or—uh, sorta-kinda.*

"I've always just been used to the way he is. My mom—she was—she was always there keeping things— or uh—*him* under control. He's nervous around people and loud noises and stuff, so that's why I'm surprised he's disappeared. He never leaves the house."

"Yeah, I see," Pete says, only I'm worried he doesn't. I'm worried he doesn't really get how great Dad is.

"He's great. He's a great father. I mean—he—I— I don't want you to get the wrong idea."

CRAZY GLUE: *Watch it. Don't oversell it, goob.*

"No, I don't," Pete says. He shakes his head; then he turns onto one of the cobblestone roads and we bump along. I keep a watch out for Dad.

"Me and my dad, we like to canoe on the canal, and this one time—it's so funny—this one time we found this torpedo, out in the woods where we had stopped to eat our sandwiches. I mean, what was it do- ing there?"

"No kidding?" Pete smiles at me, his brows raised.

"Yeah, and my dad wants to bring it home to show

my mother, so we set it long ways across the canoe, right in the center. It doesn't sink the canoe, just kind of lowers it, so we figure we're safe. Then Dad says for me to climb in the front. He climbs in the back at the same time, and the whole thing sinks. I know we looked ridiculous, sitting there with the torpedo between us going under. And that water was so freakin' cold! I thought we were going to die of hypothermia before we got home."

CRAZY GLUE (ACTING AS JASON): *"Hey, Dad, water's coming in over the sides."*

FBG WITH A MUSTACHE (ACTING AS DAD): *"It's just a bit of water. It'll level off before we sink. We'll just be paddling a little lower, eh? We've got to expect that."*

CRAZY GLUE (AS JASON): *"I don't think so. It's really coming in now. Shouldn't we start bailing or something?"*

FBG WITH A MUSTACHE (AS DAD): *"It'll be okay."*

CRAZY GLUE (AS JASON): *"Dad?"*

FBG WITH A MUSTACHE (AS DAD): *"Well, don't just sit there, son. Start swimming!"*

I watch for Pete's reaction to my story. He nods and chuckles, so I feel what I've said is okay.

"But we got the torpedo. We brought that baby home. It's still in our basement."

Pete glances at me. "Really? How?"

"We flipped the canoe and got out all the water. Then we laid the oars inside under the seats and the torpedo on top of the seats. Then we dragged it by a rope while we walked alongside it on a dirt path. We had a car back then, so when we got to the first boat-house, we called my mom and she picked us up."

CRAZY GLUE: *Yeah, you lost that car when your dad tried to see if it could float in the Potomac.*

"Cool, I'd like to see it sometime."

"Yeah, sure, cool."

CRAZY GLUE: *Oh perfect, now look what you've done. No way can you let him inside your house!*

"So, yeah, my dad's like my best friend. He's always just been my—my best friend."

"Well, you don't hear that too often," Pete says. "I hope we find him."

"Yeah, me too."

CRAZY GLUE: *Me three.*

I keep my head turned away from Pete and stare out my window. My face feels hot and my ears are burning. That sock is still stuck in my throat. Something doesn't feel right about my story, but I don't know what.

CHAPTER NINE

PETE AND I drive all over town looking for Dad, but we don't find him. By the time we pull up to my house again, the rain and sleet have stopped, but the wind has picked up and the temperature seems to be dropping fast.

"I hope wherever your father is, he's indoors," Pete says, rubbing his hands together.

I climb out of the car and turn around to face him. "Yeah, me too." I look behind me at my house. The lights are all off, but that doesn't mean anything. Dad could still be in there.

"I once found my dad passed out on top of a pile of snow in the High Street parking lot," Pete says. "You know how they shovel it all off to the sides? His toes were frost-bitten, but he didn't care." Pete lifts his hand in the air as though he's tossing a hat. Then he leans forward and peers up at my windows.

"I'll wait here to see if your dad's there. If he isn't, I'm calling Haze and Shelby."

"No. Really, that's okay," I say, waving my hand, brushing the idea away. "Really."

"Listen, you shouldn't be alone tonight. Believe me, I've been there—waiting for my dad. If it weren't for my mother and my brothers, I don't know, man—it's tough."

"Really, I'm okay," I say, sticking out my chin, trying to look confident. "Thanks again for coming, and good luck with your intervention tonight. I hope it works."

"It has to, or my dad's out on his ass. My mom changed all the locks."

"Well, good luck, then." I close the door and run up the steps of my house. I go inside and switch on the lights in the hallway and living room, calling to my dad as I go. The house feels too empty, too silent, for Dad to be here. I hate going back out to let Pete know this. I don't want Shelby or Haze coming over. I feel overexposed as it is.

SEXY LADY: *Ooh! Overexposed. Nothing wrong with that.*

I look out the window and see his VW idling there.

I go out onto the stoop and shrug to indicate that Dad isn't home. Then I smile and wave him on as if it's no big deal.

CRAZY GLUE: *Yeah, no big deal. That's why your insides feel like a thousand birds clamoring to get out.*

I watch Pete pull away, then go back into the house. I search each room again, just to give myself something to do, and finally end up in the doorway of my parents' bedroom. I just stand there for a couple of minutes. I don't like coming into their bedroom anymore. It reminds me too much of my mom with the sheer curtains with daisies embroidered on them, Mom's favorite flowers, and the chest of drawers that still holds her fancy perfume bottles and makeup and a hand-carved jewelry box. The quilt she made by hand with the date of my parents' wedding stitched into the fabric still lies across the bed, and her clothes still hang in the closet.

AUNT BEE: *It's as if you think she's coming back.*

The only time I come into this room is to clean and gather the laundry or to put laundry away.

CRAZY GLUE: *Yeah, and it's like the hundred-yard dash the way you rush in and out of here.*

I step into the room and go over to the chest of drawers. I pick up the red nail polish Dad used to paint his wound on his chest. I shake it up and stare at the bright red color a few seconds. Then I set it down and open a bottle of perfume and take a whiff.

FBG WITH A MUSTACHE: *Odors evoke memories more strongly than almost anything. Bad idea, son.*

I jam the top back in the bottle and pick up my mom's eyeliner.

AUNT BEE: *I think Haze paints those small tears on his face with eyeliner.*

CRAZY GLUE: *Don't prisoners tattoo tears on their face to show they've murdered someone?*

FBG WITH A MUSTACHE: *Haze is just trying to express outwardly what he's feeling inside.*

SEXY LADY: *Go on. Express yourself, Jason.*

I unscrew the cap of the eyeliner and pull the little paintbrush out. I stare at it for a few seconds, and a little blob of black starts to build on the tip. I check myself out in the mirror.

CRAZY GLUE: *It's been a long time since you've taken a look at that face.*

SEXY LADY: *What are you so afraid of? You're hot, a little hungry-looking, though, and anxious—your eyes give you away. You need to practice looking more relaxed, and your hair is shaggy and long, but still hot. Good strong cheekbones.*

FBG WITH A MUSTACHE: *I know what he's afraid of . . .*

Everybody, be quiet!

I lean in and place the tip of the brush at the top of my forehead, about an inch to the right of center. Carefully, with one long stroke, I paint a jagged line moving from the top of my head, along the right side of my nose, toward the middle of my lips, and all the way down to my chin. I study the line and it doesn't look quite right. I start again, this time working left of center. I draw another jagged line, down past the left side of my nose, and slowly connect it with the first line at my lips. I look at the results.

CRAZY GLUE: *Yikes, it looks like you've ripped your skull open!*

SEXY LADY: *That's not hot.*

AUNT BEE: *Oh dear, I can't look. Something might spill out. Something terrible. Don't look! Don't look!*

I grab my mom's hairbrush and strike the mirror. Jagged lines shoot out from the wound. The whole mirror splinters but doesn't crumble. My face looks fractured into a million pieces.

LAUGH TRACK: *Gasp!*

CRAZY GLUE: *What'd you do that for?*

FBG WITH A MUSTACHE: *I know . . .*

Shut up, everyone. Just shut up!

I reach for the light switch and turn out the light. I stand in the dark for several minutes, scared out of my wits.

I hear our doorbell. "Dad?"

I race downstairs and fling open the front door. It's Shelby.

"Hey—oh, whoa, what's that? Eew!" She presses a cold finger against my forehead and pushes my head back.

CRAZY GLUE: *Yeah, that's what we want to know.*

I have no answer, so I say, "I thought you were my dad." I wipe my hand over my face. Nothing comes off.

She shrugs. "Sorry, it's just me. Can I come in?"

CRAZY GLUE: *No way!*

"Oh listen, yeah, this is really nice of you, but you didn't have to come over. You don't have to stay here with me. I'm doing fine." I try to block the doorway by standing with my legs spread apart and my right hand on the door frame.

Shelby eyes my forehead. "Yeah, uh-huh, I can see that you're real fine." She barrels into my arm and pushes her way in.

CRAZY GLUE: *She's heading for the living room. Tackle her before she gets any farther. You don't want her seeing the house like this.*

AUNT BEE: *Don't you dare!*

"Look, Jason—no need to put up a front for me," she says over her shoulder. "It's no fun facing this stuff alone." She turns around and smiles, then notices the room. "Wow, you've got a lot of books! What is this, some kind of used bookstore you're running?"

CRAZY GLUE: *Say yes. Lie, goob, lie! Maybe owning so many books is crazy.*

I can't come up with a good lie, so I tell the truth. I walk into the living room and set my hands on one of the many shelves of books. "My dad's a writer and we all love to read, or loved to, or . . . uh . . ."

CRAZY GLUE: *Told you. You should have lied. Just don't let her upstairs.*

Shelby stares at the ceiling. "Wow, the ceilings are really high in this place. What are they, like twelve feet?" She looks at me a second, but before I can answer, she's marching toward the dining room, which is looking kind of empty without the table and chairs and side table, which I sold because we needed the money.

CRAZY GLUE: *Along with his bike and the canoe and . . .*

"Really, Shelby, you don't have to stay here. I mean, what are you going to do, stay the night?"

LAUGH TRACK: *(Laughter).*

She turns around to look at me. "Well, yeah. You don't want me going back out in the cold again, do you? It's freezing out there—and the roads are really icing up."

CRAZY GLUE: *(In a singsong voice) You're gonna wet the bed.*

LAUGH TRACK: *Uh-oh!*

It's only now that I notice Shelby is wearing a bike helmet.

CRAZY GLUE: *About time.*

"You mean you biked over here?" I run to the living room windows and look out to the street. Her bike is locked to the speed limit sign.

Shelby follows me. "Well, yeah, how else was I going to get here? I live way over on Vinton Street, near the school, and my dad's out of town, as usual, and my mom can't drive—duh, and my sister's away at college, and the nurse has to stay with my mom, so . . ." Shelby unfastens her helmet, takes it off, and shakes her hair out. It looks the color of cinnamon in the living room lights. It falls onto her shoulders in a mass of frizzy curls.

SEXY LADY: *What an obvious move. She's trying to come on to you.*

Shelby joins me at the window.

"You could have killed yourself," I say. "It's really slippery out there."

"Tell me about it."

I look at her and she smiles, lighting up her whole face.

I smile back at her, pleased that she's come out in miserable weather just to keep me company. We stand for a few seconds looking at each other. I notice that her eyes and even her freckles are the same color as her hair. She's the color of cinnamon all over.

CRAZY GLUE: *(Singing) You're gonna wet the bed.*

I turn back to the window. "I can't believe you rode all the way over here."

"Right, so don't be sending me out there into the cold. Show me your kitchen; I'm hungry."

Shelby sets her helmet on a stack of books and scuttles toward the back of the house.

"So tell me what happened? You just came home and your father was gone?" she asks, still aiming for the kitchen while I struggle to get ahead of her and block the entrance. I know there's nothing to eat. I don't want Shelby going through our cupboards and finding that out.

I manage to squeeze past her just as she reaches the kitchen. She looks at me standing in front of her. "What are you doing?" She pushes her finger against my forehead again, and I remember the eyeliner. I know I look crazy.

CRAZY GLUE: *But you're not, right?*

"Jason, you almost knocked me down." Shelby pushes me aside and enters the kitchen.

I follow her. "Just—just would you wait a second? I haven't done any shopping lately, so all we have is—"

"Hey, I'm a whiz at making something tasty out of this and that. Just watch me." She goes toward the refrigerator, so I give up and just let the embarrassment happen.

"Nice kitch, by the way. I really like red walls."

AUNT BEE: *We have such a nice memory of you and your dad painting it while your mom was in her coma. We all hoped to surprise her when she got better and she came home, but . . .*

CRAZY GLUE: *Aunt Bee, stow it already.*

AUNT BEE: *I was just going to say, at least someone's appreciating it.*

The kitchen does look fresh, with its red walls and white cabinets and trim. We have a pine table in the center of the room with four chairs that my mom painted in different colors: red, yellow, aqua, and green. The room looks festive and warm.

Shelby opens the refrigerator to find . . .

CRAZY GLUE: *Exactly nothing.*

"I was going to get some milk and bread and eggs—really," I say.

She nods and closes the refrigerator, then removes her backpack. She digs into her pack and pulls out her cell phone. I see her texting somebody.

"Who are you talking to? What are you saying there?" I peer over her shoulder.

FBG WITH A MUSTACHE: *She's broadcasting your empty refrigerator to the whole school.*

CRAZY GLUE: *Busy fingers are already at work all over town text messaging: The Pope-a-Dope has no food!*

"I'm asking Haze to bring some goodies when he comes over later tonight," she says.

"He's coming, too?"

LAUGH TRACK: *Gulp!*

"Yeah, the more the merrier in cases like this, right?" She gives me a puzzled expression, as if to say, what's got you all bent out of shape?

CRAZY GLUE: *Nightmares, urine-soaked sheets, crazy dad—for starters.*

"In cases like what?" I ask.

CRAZY GLUE: *Careful—your paranoia is showing.*

"You know, in cases where we're going through a tough time," Shelby says. "We're here for you, Jason. That's what 'support group' means, right?" She picks up the burned-out pot in the sink.

I lunge for the pot and grab it out of her hands. "I burned my soup," I say loudly, feeling like a little kid the way I grabbed it away from her.

CRAZY GLUE: *Your face is burning.*

"Sorry!" she says. She moves over to the cabinets and opens the only one with food in it. A bag of dry lentils sits beside a box of Lipton tea bags and a carton of oatmeal.

"Tea!" she says. "That's just what I need. Let's have some tea, okay?"

CRAZY GLUE: *Do we have a choice?*

She's already got the box down and is squatting, searching the lower cabinets for a teakettle.

CRAZY GLUE: *The teakettle is so yesterday. Your dad burned that baby four burned-out pots ago.*

"We just use a pot. Here." I lean over and grab one out of the drying rack on the counter. "Use this," I say.

"Great, okay." Shelby stands and takes the pot. She runs cold water into it and sets it on the stove.

I watch her while she putters. She's buried in layers of fleece, which hide her curves and make her look like a fuzzy black and red snowball. I notice her running shoes—Nike, no socks.

AUNT BEE: *Remember when you had a nice pair of running shoes?*

"So don't you ever wear socks? Is that how you got your nickname?"

She turns around. "Yeah, haven't you noticed? My feet sweat like crazy. I don't know what's wrong with them. I remember when I was twelve, they really started to get bad. That's when my mother was first diagnosed with ALS, and I thought maybe the sweaty feet were some kind of sign I was getting ALS, too."

CRAZY GLUE: *Careful. Your bird heart is getting jumpy.*

AUNT BEE: *Oh dear.*

What? What did she just say?

FBG WITH A MUSTACHE: *I know, but it's better that you don't . . .*

Shelby pulls the aqua chair, *my* chair, out from the table and sits down. I choose the green one across from her. "What is ALS, anyway?" I ask. I notice I'm sweating even though the room is cold. I feel the eyeliner starting to run.

"Amyotrophic lateral sclerosis," she says. She hands me a napkin from the Popsicle-stick napkin holder I made in third grade. "Here, wipe that off, why don't you."

I grab the napkin and go to the sink and wash it all off with dishwashing detergent. While I scrub, Shelby talks.

"ALS is like a wasting-away disease. People usually call it Lou Gehrig's disease because he was one of the first famous people to get it."

"Sounds scary," I say.

"My mom says it's like getting buried alive. So yeah, it's scary."

LAUGH TRACK: *Uh-oh! (Nervous laughter).*

I freeze.

AUNT BEE: *Buried alive. Oh dear, bad choice of words. We know what that's like.*

FBG WITH A MUSTACHE: *Oh, come on. Pull yourself together! Enough self-pity already. Buck up, son.*

I dry my face on a dishtowel and take my time with it. Then I take a deep breath and rejoin Shelby at the table. We both just sit there a minute, thinking, and then Shelby looks straight into my eyes. "I would never do it," she says, her voice a whisper.

I know she's talking about this afternoon when she confessed that her mother had wanted Shelby to leave her to die.

I reach for her hand across the table. "Yeah, I know," I say. I realize what I've just done and pull my hand away.

Shelby blinks back her tears. "I'd never do it on purpose. This sounds awful, especially with your father missing and all, but sometimes I just wish I'd come home and the nurse would tell me my mother had passed away while I was at school." She leans back, letting both hands drop into her lap. "Then other times I think I don't know what I'll do if she passes and I'm not there holding her hand. I hate going to school knowing that any minute she could die and I wouldn't be there." She twists up her mouth as if trying to keep from crying.

"Exactly," I say. "I know exactly how you feel." The water is boiling and I stand up to make the tea for us, glad to have my back to her, what with what I'm about to confess.

CRAZY GLUE: *You're so going to regret this.*

AUNT BEE: *Go ahead. Take a chance.*

SEXY LADY: *Ah, young love. We'll confide anything in the heat of passion.*

FBG WITH A MUSTACHE: *This isn't passion; it's fear. He's trying to shed some fear.*

Would you all let me speak already?

"My dad—he's—he's kind of a little crazy right now, and I think—I mean, I'm sure he'll get better again, but right now, it's like half the time I can't wait for school to end so I can run home and make sure he's all right, that everything's all right. But then—but then, I dread it, too. I don't want to go home. If it weren't for school and the break I get from dealing with my dad, I think I'd go crazy. Ha, ha, ha."

CRAZY GLUE: *You're so lame.*

"Yeah, that's it," Shelby says. "I know exactly what you're talking about."

I bring the two mugs of tea over and set them on the table. I feel relieved that she's taken what I told her so casually.

CRAZY GLUE: *Pretty cool.*

"Thanks," Shelby says, drawing her mug closer. She dunks her tea bag in and out of the hot water, then leans forward and takes a deep breath. "Ah, tea," she says, smiling and closing her eyes.

She looks as though I've just handed her the most wonderful meal in the world, the way she smiles. She looks like an angel, an angel with freckles. I smile back, and I realize I'm glad she's here.

CHAPTER TEN

SHELBY AND I are in the middle of an argument. It started in my dad's study. I took her there to show her the books my dad wrote.

Shelby looks at the Cretan scenery on the covers, both photos my mom took, and asks, "Have you ever been to Greece? It looks beautiful."

"Yeah. Yeah, I used to want to live there when I grew up. It's cool the way the mountains rise straight up out of the sea. My dad told me about this runner during World War Two who ran up and down and all over those mountains delivering messages between the Greeks hiding out in caves and stuff. He's a real live hero there. I—I'd like to do that someday. Live and run in the mountains, I mean, and take pictures, too, like my mom used to. She—she was a photographer. Now I have her camera and stuff."

Shelby looks around. "There aren't any pictures on your walls anywhere. That's the first thing I noticed when I came in the house."

"Oh yeah, well, my dad's kind of funny about stuff on the walls."

CRAZY GLUE: *Funny? Don't you mean crazy? He thinks the pictures are talking to him.*

Shelby sets my dad's books down, then looks into my eyes and says in that too-honest way of hers, "You know you're going to have to put your father in a mental hospital, don't you? I mean, yanking his tooth out like that, almost electrocuting himself, no food in this *freezing* house—he needs help. You both need help."

CRAZY GLUE: *I warned you, you were talking too much.*

LAUGH TRACK: *We all warned you.*

FBG WITH A MUSTACHE: *But you ignored us. Told us to shut up.*

SEXY LADY: *You fell for her feminine wiles and the intimacy of the moment and made a full confession.*

AUNT BEE: *Oh dear.*

CRAZY GLUE: *Stupid! Stupid! Stupid!*

"Jason, are you listening to me? He needs to be in a hosp—"

"No way! I can't do that to my dad. You don't know. You don't understand. Anyway, we have no money. He'd have to go to a state institution. Do you know what they're like?"

"No, do you?"

"Last time, they tied him down. They locked him up. No way! And what do you mean, *I* need help? *I'm* not crazy, if that's what you're thinking. Just because of a little eyeliner . . ."

"And you should call the police," Shelby says, as

if she hasn't heard a thing I've said. "What if he's out there somewhere in this cold, freezing to death? The police could be looking for him right now. They might have found him by now. They could get dogs out looking . . ."

"Stop! Just stop it, will you?" I storm out of the room with my hands over my ears, just like a kid—just like Dad blocking out the Furies. A moment later I spin around and glare at her. "If they did find him, what would they do to him? Put him away? No! I'm not calling them."

Shelby sets her hands on her hips. "What exactly are you so afraid of? So, you'd rather find him frozen to death somewhere than have the police find him and discover that maybe, just maybe, he's a little nuts?" She widens her eyes and shakes her head.

"Just shut up, Shelby!" I shout. "I don't want to hear it."

The doorbell rings.

AUNT BEE: *Oh, thank goodness.*

I go to the door and fling it open, hoping against hope to see my dad, but it's Haze, standing on the stoop with a grocery bag in his arms.

"Whoa, man, I could hear you guys yelling all the way down the block."

"Did you drive here?" I ask, not even bothering to say hello.

"Yeah, what do ya think? I had to park down the street a ways, though."

"Good," I say. "Let's go." I brush past him and trot down the steps, not caring if they're slippery and I fall and break my neck.

"Okay," Haze says, turning around and following me. "But where are we going, dude?"

"To look for his father," Shelby says. I turn and see her in the doorway. She smiles at me and shrugs.

"Right." Haze nods.

"Come on—close the door and let's go," I say, trying my best to return the smile.

Haze has to be the worst driver in the world. He owns a 1967 eight-passenger cargo van with a major muffler problem. He tears up the roads like he's driving a Porsche. Every time I tell him to slow down because I want to check someone out, he slams on the brakes and we skid like a hundred feet before stopping. Then he goes slowly for a while but gradually picks up speed again, getting right on the tail of any car in front of us until they move out of his way.

CRAZY GLUE: *Dude doesn't know the meaning of the words "slow down." We're gonna get killed in this tin can of his.*

Shelby is sitting in the one back seat that has a seat belt and is rummaging through the sack of food Haze brought with him. She calls out, "Anyone want some Doritos?"

"Most definitely," Haze says. She tosses the bag up to the front. I catch it, then open and hand it to Haze. He takes a few and hands it back to me. "Here, take some."

"No, thanks. I'm not hungry."

CRAZY GLUE: *The way he's driving, you'd be tossing them right back up, anyway.*

"Dude, you gotta eat. You'll feel better. I bet you haven't eaten since that stale burger you had at lunch today, and it's almost seven thirty, so eat, eat!"

I take a chip just to shut him up, but it tastes so good, I take another one and then another. By the time we reach downtown Washington, D.C., I've finished the bag along with some Twizzlers and a can of Pepsi.

CRAZY GLUE: *That's it, swallow that burp down, goob. There's a lady in the car.*

I haven't had much in the way of junk food in forever. It tastes like heaven.

My parents used to love to visit the Smithsonian, so even though it's closed, we drive around the area just in case Dad's there. Then we drive over to Georgetown, where he and my mom first lived as newlyweds. They rented the basement of a townhouse near Dumbarton Oaks Park, so we drive over there to look and then to the Georgetown University campus, where my parents first met and went to school. I don't know where to go after that, so we just wander the streets, stopping and speeding up, stopping and speeding up in Haze's old van while Haze tells us about his father's latest trick of spray-painting the word "whore" on the front of their brick house.

"It's in big black letters, right? A story and a half high, at least—spray-painted right on the front of our house. Whore! So my sister calls my dad on his cell, and she's screaming at him for calling her a whore, because she lives there, too, and so maybe he meant to call her a whore and not my mother, or maybe he meant it for the both of them. And my dad's trying to explain that it was just meant for my mother, like that makes it okay. And he's a lawyer!" He shakes his head. "What an asshole. Anyway, who's gonna know who it was meant for? Right? Sooo, the school bus stops in front of our house and like, man, everybody's howling when they see the house, and when my sister gets on, they start calling her a whore. She's in the fifth grade. She doesn't need that shit, man."

"Yeah, for sure," I say, remembering my fifth grade.

CRAZY GLUE: *Jason got a swirlie! Jason got a swirlie!*

It's ten o'clock and Haze is almost out of gas, so we head back to my house. Haze pulls into the same spot he had parked in before and turns off the engine. The whole van shakes and rattles and coughs so much, we're sure it's going to explode. The three of us leap out of the car and make a slippery run for my house. It's freezing out, so we run huddled together.

As we draw closer to the house, I notice my dad's bedroom light is on and I stop and just stand there, staring, not believing my eyes.

"What? What is it?" Shelby asks. She and Haze have halted beside me.

"My—my dad's light." I point to the front room upstairs.

"He's home?" Shelby asks.

"I—I think, maybe."

CRAZY GLUE: *Well, don't just stand there getting all choked up. Move, goob. Move.*

I can't bear to be wrong. What if he's not there?

Haze slaps my back. "Come on, dude—let's go find out if he's in there."

Shelby grabs my arm and pulls me forward, and the three of us run down the street and into the house. I call out to my dad as soon as we cross the threshold. "Dad? Dad, are you here? Where are you?"

I hear violin music coming from upstairs. It stops, and then I hear a voice: "Is that Apollo home from the war? What news have you from the front?"

The music starts up again, and I feel something in my chest give way, as if my heart, my bird heart, so pumped up with fear and dread, has at last collapsed back to its normal size. My dad has come home.

CHAPTER ELEVEN

I TACKLE THE STAIRS two at a time with Haze and Shelby right behind me.

AUNT BEE: *Ah, what a relief.*

FBG WITH A MUSTACHE: *Buck up, son. He's all right. Everything's back under control.*

I run to my dad's room and there he is. He's standing in front of the full-length mirror built into his closet door, wearing a wool scarf tied around his head with bits of aluminum foil peeking out from his ears. He's in Greek costume, wearing a dark blue shirt and embroidered vest, red sash, a pair of funny-looking, baggy black pants, and tall boots that come up to his knees. I know this outfit came from his Greek memories box. He looks noble in it, and very Greek with his beard and olive complexion. He's holding a violin, which must have come from the box as well, and he's playing it. We used to have, hanging on our walls, pictures of Dad playing the violin. He even won a major competition once, but that was before he got sick. That was before I was even born. This is the first time I've ever heard him play, and I'm surprised because he sounds pretty good—actually, really good. He's staring at himself, as though he's trying to recognize the person he sees in the mirror. As I rush toward him to give him a hug, I catch sight of the mirror over the chest of drawers still in a million splinters.

CRAZY GLUE: *Did you think they'd magically glue themselves back together?*

AUNT BEE: *Oh dear, you're so ashamed.*

FBG WITH A MUSTACHE: *He's frightened by it.*

"Dad!" I give him a hug and squeeze my eyes shut to keep from crying. "Jeez, where have you been? I've been looking everywhere for you."

AUNT BEE: *Now, don't be angry with him.*

SEXY LADY: *Of course he's not angry. He's a good son.*

Dad holds the violin above his head while I hug him. I let go and he starts to tuck the violin back under his chin, when he notices Shelby and Haze, and in a flash he drops to the floor behind the bed. He tugs on my pants leg. "Apollo, they're here. The Furies. Get down," he says in a loud whisper. He moans and begins his chant:

"Now by the altar,
Over the victim,
Ripe for the ritual,
Sing this enchantment:
A song without music,
A sword in the senses . . ."

"Whoa!" Haze says. "We can just wait down-stairs, dude."

I squat down. "No, Dad, it's okay. These are my— my—these are the Argonauts, here to help me capture the Golden Fleece. They're our friends."

Dad sets his violin and bow on the floor, then cov-ers his ears. His voice trembling and his face turning red, he continues:

"*A storm in the heart,*
And a fire in the brain;
A clamour of Furies
To paralyse reason . . ."

"Come on—let's go down," Shelby says.

"It's—it's Athena, here to help you," I say. "She's here to defend you against the Furies."

Thankfully, Dad stops chanting. He looks at me a second and I nod. His eyes are bloodshot, his nose is running and red, and his cheek is bruised and swollen on the side where he had pulled his tooth. He wipes his nose on the sleeve of his shirt and peeks over the top of the bed at Shelby and Haze, who are standing just inside the door of the room.

He picks up the violin and bow and slowly stands. I stand, too.

Shelby steps forward and I can see doubt in her eyes. She says hello. Then Haze says, "Yeah, hey, man," and steps into the room. "Cool violin. You sound real good." Haze coughs and shrugs, and I see him glancing at all the buckets and wastepaper baskets we have placed around the room to catch the water when it rains.

AUNT BEE: *It's all right. So what. Now they know the worst of it.*

FBG WITH A MUSTACHE: *Buck up, son.*

Dad hides behind me. I feel his breath on the back of my head.

Haze looks at the ceiling. He points at the missing plaster. "I could fix that for you if you wanted. I'm pretty good." He looks at me. "I work with my uncle's construction crew in the summers."

"Our whole roof leaks," I say. "If you fixed the ceiling, it would only leak through again." I reach back for Dad's hand. I know I need to comfort him, reassure him, so he doesn't get all worked up. His hand feels ice cold, but he's home and he's alive; that's all that matters.

"Well," Shelby says, her voice a little too loud, "I'd love to hear some more violin music. Mr. Papadopoulos, would you play something for us?"

CRAZY GLUE: *She thinks your dad's crazy and deaf.*

LAUGH TRACK: *(Laughter).*

Dad steps out from behind me, hugging the violin to his chest. "I found it. I thought I lost it, but I found it in the maze of quadraphonic sound." He turns around to face the mirror again, and tucks the instrument under his chin. He lifts the bow, hesitating for a minute, then plays his music, and he sounds so—so . . .

CRAZY GLUE: *Sane. The word is sane.*

AUNT BEE: *I forgot he could play the violin.*

SEXY LADY: *You should play, too, Jason. You'd be so hot.*

Looking at Shelby and Haze, I smile and shrug. They smile, too, but I catch Shelby checking out the broken mirror, and I know she's thinking my dad broke it. I know she's thinking he's so crazy.

CHAPTER TWELVE

I'M SURPRISED at how comfortable it turns out to be with Haze and Shelby and my dad. Maybe because they're used to dealing with difficult parents themselves, they aren't freaking, and Dad just seems calmer with the violin. He uses it like a shield. As long as he has it in his arms or on his lap, he's quiet; when he gets nervous about the Furies, he plays, and he feels better. Maybe the meds are starting to work, too. Maybe he really will be okay.

CRAZY GLUE: *And maybe you won't have a bad dream and maybe you won't wet the bed and maybe . . .*

LAUGH TRACK: *Shut up!*

CRAZY GLUE: *Are they allowed to say that? That's not in their script.*

Shelby and Haze offer to order Chinese take-out. I try to protest, but they insist.

CRAZY GLUE: *Yeah, we all notice how lame your protest is.*

AUNT BEE: *He's starving, poor boy.*

Okay, so I don't put up much of a fight. Who can resist? We have sweet and sour soup, fried rice, beef and broccoli, moo shu pork, Kung Pao chicken, and lots of egg rolls and oolong tea.

Dad eats so much, I'm sure he's going to get sick since he's unused to so much food, but except for a few burps he holds it all in.

It's almost midnight by the time we've finished eating, and even though I tell them they don't have to stay, Shelby and Haze insist on spending the night with us.

LAUGH TRACK: *Uh-oh!*

Haze, Dad, and I will sleep in Dad's king-size bed and Shelby will sleep in mine. I show Shelby my room.

She looks around. "All right! I like it. You sure like the color blue, don't you?" Before I can say anything she says, "Who took all the pictures in here? Your mom?"

I have black-and-white photographs of Greece on the walls all around the room. Most of them are of Crete, where my dad's family is from. I go over to the wall. "I did these. My mom mostly liked photographing faces." I point to one of the photos. "This cave here is supposedly where Zeus, the Greek god, was born. There's another cave where he's supposed to have been born, too, but I like this one because it's not all touristy the way the other one is. I love caves. I love black-and-white photos of stones, like stone walls and these rocky mountains, and the caves. Oh, and I love taking pictures of snow. It's all about light and shadows with black-and-white film and snow. It's really cool. I only use film. I don't do digital. My mom has—had a darkroom in our basement. I haven't been down there since . . ."

I turn from the pictures and see Shelby just staring at me. She has this look on her face that I don't understand.

SEXY LADY: *She thinks you're hot.*

I press my tongue to the roof of my mouth.

CRAZY GLUE: *Goob. You talk too much.*

"Well," Shelby says, "I love these! I didn't know you were an artist."

"Oh no—I'm not. I just . . ." I shrug.

"You're an artist, like me. No wonder you're so sensitive."

"I am?"

"Well, yeah," Shelby says in this voice that makes me wonder if she's annoyed with me. Maybe she doesn't like sensitive.

SEXY LADY: *Maybe she does.*

Haze comes to the door asking for more blankets and I leave, but I don't want to. I kind of wish I could stay the night there in my room, with Shelby.

CRAZY GLUE: *Aw, how sweet. Is it love or is it indigestion?*

LAUGH TRACK: *(Laughter).*

FBG WITH A MUSTACHE: *I just have one word to say: Pee!*

I try to stay awake all night. I'm lying between Haze and Dad, and I know if I fall asleep and have that suffocating/drowning dream, I'll wet the bed, and both Dad and Haze will get wet. What would Haze do, I wonder? How would I ever live it down? I'd have to run away. I imagine myself in Greece with Dad. Would it be easier to take care of him in a cave somewhere? My mind drifts to Shelby. I think of her lying in my bed beneath all the glow-in-the-dark stars my mom and dad and I stuck to the ceiling when I was younger. I had insisted they be accurate, just like a winter sky, with Orion, the mythological hunter, directly above my bed. I wonder if Shelby is staring at them now, thinking of me. Does she like me? Do I like her?

CRAZY GLUE: *Dumb question.*

I like how sure she is about everything. I can't imagine what that would feel like, to be so sure.

AUNT BEE: *You sound so sure in your Dear Mouse letters.*

FBG WITH A MUSTACHE: *He's faking it. It's all a sham.*

I return to thinking about Shelby and they're the last thoughts I have before I fall asleep. I guess I was too exhausted to pull an all-nighter. I'm unconscious until morning. I awaken to the smell of coffee and maybe bacon coming from below. For a moment I forget where I am and I think my mom's in the kitchen cooking breakfast the way she always used to do. I roll over and smile to myself. Then, when my leg kicks up against someone else's, I open my eyes and see Dad still asleep beside me, and everything comes back to me. The radio is playing softly on the chest of drawers and the violin is propped up against the chair facing him so that he could keep an eye on it through the night. When I see this and remember how Dad wouldn't go to bed until he had set the violin just so in the chair, I feel a deep sadness. Then I remember Haze and my fear of wetting the bed, and I freak. I spring away from the spot where I'm lying and feel around for any soaked patch.

"What are you doing, Pope-a-Dope?" The loud whisper comes from behind me.

I flip myself in the other direction and find Shelby staring at me from the doorway with one of my blankets wrapped around her shoulders. Her hair appears to have doubled in thickness overnight. It sticks out all over her head, a fat nest of a mess. I try to look relaxed, calm, now that I know I'm safe, no nightmare, no wet patch.

CRAZY GLUE: *Oh yeah, you look real calm there, goob.*

"I uh—was still dreaming—uh, I think. So, you've been cooking breakfast?"

She scratches her head. "Must be Haze." She yawns and stretches.

I check the clock on the chest of drawers. It's six thirty.

I climb out of bed, careful not to wake Dad, and follow Shelby downstairs to the kitchen. She stumbles on her blanket a couple of times, but I steady her from behind.

"Thanks, it just takes me a while to wake up in the mornings," she says the second time I catch her.

SEXY LADY: *I bet she's doing it on purpose just so you'll catch her.*

We reach the kitchen together and find Haze and Pete standing over the stove.

"Hey, what's going on?" I ask. "Pete, when did you get here?"

Pete glances up. "Haze came by and got me this morning." He flips the bacon frying in the skillet with a fork one by one, careful not to splatter.

"Mmm, bacon," Shelby says, shuffling to the table and flopping down in a chair.

"Don't get too excited," Haze says. "It's soy bacon. Pete, the Buddhist, is a vegan."

"It's just after six thirty. What time did you get up?" I ask Haze.

"Yeah, well, I don't sleep much, you know? Sooo, I was up at four and I called Pete just to talk, and he said to come get him, so I did. Then he suggested we go to the twenty-four-hour Safeway and pick up a few things." He opens the refrigerator and I see a gallon of milk, two loaves of bread, peanut butter, two kinds of jelly, some broccoli and cauliflower, and a store-bought chocolate layer cake.

CRAZY GLUE: *Jackpot!*

"Wow! I don't know what to say. I—I—thank you."

Pete holds out a spatula with a pancake on it. "Somebody get me a plate for the pancakes. The first ones are done."

Haze shuts the refrigerator and reaches for a plate.

"Those are vegan pancakes, everybody, so don't start salivating yet."

"Coffee," Shelby says. "I need coffee." She lets go of the blanket she has wrapped around her and holds out her arm, her hand poised to receive a cup. Glad to be useful, I step over to the sink, grab the mug I had given her yesterday, and pour her a cup from the Mr. Coffee maker. I place the mug in Shelby's hand. She mumbles thanks and sits straighter, scooping the blanket back around her. Her eyes look puffy, and she opens them just enough to see.

Haze sets a bottle of maple syrup on the table, and noticing Shelby, he says, "Whoa, that's a lot of hair there, Socks. You poke your head in a cyclone or something?"

Shelby scratches her head, then scoops her hair up and twists it somehow, grabs a wooden chopstick left on the table from last night's take-out, and stabs it into the wad of hair. Amazingly, it holds. "There," she says, "you happy?" She leans forward and takes a sip of her coffee.

"Cool." Haze nods.

"Anyway," Shelby says, pointing her pinky at me, "Jason's hair isn't much better. Ever think about getting a haircut there, dude?"

I press my tongue to the roof of my mouth. It's such a pain to cut my own hair and after a while I figured it was just easier to let it grow out, so I did, and now it's grown to my shoulders. Before I can re-spond, Pete says, "Order up." He places two pancakes and four slices of soy bacon on a plate and sets it down on the table. "There you go, Pope-a-Dope. You first; it's your house."

I don't know what to think.

CRAZY GLUE: *Don't look at us. Neither do we.*

AUNT BEE: *Just eat and be thankful.*

I see the jar of coffee, a carton of orange juice, and a bowl of fresh apples, bananas, and pears sitting on the counter. I shake my head. "You guys hardly know me and"—I swallow—"and look what you've done. I don't know how I'm ever going to repay you. I don't even know why you'd do all this for me and my dad. I don't understand."

Pete slaps my shoulder and shakes it. "You're one of us, man."

"I am?" I feel a flush of pleasure spread across my chest.

"Sure. We look after one another, don't we, guys?"

"Wuh-huh," Shelby says, nodding.

"Hey, are you kidding, man?" Haze joins in. "We're having a blast. Your father may be nuts, but at least he likes you, right? Right? My dad, whoa! I'm just *sooo* glad to be out of the house." He takes the second plate of food Pete holds out to him and sets it on the table. "Come on—eat up before it gets cold."

Shelby grabs the plate and drags it toward her. "Great, I'm starving," she says. She picks up a slice of bacon and bites into it. She shrugs. "Not too bad."

"Man, you sure can scarf down a lot of food," Haze says. "You should have seen her last night, Pete. Total pig-lady."

I sit down next to Shelby and pour some syrup on my pancakes. I close my eyes and take a bite. Vegan or not, it's delicious.

CRAZY GLUE: *Too bad we're just a figment of his imagination. Why don't we get to eat anything?*

I open my eyes and all three of them are staring at me. Did I just say that out loud?

"What? What?" I look at them, worried.

They laugh.

"It's just I've never seen someone enjoy his food so much," Pete says. He sets the third plate of food down on the table and Haze sits down.

"All right, I'm looking forward to this, man," he says. "It's freezing in this house." He rubs his hands together. "Gotta stoke."

I look at Pete and Haze, still in their jackets and with their hats pulled down over their ears, and Shelby, my blanket wrapped around her, and I'm embarrassed. "Sorry about the cold, guys."

"Yeah, no probs, no probs," Haze says, nodding and shuddering at the same time. He stuffs a whole pancake into his mouth and the syrup runs down his chin.

"That's so gross!" Shelby says, wrinkling up her nose. "Try eating like a human, why don't you."

"Grouch," Haze says, getting right up in her face. Shelby swats him away.

Pete comes over to the table and sits down with his plate of food and a mug of tea. I remember that he was supposed to have had the intervention with his father last night, so I ask him how it went.

Pete nods and takes a sip of tea. "It went okay. What can I say? We had the intervention coach there, and my mom and my two brothers and I, and then my dad's parents and his sister and brother. We each told my dad how his doing drugs was affecting us, so he's crying the whole time and saying how sorry he is and that he's going to stop; he doesn't need to go into rehab, blah, blah, blah."

Shelby smacks her coffee mug down on the table and some of the coffee sloshes out. "What? I hope you told him to get his ass in rehab, and fast. He so doesn't get it, does he? You told him, didn't you? You told him he's out, right?"

Pete shrugs. "Yeah, we told him. We said we loved him, but he either went with Charley, our intervention coach, right away to rehab, or he was on his own. We said we would have nothing to do with him until he got clean." Pete stares into his mug of tea and his far-away expression makes me think he's reliving the whole intervention scene.

Shelby slaps him on the back. "Way to go."

Haze says, "*Sooo*, did your old man go, or didn't he?"

Pete looks around at the three of us, his face blank; then a smile spreads across his face. "He's in. Went into rehab last night around nine."

We all slap his back and congratulate him.

I'm pleased for Pete; I really am.

CRAZY GLUE: *But . . .*

But I feel strange. I know it's a good thing his father's in rehab, but he's in an institution. They'll lock him up. Maybe they'll tie him down. He won't have any control. No. I don't like that. If anyone ever tries to take Dad from me and put him away, I'll kill him. I'll just kill him.

CHAPTER THIRTEEN

LAST NIGHT when I heard my dad tuning his violin, he stretched the strings so tight I thought they'd all bust. They made little screeching and scritching sounds that set my teeth on edge. This morning, sitting with Shelby, Haze, and Pete around the kitchen table, I feel like that violin, only my strings are loosening, unwinding from the pegs, and I feel strange this way. I feel that maybe it isn't safe to laugh, to let go of my vigilance over my dad, and myself, but I can hardly help it because it feels so good. It just feels so good.

The four of us finish our breakfast, and then everyone prepares to leave for their own homes to get ready for school. Shelby and her bicycle are hitching a ride with Haze and Pete in Haze's van.

I tell them I'm going to stay home with my dad, and Shelby says, "You know you can't exactly lock him inside the house all the time, so what are you going to do, stay home every day and guard him? You need a better system, Jason."

I don't feel like fighting with Shelby, whose family can afford a private nurse to look after her mother, so I just wave her out the door, thank them all again, and head up to my dad's bedroom with a cup of hot coffee in my hands. He's still asleep when I get there and I'm glad. He sleeps as little as I do, so I'm glad he's getting some rest. I leave the coffee on the bedside table along with the two pills he's supposed to take each morning. Then I go to my room to work on the Dear Mouse letters. I'm not sure when I'll find time to take my laptop to the library to send them, but I know I'll have to or someone might notice that every time I'm missing from school the letters stop.

CRAZY GLUE: *Yeah, and then you'd be up to your neck in some major doo-doo.*

Exactly.

Dear Mouse:

You little puke face! Why don't you show yourself? When I find out who you are, I'm gonna shove . . .

CRAZY GLUE: *I thought you deleted all of those kinds of letters.*

Yeah, me too. I sure didn't mean to save that one. I delete it and move on to the next one.

Dear Mouse:

My best friend copies everything I do, and I mean everything. She dresses like me and talks like me and even laughs like me. She got a job at the same place I did, even though she doesn't even like horses, and she blamed a big

114

mistake she made on me, so I got fired. I could tell the boss that she did it, but she so sucks up to him she's like the favorite, and I know the boss wouldn't believe me. We've been friends since always and we have lots of fun hanging out together when it's just us, but around everybody else she's such a phony. She competes with me for grades and attention and stuff, and now she's taken my boyfriend. She didn't even like him until I did. Now they're all over each other. I told her how I feel and she acts like she gets it, but then she does something else, so I know she doesn't. What's scary is that I think she's better at being me than I am. What should I do?

Cloned

Dear Cloned:

Here's a clue. She's not your best friend. She's not even your friend. She's a soul stealer. I mean, a little imitation might be flattering, but it doesn't seem like she even thinks about your feelings. It's all about her. Sounds like she doesn't really know herself and so she has to glom on to your life. She's a vampire just sucking the lifeblood out of you. Anyway, get a better friend. So what if you've been friends for always and sometimes have a good time. Dump her! Oh, and she'll never make a better you. You're the original.

Mouse

I'm in the middle of rereading my letter to see if it makes sense, when I hear the doorbell ring and loud banging. I figure it's one of the neighbors coming over to complain because my dad is awake now and in his room playing the violin. Since our house is a townhouse, we share a wall with our neighbor and they must be hearing the music.

On my way to answer the door I poke my head into Dad's room. "Hey, the neighbors are complaining. It's too early in the morning to be playing the violin."

"I must play furiously to rid the Furies. I think they might try to kill me today," my dad says, not stopping.

I hear more loud banging, so I hurry downstairs to answer the door. I open it, bracing myself for the rage of the guy who lives next door. Instead, I find Haze, Pete, and Shelby standing in front of me.

I start to smile, feeling relieved it's just them, but then I see their anxious faces and I stop.

LAUGH TRACK: *Uh-oh!*

"Hey, guys, what's up?"

Shelby pushes me back into the house and the three of them come inside and close the door.

"Bad news, Jason. It's bad news," Pete says.

CRAZY GLUE: *Major uh-oh!*

"What? What's happened?" I stare at the three of them. They look upset and even frightened, like our school has been bombed or maybe there's been a shooting.

"Guys, come on—what's goin' on?"

Shelby glances up the stairs where my dad's still playing, and then the other two do the same thing.

"Let's get out of the hallway," Pete says. "Let's talk in the living room, okay?"

"What? What is it? I don't like this," I say as Shelby and Haze push me back toward the living room. "Stop it, guys! Just tell me. What?"

CRAZY GLUE: *Don't panic.*

"That violin your dad's got? He stole it," Shelby says.

"What? No, he didn't. What do you mean? How do you know?"

"Dude, we heard it on the news on the way to school," Haze says. "It's all over the news, man."

"They said a guy's violin was taken from the Kennedy Center yesterday," Pete adds, looking pained and almost green in the face with having to tell me.

Shelby nods. "Yeah, it belongs to a guy from the Walden String Quartet. They're performing at the center."

"It's a way-expensive violin, man," Haze says. "Like worth millions. Dude said he always kept the violin with him. He had it backstage. He left it there for five minutes and it was gone. It's a Strasselburg or something—made in the sixteen hundreds, so like whoa, it's way old."

Pete elbows Haze's arm. "It's a Stradivarius, bozo, not a Strasselburg."

"Ouch, I didn't know." Haze winces and rubs his arm.

"Anyway," Shelby says, bugging her eyes out at the two of them, then looking at me, "the police think one of the guys who cleans up around there might have taken it, because they found out he has a criminal record, and this guy, the one who owns the violin, is making a big stink, saying he's going to sue the center and everybody. He was asking the news people, like they had something to do with it, how they could let a guy with a criminal record clean the building."

Shelby stops talking and the three of them wait for me to say something. I blink several times and try to figure out what to say.

CRAZY GLUE: *How about "oops"!*

"It sounds like this stagehand guy did it, then," I say. "It's not the same violin. My dad brought his violin over from Greece. I—I saw the box—his Greece box open on the bed."

CRAZY GLUE: *That's right, grab at anything you can.*

FBG WITH A MUSTACHE: *You know the truth.*

"No, I don't."

Haze, Pete, and Shelby look at one another and then at me. " 'No, you don't,' what?" Pete asks, while at the same time Haze says, "Huh?" and Shelby just gives me her "you jerk" look.

CRAZY GLUE: *Yep. You said it out loud.*

AUNT BEE: *Oh dear!*

"Oh, uh, I was just thinking out loud, kind of— I—uh, I mean I don't know really if it's his, I guess—

really." I press my tongue to the roof of my mouth so hard I think it might burst through to my nasal cavity.

CRAZY GLUE: *T-M-I, goob.*

"I really doubt it's his," Pete says.

Haze adds, "They held a big press conference on TV and everything, and they said it's got that Stradi—Stradi—whatever, label inside the violin and three cherubs on the tailpiece, just like the ones on your dad's violin, right?"

Pete shakes his head and makes this sorrowful face. "I'm sorry, Jason."

It reminds me of the doctor's face when I came to see my mom the day she died. He said the same thing. I was too late. She had died in the night while Dad and I were at home sleeping.

FBG WITH A MUSTACHE: *Maybe that's why you don't sleep well anymore. The guilt.*

I feel sick. Really sick, like I might throw up. The floor beneath me tilts sideways. I struggle to make Dad's violin be all right. This has to be all right.

AUNT BEE: *He could go to jail.*

FBG WITH A MUSTACHE: *That might be the safest place for him.*

"No!" I realize I've said this out loud, too. "Oh, I mean, no, how could my dad have taken a violin from the Kennedy Center?" I drop to the floor and sit with my head in my hands. "He'd have to take a bus. He hates buses, and people and noise, and anyway, don't they have guards there?"

I look up at the three of them standing above me, all of them with pitying looks on their faces, looking like the nurses at the hospital, the nurses who couldn't revive my mom for even just one more minute, just one minute so I could say I loved her and goodbye.

I can't stand it. My dad is playing scales in the room above us—up and down, up and down with the scales. Crazy. It suddenly just sounds crazy—like him.

AUNT BEE: *It's all right. It's just your friends, not the nurses. They're your friends. It's going to be all right.*

Shelby kneels beside me and puts her arm around my shoulders. "What do you want to do, Jason? How can we help?"

"I don't know. I don't know." I shake my head and try to get a grip on myself.

FBG WITH A MUSTACHE: *Atta boy.*

Haze and Pete join us on the floor. They kneel in front of me, looking concerned, and I'm both embarrassed and grateful they're here. I had forgotten that about friends, that they could be a blessing and a curse at the same time. I'm not sure I'm ready for friends. It's safer to be on my own.

FBG WITH A MUSTACHE: *But is it saner?*
SEXY LADY: *Shh.*

I force a smile as a kind of thanks to them for being here for me. "I know we've got to return the violin," I tell them, "but—I guess I'll just say *I* took it. I can't tell anyone my dad took it or they'll put him away."

CRAZY GLUE: *And what would they do to you, exactly? Throw you a party?*

"Is that really such a bad thing for your dad?" Shelby asks. "He'd get the help he—"

I jump to my feet. "Yeah, it's a bad thing," I shout. I pace the floor. "Are you kidding me? Don't you get it? Where would I live? What would happen to us? He's all I have. I need him and he needs me. And I promised my mother that if anything ever happened to her, I'd—I'd—you don't understand." I stop pacing. I want to run. Hide. I'm scared. I'm so scared and I'm tired, just so tired of it all.

AUNT BEE: *Hold on. It will be all right.*

Pete stands and puts his hand on my shoulder. "I've got an idea."

The other two stand and join us.

"What? What idea?" I ask.

"What if we go to the police and say we found the violin somewhere. I mean, it's the truth. We did find it, in your father's hands maybe, but we found it."

"I don't know," I say, thinking the idea over.

Haze says, "Yeah, we could tell them we found it on a bus, or maybe in the park. We could say we were—"

"You guys are insane." Shelby clicks her teeth. "Look at you two. Haze, you've got eye makeup on and that funny-looking beard and those teardrop things, and Pete, you shave your head and look weird—no offense, guys—and besides all that, do you really think

121

the police would believe we just found it? They'd lock us all up."

"You look pretty tame," Pete says. "And you're a girl. You could turn it in."

Shelby raises her hands and backs away. "Hey, no way."

I step forward. "Look, if anyone's going to do this, it has to be me. I couldn't let any of you risk it."

"Look, you guys," Shelby says. "Why don't we just tell the truth? It's bound to come out, anyway. We'd all look guilty trying to pretend we took it or found it or whatever. Your father stole it; he should take the blame."

CRAZY GLUE: *Could we just tape her mouth shut or something?*

"No!" I shout. "Forget it. I'll take care of it. You all just go on to school. Thanks for letting me know and all." I try to herd them out into the hallway, but they don't budge.

CRAZY GLUE: *Note to Jason: Nix the friends. It's not worth it.*

"Hey!" Haze slaps his forehead. "Why don't we just leave it somewhere? I mean, why do any of us have to confess to anything? Just leave it and let someone else find it, right?" He looks at us. "Right?"

"That's not a bad idea." Pete smiles this devilish smile and nods. "We just have to make sure we leave it somewhere safe. And we need to be sure the person who finds it is reliable and honest. I mean, they said the violin is worth millions, so we can't just leave it sitting out anywhere."

"Yeah, you're right," I say. "Who could we trust besides the police?"

"Who says police are always trustworthy?" Shelby asks.

CRAZY GLUE: *Why does she always have to be so contrary?*

Haze gets this strange look in his eyes and says, "Maybe," and we all wait.

"Haze?" Pete says. "You got an idea?"

Haze studies the ceiling. "Maybe," he repeats.

Shelby punches his arm. "Maybe what?"

Haze smiles at all of us. "Maybe we could leave it with my mailman."

"What?" Shelby and I say in unison.

Haze holds up his hands. "No, hear me out, man. We've got this mailman, and he always parks his truck on the side of the road, gets out, leaves the door of the truck wide open, and then he goes walking through the neighborhood. He goes like two miles before he returns to the truck. You should see him. The dude's so loaded down with catalogs and shit. It's a riot. Anyways, the houses are all far apart and everybody works. Believe me, nobody's home. Nobody will see us."

Pete shakes his head. "Mail trucks are supposed to be locked when they're unattended. I think it's the law or a rule or something."

"Well, I'm telling you, the dude never locks it. It's wide open."

After some more discussion, we get excited about

the plan. We agree that I will get the violin from my dad, and then we'll wipe the fingerprints off it, put it in a bag, and put it in the mail truck. Haze says the mail usually arrives at his house at around three thirty or a quarter to four, so we plan to meet back at my house right after school. Then we'll ride over in Haze's van and just pull up, pass the violin out through the window to the mail truck, and drive away.

After we've worked out the details of the plan, Shelby puts her hands on her hips and studies us. "Look at you guys. You're all hyped up like we're pulling off some caper for the FBI or something. We could still get in a lot of trouble. This plan isn't foolproof, you know." She glares at us with a sour expression on her face, and Haze gently pounds his fist on her head.

"Party pooper," he says.

"Well, I'm just saying."

"No fears, Socks, it's gonna work, you'll see," Haze says. He looks at his watch and heads toward the door. "Come on—let's get to school. Jason, see ya later." He opens the door and the three of them leave again.

"See you this afternoon," I call after them, hoping my voice doesn't give away my anxiety about our plans. I watch them pile into Haze's van and pull away from the curb. Then I close the door and realize I feel sad I'm not going with them—my new friends.

CHAPTER FOURTEEN

I KNOW IT'S WRONG that my dad stole this expensive violin, but I can't help wishing he could keep it. He's calmer now that he has it and I almost think he could really get well if he could just play it long enough. I believe he could play himself well. People do that, don't they? It's a kind of therapy, isn't it?

I even think I could have gone to school today, since all my dad wants to do is play. I poke my head into his room and find him standing at the window with his back to me. He doesn't even acknowledge that I'm here. He's dressed in his Greek outfit again and even from the back he looks very Greek somehow, very old country, but his long hair is all matted and instead of holding himself in the straight, proud way he always did before Mom died, he's bent, hovering over the violin protectively as he plays, as though he fears the Furies might grab it away from him. He has aluminum foil wrapped around his ears, and I feel a twinge of guilt that I've hidden the helmet.

I leave him and go down to my bedroom and look

at the walls with my photographs, and I remember my conversation with Shelby.

"I did these," I say, remembering. "I like taking pictures of stones—of walls and mountains and caves and snow . . . the play of light and shadow."

"You're an artist," I hear her say, as clearly as if she were right here with me, still. "You're an artist, like me."

I want to live in that moment forever. I don't want to ever step out of it. I know it's not much of anything, really, but on either side of that moment is a pile of worry and hunger and other stuff I don't want to think about, but I was full and happy and I felt . . .

CRAZY GLUE: *Sane. The word is sane, goob.*

Yeah, and normal. It's just that I shared something important about myself, and Shelby got it. I think she got it.

"You're an artist, like me," she said.

I think I have friends—real friends this time. They want to help me.

CRAZY GLUE: *Careful, goob.*

AUNT BEE: *I've always said you needed a good friend.*

SEXY LADY: *And I've always said your photographs were hot.*

I'm in my room, trying to catch up on some overdue homework, when I hear a bloodcurdling, hair-standing-on-end scream.

I run to my dad's room and I see blood on the window where he had been standing. I see the violin and more blood on the bed.

"Shit! Dad?"

I hear him muttering. I stoop down and look under the bed. I find him curled up in a tight ball, chanting his Furies chant. His whole body is shaking.

"Dad, what is it? What's happened?"

"Evil! 'A clamour of Furies'! They have torn off my fingers so I can't play." He holds his left hand out so that I can see, and his fingers are all bloody but still attached.

AUNT BEE: *Well, thank goodness for small miracles.*

SEXY LADY: *He's crazy.*

CRAZY GLUE: *He's dangerous.*

FBG WITH A MUSTACHE: *He's dangerously crazy.*

I don't understand what he could have done to himself, and then I remember the violin strings.

"You've been playing nonstop for hours, Dad. You've probably cut your fingers on the strings. You have no calluses, that's all. Come on—come on out and let me look at them."

"They've cut off my fingers so I can't play. They seek revenge. They won't stop the torment. How do I stop the torment? Stop it! Stop it! They want to tear me to shreds." He grabs at his hair and pulls and lets out another bloodcurdling scream.

CRAZY GLUE: *Yow, mama! That's killer.*

I run around to the other side of the bed so I can crawl under and grab hold of his legs and pull him out. I pull on him and Dad kicks me in the face with his boot. Blood comes gushing out of my nose.

"Ow! Jeez, oh jeez! Oh jeez!" I back out from under the bed and race to the bathroom to get some tissues and run cold water on my face to stop the bleeding. Dad keeps on screaming. I tilt my head back and press the tissues against my nose.

CRAZY GLUE: *Tell me again why you won't get him help. This is crazy.*

I can't lose him. He's my dad. He's all I have. And what would happen to me? Anyway, it's not really that bad. He's okay. He's doing all right.

CRAZY GLUE: *Oh yeah? On what planet?*

FBG WITH A MUSTACHE: *Jason's afraid.*

Shut up!

FBG WITH A MUSTACHE: *He's afraid he—*

I cover my ears. "Shut up! Shut up! Shut up! I'm not afraid and I'm not going crazy, if that's what you're thinking."

FBG WITH A MUSTACHE: *It's what you're thinking that matters.*

"No! Shut up!"

I catch sight of myself in the mirror with my hands over my ears.

CRAZY GLUE: *That's right, goob. Next thing you know you'll be digging that helmet out from under your bed and putting it on.*

No! Everybody, just shut up!

I tear out of the bathroom and storm down to my dad's room. I reach under the bed, grab his leg, and yank him out. He hits his head on the bed frame. He's still screaming and I shake him. I'm on my knees with my dad, and I'm shaking him and I can't stop.

"Just shut up, Dad! Shut up. Shut up. You've got to shut up!"

I can't stop shaking him and it takes me a few seconds to realize he's stopped screaming. Instead, tears are streaming down his face. He's staring into my eyes with this horrible, hurt look. He sees me. He knows it's me, his own son, hurting him. I stop shaking—finally I stop—and I grab him and hug him, and I cry. I cry so hard, it hurts my face. I cry and I rock my dad in my arms and I hear my mother's voice in my head. "Everything's going to be all right, Jason, I promise." But I know everything is not going to be all right. Not anymore. Not ever. She took care of that.

I rock my dad and I feel so small in this room, in this wide world, with all its people with their busy, happy lives, going to and fro—so small, and so alone.

CHAPTER FIFTEEN

I WASH MY DAD'S HANDS and put Band-Aids on his fingers. I wash the blood off the window, and wipe it very carefully off the violin, and change the bedspread, and check my nose, which looks a little red and swollen, and I try to recall a good memory of my dad.

I remember the time we hiked for a week along the Appalachian Trail. A storm came up one day and we were running for shelter. I got so tired, I didn't want to run anymore. I just sat down on the trail—sat down right in the mud.

FBG WITH A MUSTACHE (ACTING AS DAD): *"Come on, Jason. Climb on my back. It's not much farther."*

CRAZY GLUE (ACTING AS JASON): *"Can't we just stay here? I'm tired and it's cold."*

Dad took off his jacket and wrapped it around me and my pack and lifted me onto his back. He ran with me like that for at least a mile, his pack, my pack, me, the thunder and lightning. Then at night at the shelter, it was just the two of us eating oatmeal and sitting around the fire. We sang songs and told stories and looked at the stars. It was like we were the only two people on the planet, but it felt safe then—like a good thing.

FBG WITH A MUSTACHE (AS DAD): *"Hey, Jason, did you hear the one about the mortal who asked the great god Zeus, 'What is a million years like to you?' Zeus says, 'Like one second.' So the mortal asks, 'What is a million dollars like to you?' And Zeus says, 'Like one penny.' So the mortal says, 'Hey, Zeus, can I have a million dollars?' And Zeus says, 'Sure, wait just a second.' Ha! Now, that's funny, huh?"*

CRAZY GLUE (AS JASON): *"That's so lame, Dad."*

But I loved his lame jokes. I loved when he laughed. It sounded like a dog barking. I miss it.

AUNT BEE: *That's a nice memory, Jason.*

Dad is in his room playing again and I'm doing laundry when Pete, Haze, and Shelby arrive.

"We would have come sooner," Shelby says, brushing past me and into the house, "but I had to check on my mother. Is everything okay here?"

"Yeah, sure," I say, trying to look cheerful.

CRAZY GLUE: *Talk about lame.*

"My dad's upstairs playing—well, I guess you all can hear him."

"Yow! What *is* that?" Haze asks. "That's some weird music, man." He starts to take off his jacket, then changes his mind and zips it back up.

I shrug. It's crazy music—that's what it sounds like.

"So, let's get this show on the road." Haze rubs his hands together and grins at us, clearly excited.

131

"Right," I say. "I'll go get the—the uh—"

LAUGH TRACK: *Uh-oh.*

I realize I haven't figured out how I'm going to get the violin away from Dad. I scratch my head and look at the others, who look back at me expectantly. "Uh—I'll be right back."

I run up the steps, wondering what I'm going to say to my dad. I find him back in front of the mirror. He's wearing a fresh set of aluminum ears and four bandaged fingers. "Dad, it's time to—time to take the violin in for repairs, now," I say, shifting from one foot to the other, hoping my voice sounds bright and cheerful. "We need to drop it off at the shop."

"Jason, it's Danse Macabre," he says.

"Yeah, nice." I walk over to him and touch his arm. "Dad, I need the violin now."

We look at each other through the mirror, and I see that I look like a younger version of him. I'm even almost the same height now.

SEXY LADY: *Don't look.*

CRAZY GLUE: *There goes your bird heart. It's just flapping and beating its wings like crazy.*

Dad twists away from me. "I have to play." He speeds up his playing, almost poking me in the eye with the bow.

"Look, Dad—the Argonauts are here again. They want to see you. They're downstairs."

He stops playing and lifts his head. "They are? Am

132

I to stand trial for murder? Are the Furies with them? And what of Athena, my defender?"

"Yeah, she's here, too. So come on—they're waiting for you."

"Okay, if the Furies aren't there." My dad nods and follows me, and I breathe a sigh of relief. I figure if I can distract him with my friends somehow, I can get him to set down the violin and we can take it.

We reach the top of the stairs and Dad stops. He sees everyone in the hallway below and he panics. He grabs me by my shirt and I'm pulled off balance. I'm too close to the edge of the staircase; I lose my footing and fall backwards down the steps, my back, shoulders, head, elbows, and shins hitting the wooden treads, the wall, and the balusters on the way down. As I tumble, I hear Shelby cry out; my dad's playing his Danse Macabre; Haze shouts, "Hey! Hey! Hey!"—and it all feels as if it's happening in slow motion.

I land sideways with my legs tucked into my chest at the foot of the staircase, staring up into the stunned faces of my friends.

Shelby's the first to react. "Are you okay, Jason?" She kneels down beside me and takes my hand in hers.

CRAZY GLUE: *Ah, nice!*

The others join her by my side. "Don't move him; something could be broken," Pete says.

For a few seconds I feel a little loopy, but then I realize Dad's still playing, and I know how this has to look with him practically pushing me down the stairs. "I'm okay," I say. I sit up and feel a sharp pain in my shoulder—it kills, but I ignore it. "I'm great," I say. "I'm used to it. I—I've always been clumsy around stairs." I laugh.

CRAZY GLUE: *So lame.*

Shelby shakes her head and gets to her feet. She shouts at Dad, "Hey, look what you did. Hey you! Mr. Papadopoulos! Look what you did to your son. You pushed him down the steps!"

Dad keeps playing.

I try to get to my feet, pushing off the floor with my hands, but an excruciating pain shoots into my shoulder, stunning me for a moment so I can't rise or speak fast enough to defend my dad and shut Shelby up.

"Stop that playing!" she shouts at him, clapping her hands like a teacher.

CRAZY GLUE: *Remind me again why you like her.*

I raise my arm and grab Shelby's hand. "*You* stop it! It's all right. I'm okay. Leave him alone."

Shelby and Pete are about to say something, when Dad notices me on the floor and stops playing. "Jason? What happened? Are you hurt? Why did not the Argonauts defend you?" He trots down the steps to see me. "Did you fall?"

"Yeah, you pushed him," Shelby says, her voice angry, her eyes blazing.

My dad kneels beside me. "Uh-oh, Jason. My poor son." He sets the violin and bow on the floor, takes my head in his arms, and pulls me toward him. It kills, but I don't holler like I want to. I say, "It's all right, Dad. It was an accident."

Just a couple of hours ago I was rocking him and now he's rocking me. The thought makes me uncomfortable.

He tries to rock my head in his arms and kiss it at the same time. "Poor boy, poor little boy," he says, and I suddenly feel embarrassed. Everyone is looking at us.

FBG WITH A MUSTACHE: *Get up, son! You're making a fool of yourself.*

"Dad, let me get up, okay? I'm all right. Really, I'm all right." Dad lets go, and with Pete's help I stand. I brush myself off just to have something to do because I'm still so embarrassed, and then I notice Haze staring wide-eyed at me, raising his eyebrows up and down and signaling something. He backs away toward the front door with an odd shuffle and his arms behind him. I glance at the floor where Dad had set his violin and bow and see that they're gone. I nod at Haze, then grab on to my dad with my good arm. "Help me walk a second, will you, Dad? I need your help."

"He's helped enough, if you ask me," Shelby says, still angry. She obviously has no sympathy for my dad's condition, and that irritates me.

FBG WITH A MUSTACHE: *Too much sympathy can be as harmful as too little.*

AUNT BEE: *I'd rather have too much than too little. Poor Jason.*

I want to say something to Shelby, to explain a few things, but I'm in too much pain to say much of anything, what with the way Dad and Pete are pulling on me as they help me walk around the room. I bite down on my lower lip to keep from yelping and lean into my dad, hoping to keep him distracted. I hear the door open and Haze says, "Be back in a min."

"Help me sit down, okay, Dad?" I say, blocking his view of the door.

"I'll carry you," Dad says, bending down and trying to lift my legs.

Shelby panics. "You're going to trip him! You're going to trip him! What are you doing?"

"It's okay," Pete says, grabbing me under both arms to support me. "We've got him."

"I can walk," I say through gritted teeth. "Just let me get to the kitchen."

The three of them huddle close as I hobble my way toward the kitchen, all three talking to me at once, giving me instructions to be careful, and asking where I hurt.

Before I even reach the kitchen, though, Haze returns and says, "Everything's wiped clean and in the bag. Let's get going, man."

"Where? Where are we going?" Dad asks.

We all stop and look at one another.

CRAZY GLUE: *Yeah, goob, where are we going?*

I recover first. "We have a musical mission to accomplish, Dad. Do you want to come with us?"

"What? Are you kidding me?" Shelby says, and Pete sets his hand on her shoulder.

136

Dad smiles, exposing his yellowed teeth and swollen gums. "A musical mission? Will the Furies be there? The horrible Alecto, Megaera, and Tisiphone?"

"Cool," Haze says. "Who are they?"

"No, we're safe, Dad. Come on—let's get our coats on." I turn around and we all go back to the entrance hall, where Dad and I grab our coats. I try putting mine on, but it hurts to lift my arm, so I just carry it and tell everyone I feel kind of warm.

We step outside, the first time I've been out all day, and I'm hit by the brightness of the sun. It cheers me even though it's only about ten degrees out. I shiver and limp with the rest of the gang toward Haze's van, holding on to my dad's arm. I feel bruised about the body and still a little shaky.

We reach the van and we all climb inside. I tell my dad to get in the far back and I push him from behind. Then I climb in and sit down next to him. I look to the front of the van and spot the two grocery bags holding the violin and bow in the passenger seat, one turned upside down on top of the other.

We all get settled, Dad and I in the back, Shelby and Pete in the center, and Haze and the Stradivarius up front.

As soon as Haze turns on the ignition, the car explodes with the sound of hip-hop and it rocks the van. Our musical mission has begun.

137

CHAPTER SIXTEEN

HAZE LIVES IN ONE of the new neighborhoods around here that have these gigantic houses and acres of fancy lawns. The roads are really wide and there are all these young trees planted at evenly spaced distances along the grassy strips running between the houses and the streets. It all looks well tended and perfect—like a fantasyland. Looking at Haze in his rumpled clothes and bizarre makeup and driving around in his industrial-size van, it's hard to imagine he actually lives in one of these homes.

We turn onto his street, Honeysuckle Circle. Haze shuts off the radio and says, "Well, there it is." He points to a four-story brick mansion with porches and balconies jutting out from both sides. "That's the whorehouse."

CRAZY GLUE: *Yup, hard to miss. Looks like there's more than one loony-tooney parent on the loose.*

Spray painted in large black block letters across the front of Haze's house is the word "whore," and I notice as we pass the huge, four-car garage that the center door has a Hummer-size hole in it.

Pete laughs. "You don't lie."

"Yeah, right? I told you." Haze chuckles.

AUNT BEE: *How nice to have a sense of humor about it.*

SEXY LADY: *Jason has a sense of humor; it's just that nothing's funny.*

We drive for a minute or two more, and then Haze slows down and says, "Shit!"

We look up ahead and see the mail truck. "What's wrong?" Pete and I both ask.

Dad says, "Is it the Furies?" He grabs my sore arm and I wince.

"The open door is on the sidewalk side," Haze says. "We can't just roll up and drop it in. Shit! Someone's got to get out and walk past the truck."

Pete and I both volunteer. "I'll do it," we each say.

I repeat more firmly, "*I'll* do it."

CRAZY GLUE: *Way to go. You've got a busted arm, goob. Why can't you just shut up sometimes?*

AUNT BEE: *He's doing the right thing.*

Haze pulls up alongside the mail truck and looks inside as we drive by. "Good, he's not there. Let's drive around and find out where he is, first."

"Where's the music?" Dad asks. "Just, where's the music? Have we lost the music? This is very dangerous." He puts his hands over his ears.

Haze turns the radio back on but keeps it down low. We ride about half a mile and find the mail carrier turning away from someone's bricked-in mailbox. Haze continues driving, but we all look back to see in which

139

direction the carrier is headed. Unfortunately, he's moving toward his truck.

"That's okay. It's okay—we've still got some time."

"Let's just hope you don't have any nosy-bodies poking their faces out the windows around here," Shelby says, speaking for the first time since we got into the van.

"So what," Pete says. "Let's just do it."

Haze speeds up. "This street makes a full circle, so I'll just keep going. Jason, get up front and get ready to jump out with the vi—vi—viceroy," Haze says, shrugging and looking at Dad for his reaction in the rearview mirror.

Dad doesn't notice the slip-up. He's too busy keeping an eye out for Furies lurking in bushes and behind houses.

I get up from my seat and make my way to the front of the van, my shoulder throbbing with sharp stabs of pain and both my hips aching.

FBG WITH A MUSTACHE: *I bet you anything your collarbone is broken. Give the job to someone else. Have some sense.*

I catch Pete watching me. "Really, Jason, I don't mind doing it," he says, but I shake my head.

"I got it."

CRAZY GLUE: *You had your chance, goob, and you just blew it.*

He's *my* dad. He stole the violin, remember.

I climb into the front passenger seat, making sure I don't step on the violin that now sits on the floor of the van. I take a deep breath and let it out. I feel light-headed from the pain, and I lean back in my seat and brace myself with my right hand as we speed around a curve, wheels screeching.

"Great way to not draw attention to us," Shelby says. "Your broken muffler's bad enough—think you could slow down?"

Haze shakes his head. "No can do. If he comes around that corner, he'll see us, so I don't think we've got too much time."

I see the mail truck up ahead again, and Haze slows while I lift the bags into my lap.

"I'm going to pull in right behind the truck. You jump out, put the—*it* in the seat, and hop back in, got it?"

CRAZY GLUE: *Roger Dodger.*

"Yeah, yeah, I got it. I got it." I feel dizzy now and my heart's pounding. My hands are sweating and wilting the sacks where I'm holding on to them. I swallow hard and Haze slows to a stop. I open the door and slide out of the van, leaving the door open. I look down the sidewalk in front of me. No mail carrier. I look at the nearest house diagonally across the street from where we're parked. I study the windows a second, but most all of them are covered in some gauzy stuff, so I can't tell if anyone is standing behind one of them watching me or not.

"Go! Go!" Pete says in a loud whisper.

I jog up to the truck with the violin held out in front of me. I get to the door and it's closed, not open the way Haze claimed it would be. "Shit!"

I hold the bags in my bad arm and try to open the door with my good one, praying it isn't locked. The door slides open with a bang and the bag slips out of my hand so that all I'm holding is the empty, top grocery bag. The bottom one hits the sidewalk with a *thunk* and the violin falls out of the bag. I hear Dad call out, "My violin! Jason, my violin!"

I glance back at the van and see Pete get up out of his seat and go toward my dad. I hear Dad call out to me, and then Haze and Pete are yelling at him. I turn back to the violin and grab it off the sidewalk.

CRAZY GLUE: *Fingerprints, goob!*

Jeez! There's no time to wipe it down or examine it for damage. Haze, Pete, and Dad are yelling at one another and I can see the mail carrier coming around the corner. "Don't look up. Don't look up," I warn the carrier under my breath.

I thrust the bow and violin, with its neck now exposed, into the truck and run back to the van, still holding on to the empty grocery bag.

I jump back into the van and yell, "Come on, let's get out of here!"

That's when I notice Haze has left his seat in order to help Pete calm my dad down and hold him in the van. I look back and see arms and legs flailing; then I

142

scramble over to the driver's seat, ignoring the screaming pain in my shoulder.

AUNT BEE: *But you can't drive! You don't know how!*

LAUGH TRACK: *Uh-oh! (Nervous laughter).*

The motor's running, so I put my foot on the
brake.

CRAZY GLUE: *Brilliant!*

I mess with the gearshift a few seconds trying to
get the thing to shift, and I finally move it into gear. I
press the accelerator and we shoot backwards. I slam
on the brake and we jerk to a halt with a screech.

CRAZY GLUE: *We're all gonna die!*

I look through the rearview mirror and see
everyone except Shelby picking themselves up off one
another. Then I look out the windshield and see the
mail carrier watching us.

"He sees us!" I yell. I jam the gearshift into drive
and floor it, and we shoot forward. I turn the steering
wheel just in time to keep from hitting the mail truck.
I keep going, weaving left, then right. I don't know
what the hell I'm doing.

CRAZY GLUE: *Not quite the piece of cake you thought it would be,
huh, goob?*

We roll up onto the sidewalk, then back onto the
road. I see the mail carrier dart behind one of the
brick-post mailboxes and hear Shelby scream, "Don't
hit him!"

I'm driving mostly with my right arm because

my left arm is killing me. We ride up onto someone's grass, just past the driveway where the mail carrier is hiding.

FBG WITH A MUSTACHE: *Watch the road, son, not the mail carrier.*

"Shit!" Shelby yells.

"Shit!" I yell, bumping off the lawn and taking the curve too fast.

"Slow down! Slow down!" Pete yells.

"Keep going. Hurry up!" Haze yells.

I hear Dad crying and mumbling something about his violin.

"Shit!"

I keep driving, weaving all over the place.

FBG WITH A MUSTACHE: *Get it under control, son. Do it now.*

CRAZY GLUE: *We're gonna do a rollover at the speed you're going.*

I take another curve and Haze, who has managed to get to the row of seats just behind me, tells me I can slow down now. "Stop and I'll take over," he shouts.

I keep going. I don't know what I'm doing.

"I said, stop the van!"

I slam on the brakes; Haze falls forward and we conk heads. The hit just about knocks me out. I see stars circling my head—I swear I do, just like in a cartoon.

"Oh man!" Haze says, shaking his head, trying to shake off the pain. He rubs at his temple. "Oh man, that kills!" He shakes his head again and tells me to move over, his voice still whiny with pain.

"Yeah, gladly," I say.

I start to slide over, and everyone yells, "Put it in park!"

"Shit!" I put the car in park and scramble to the passenger seat, not caring if I rip my whole arm off in the process. I know that at any minute the mail truck is going to come careening around the corner after us.

Haze jumps into the driver's seat, puts the pedal to the metal, and tears out of there. When we turn out of the neighborhood and no truck is following us, I look into the back of the van and see peace-loving Pete sitting on my dad's lap with Dad squirming beneath him. "Oh, the indignity!" he cries, pushing against Pete's back.

Pete braces himself against the bench in front of him. "Are you going to be still now, or do I have to sit on you all the way home?"

"I am in possession of secret and mystical powers on loan from Zeus himself! Get off me or I will be forced to use them!" Dad pushes again, but Pete doesn't budge.

I smile, happy to let Pete deal with Dad for a minute; then I glance at Shelby staring out the window, her mouth set in a straight line, and she seems deep in thought. I know all this mess has taken her away from her mother for the past two days, and I feel bad for this.

CRAZY GLUE: *Maybe you can comfort her—hmmm?*

Well, I need to find some way to make it up to her. I face forward and nod to myself. Yeah, I'll find some way to make it up to all of them. That is, if the police don't haul us in first.

CHAPTER SEVENTEEN

Dear Mouse:

Don't print this in the paper. Just answer me by e-mail, ok? If you do print this, I swear I'll kill you.

So, I'm in a sort of gang—well, yeah, I'm in a gang, and I want to get out, but they'll crucify me if I even try. I've done some bad shit, okay, and I had to do it, but I don't feel good about it anymore. I never felt good about it. I don't think anybody—well, we're all scared, you know? Well, you probably don't. But I figure I got two career choices, prison or death, unless you know of something else. So what do I do? You can't answer that, can you? Didn't think so. You're not so smart, are you, Dr. Gomez?

DOA

Dear DOA:

You're right. I can't answer that, 'cause if I did, I'd tell you to run away, which is probably not the right answer. If I were you, or if I were me in your situation, I'd fake my death somehow, so no one would come after me or my family, grab some money, and run away to some whole other state. Maybe I'd take off for the woods, live up in the mountains in a cave. But I'm not you and that's probably a dumb idea. If I were Dr. Gomez, I'd know what to tell you to do. Maybe you should ask her. She's all right as far as shrinks go.

Mouse

I stare down at my answer. What a dumb answer. What am I doing? I can't even run my own life and here I am telling people what to do. Run away? How can I tell DOA to run away? Man, how did I get into this, anyway?

CRAZY GLUE: *So what. At least you know you're not the only one with problems.*

AUNT BEE: *You're not so alone anymore. You have friends. You have these letters.*

FBG WITH A MUSTACHE: *Maybe you think you can save yourself by helping others.*

Do I need saving?

LAUGH TRACK: *Yes! (Laughter).*

SEXY LADY: *He's hot no matter what.*

A whole week goes by and there's no news about the missing violin. I stay home with Dad and call the school every day, pretending to be sick. I say I have mono. Everybody gets mono. It lasts a long time, so I figure I can get away with missing a lot of school.

AUNT BEE: *For shame! There are people who really are sick.*

147

CRAZY GLUE: *Yeah, you might be creating bad mojo for yourself, and you'll get really sick some day as a payback for the lie.*

Well, I don't know what else to do.

Dad keeps leaving the house and disappearing—sometimes naked—and he claims the Furies have poisoned his meds, so I have a royal fight with him every day trying to convince him that I've removed the poison so it's safe to take the pills.

I'm spending a lot of time down in the basement in my mother's darkroom. I've stored all her photos in here, all the pictures of faces she's taken, all the brides and grooms and their families—so many smiling, happy faces. I look at them and wonder how many couples are still together? How many have had a serious illness in the family? How many have died?

CRAZY GLUE: *A little morbid, don't you think?*

I've put the photographs we have of my mom down here, too, in folders, stacks of them, but I can't bring myself to look at them—at her.

AUNT BEE: *Because you miss her, of course. That's all.*

I keep my back to the folders while I develop a roll of film, but I can feel them behind me. I feel them like a cold hand on my back. It gives me chills, makes me squirm, but I keep working. I've found a bunch of film in the dorm-size refrigerator inside the darkroom. I load a roll into her camera and take it upstairs to get some pictures of Dad.

It's a little awkward handling the camera because I've made myself a sling for my sore arm and I have to take my arm out of the sling to take the pictures, which kills, so some pics are out of focus.

Haze and Pete dropped by during the week and I took their pictures, too, but Shelby hasn't come once.

CRAZY GLUE: *The one pic you really want, too bad. That's what you get for calling in and pretending to have mono.*

I didn't capture anything special in my pictures the way my mom did when she made portraits. I'm better with photographing stone, but I develop the roll, anyway, and I laugh at the picture of Haze all decked out like he's some kind of rock climber with a bunch of different-colored carabiners hooked on all his belt loops. Then I hold up the one I took of Pete yesterday and he looks . . .

CRAZY GLUE: *Guilty! He so doesn't want you to know something. It's written all over his face.*

AUNT BEE: *Or maybe it's shame.*

LAUGH TRACK: *Uh-oh!*

I don't know what it is, but it makes me nervous—very nervous.

I hear the doorbell ring, so I leave the darkroom and hurry upstairs.

I open the door and it's Pete.

CRAZY GLUE: *Speak of the devil. And look at his face—he's still guilty of something.*

"Hi, Pete," I say, stepping back to let him in.

"Pope-a-Dope, any news on the violin?" He steps inside and we automatically head back to the kitchen, and I like how natural—comfortable—this feels.

CRAZY GLUE: *If only he didn't still look so guilty.*

"No. No news, yet," I say. "I don't know what's going on. Maybe the mail carrier is a violin virtuoso and he thinks somebody gave it to him as a gift."

"Or he's trying to sell it for millions," Pete says.

"Yeah, or he went to the police and they're trying to trace the fingerprints I left." I whisper this because we're passing through the living room and my dad's asleep in the tub upstairs. He fell asleep trying to stay warm again, so I drained it and put a pillow under his head and several wool blankets on top of him. I tell Pete he's asleep. He nods and kind of tiptoes the rest of the way to the kitchen.

We sit in the kitchen and drink tea—the cheapest way I know to keep warm in our house. Pete has brought over a tin of some kind of homemade herbal tea concoction that smells like candy and tastes kind of sweet and mellow. He mixes the herbs himself, which I guess is weird but definitely a Pete kind of thing to do. He tells me the tea is an amazing health elixir and that I should get my dad to drink it, too.

CRAZY GLUE: *Come on. He's stalling. It's so obvious he's got something on his mind.*

AUNT BEE: *Oh dear. I don't like this.*

"Someday I'm going to live in Hawaii and grow all my own tea," he says, "and medicinal herbs, too. I think I'll become an herbalist—you know, a healer."

"Oh yeah?" I stare into my mug of tea, only half listening.

CRAZY GLUE: *It's the police. They know who stole the violin. That's got to be it. You and your dad are in big trouble now.*

FBG WITH A MUSTACHE: *Now, let's not jump to conclusions, everybody.*

"I'm starting with my dad," Pete says, and I try to remember what he's talking about. "I'm planning on using herbs with special properties that help curb cravings and addictions. I can't give him anything while he's in rehab, though—of course."

I nod and think maybe this look on his face isn't anything about me. Maybe it's just something about his dad.

CRAZY GLUE: *Doubt it, but nice try.*

"Yeah, so how's that going with your dad?" I say.

Pete shrugs and flicks his fingers at a barrel-shaped bead he's wearing on a hemp cord around his neck. "All right, so far, I guess. We're not allowed to see him, but he's still there sweating it out. He keeps saying on the phone he's miserable, but he's saying it with less and less conviction, if you know what I mean." Pete rocks back in his chair and rubs his hand over his bald head. "The important thing is he's there. In time he'll come around." He looks at me; then he looks at his watch. It's the third time in about ten minutes that he's looked at it.

"You need to be somewhere? If you do, that's okay. Go on—don't let me keep you." I wave him away and smile to show I don't mind.

CRAZY GLUE: *You're so lame. Just ask what's going on.*

FBG WITH A MUSTACHE: *I'm with Crazy on that one.*

Pete lets the chair fall forward and goes back to flicking at the bead around his neck.

"Yeah—uh, no, uh—I'm just waiting for the others." I feel my body tense. "The others? Who others?"

"Haze and Shelby." Pete's face, usually so calm, is tomato red and his eyes are looking everywhere but at me.

CRAZY GLUE: *Shelby's coming!*

"Hey, what's going on, Pete?" I ask. "Is it about the violin? Did they find it and you're just not saying? Are we in trouble? Did the mailman turn in Haze's license number or my fingerprints or something?"

Pete waves his hand and takes another sip of his tea. "Nah, not that I've heard."

He shrugs and acts like what he's about to say doesn't mean much, but his face says otherwise. "Anyway, Dr. Gomez isn't buying it that you've got mono."

CRAZY GLUE: *Oh, is that all.*

AUNT BEE: *What a relief. I was so worried.*

SEXY LADY: *I wasn't. I knew it all along.*

I straighten my back and adjust the homemade sling on my sore arm to keep the knot of the sling from cutting into my neck. "Oh yeah? Why? What do you mean? Why couldn't I have mono?"

Pete twists his mouth and doesn't answer me. He checks his watch again.

"Hey, come on—what's going on? Come on—tell me." I get to my feet. "Why are Haze and Shelby coming over? I haven't seen Shelby since that day with the violin. So why is she coming over now?"

AUNT BEE: *Don't get your hopes up.*

CRAZY GLUE: *Too late.*

Pete looks over his shoulder at the entrance to the kitchen, and, as if on cue, the doorbell rings. I glance at Pete and he's even more nervous, almost frightened. I hurry out to the door before Haze and Shelby ring it again and wake Dad. I open the door and find Haze on the balls of his feet, shifting from one foot to the other, flakes of snow melting in his hair. He looks ready to spring straight to the sky, he's so nervous. Shelby looks her usual self, though. She bursts in. "Is Pete here?" she says, too loudly. "Who's here?" She pulls off her hat, setting free her pile of hair, and strides into the living room.

SEXY LADY: *She always needs to make such a grand entrance.*

I tell them to keep it down and lead them back to the kitchen. My kneecaps are jiggling up and down as I walk. What's going on?

We all take chairs around the table and the three

of them give one another these anxious looks, like they're signaling something to one another.

FBG WITH A MUSTACHE: *Oh, this setup doesn't look good, Jase.*

"Okay, is someone going to tell me what's happened or what?" I say. My throat constricts and my voice comes out sounding thin and high.

"Look—it's like this," Shelby says, scooping up her hair and releasing it. "Well, you're in bad shape, Jason. Your father's nuts, I mean, let's face it, and dangerous . . ."

"Hey, wait a minute," I say. "He may be a tiny bit crazy, but he isn't dangerous." I shake my head. "He is *not* dangerous. No way."

Shelby touches my bad arm. "You're wearing a rigged-up sling and your hand is swollen and bruised. You could have broken your back, you know."

"That was an accident."

Shelby shrugs. "Whatever, okay?"

"I wouldn't have said anything, man," Haze says, speaking for the first time since he got here. "But you know she asked us in group the other day and we"—he looks at Pete—"we had to tell. Sorry, man." He leans forward and sets his elbows on the table, resting his head in his hands.

LAUGH TRACK: *Uh-oh.*

I break out in a sweat. "Tell what?" I say. "What do you mean?" I pound the table, and Shelby draws back and sucks in her breath between her teeth.

"Tell him what you did, Socks," Pete says.

Shelby leans forward again. She looks miserable and this scares me. "Okay." She closes her eyes. "You have no food, no heat, your dad's crazy, he pushed you down the stairs, stole a three-million-dollar violin, the house is falling apart, and you can't even get out of the house to go to school. So—you need help." She opens her eyes.

I'm standing over her. I don't know when I stood up, but here I am, standing over her, glaring, panting, fuming, gripping my one good hand into a fist that very much wants to plow into her face.

AUNT BEE: *Careful, now.*

"What did you do?"

Shelby raises her shoulders and leans away from me. "I told Dr. Gomez," she says, her voice barely a whisper.

I knew she was going to say that. I knew it! I knew it was coming, but I explode as if I didn't know. I slam my fist on the table and get right up in her face. "You did what?"

FBG WITH A MUSTACHE: *You're fighting a losing battle, son. The word is out—too late. Dr. Gomez will have to report you.*

CRAZY GLUE: *She totally torpedoed you, goob.*

Shelby rams the palm of her hand into my forehead. "Back off me!" she shouts. "Don't you dare touch me!"

I stumble backwards, feeling stunned by the blow, and she springs from her chair and backs away from me, huddling against the wall as though she expects me to pound her. Tears are running down her face.

AUNT BEE: *Don't you touch her. Your mother raised you better than that.*

Mother? What mother? Where is she now when I need her?

FBG WITH A MUSTACHE: *Just stay calm, son. Buck up.*

Pete gets to his feet and jumps between us. He holds out his arms as though he's playing defense in a game of basketball. "She told because she cares about you, Jason—we all do. Your father needs help. So do you. You can't do this on your own, man. Come on— you know it. You can't do it. Not anymore."

"What is this?" I shout, no longer caring if my dad wakes. "Is this one of your interventions? Is that what this is? Huh?" I glare at the three of them. "You playing psychologist now, Pete? Mr. Healer, Mr. Peace Buddha?" I sneer at him. "I—I tell you guys everything and this is what you do? You tell Gomez? You ruin my life?" I'm gasping and choking on my words, but I refuse to cry. Here it is again, the betrayal, just like in fifth grade with the swirlie and my best friend—only worse, much worse. When will I ever learn?

CRAZY GLUE: *Never trust a soul ever again.*

SEXY LADY: *Just us.*

LAUGH TRACK: *We're here for you. We're all you need.*

"You three admitted it," I say. "You've wanted your

parents dead. Well, I never did. I know what it's like to lose . . . I know, okay? My dad is all I have. How could you—how dare you try to take him from me?"

I move left, then right, trying to yell specifically at Shelby, who stays behind Pete with her arms wrapped around herself for protection.

I glare at Haze, then back at Shelby. "Remember Haze once asked you if you could ever leave your mother helpless and—and gasping for air? Remember? You couldn't do it! You know you couldn't do it, and yet you're trying to force me to do that—to leave my dad. I won't! He's helpless, too—without me."

I turn to leave. "Dad and I are getting out of here. We're leaving this house."

Pete calls after me, "But, Jason, where will you go? It's snowing, it's cold, your father is crazy, and you have no money. Come on, man—think it through. How are you going to handle him when he's loose on the streets?"

I keep walking, trying not to let his words reach me.

CRAZY GLUE: *You'll live in the woods, in a cave.*

I hear the three of them hurrying after me and they stop at the bottom of the steps while I charge them two at a time, leaping over a broken tread.

I hear Haze say behind me, "Come on—we need to tell him, man. We need to tell him now."

I turn around at the top of the stairs. I see the three of them looking up at me with anxious expressions—

Pete's face, always so open and friendly, and Haze's bearded face with the drawn-on teardrops, and freckled Shelby—and all I feel is hate. I hate them more than I've ever hated anything or anyone. I *hate* them.

AUNT BEE: *Oh dear.*

"Tell me what?" I ask. "What more could you have to do to me?"

"Dr. Gomez . . ." Shelby starts, but the doorbell rings.

"Oops, too late," Haze says, and I know that Dr. Gomez, and whatever authorities handle the removal of crazy people, are standing on the other side of the door.

I back away from the stairs and down the hallway toward the bathroom, where my dad is still sleeping, and I shout, "No! No! No! No! No! No! No!"

I just can't stop. The day, the moment I have feared and fought against ever since my mom died, is here. I need to escape. I need to think, but all I can think of is "no"—the same word that's been screaming inside my head every day for the past eight months.

CHAPTER EIGHTEEN

I KNEW THAT IF ANYONE found out about my
dad, he'd get taken away and I'd never see him again. I
knew it. I should have kept my mouth shut. I should
never have told Pete, or Haze, or Shelby. I should never
have let them in my house. How could I have let my
guard down like this? I knew better.

AUNT BEE: *You just wanted some friends.*

FBG WITH A MUSTACHE: *You didn't want to feel so alone in the
world.*

CRAZY GLUE: *Yeah, well look where that idea's gotten him. Stick
with us, buddy. You don't need anyone else.*

The doorbell rings again. I stand in the doorway
of the upstairs bathroom and yell for everybody to get
out of my house. I back into the room and close and
lock the door. I stand with my good arm pressing
against the door, trying to get my breathing under control. I hear the door open down below.

FBG WITH A MUSTACHE: *Don't panic. Just don't panic. Think! Think!*

I take a deep breath and turn around to check on
Dad, realizing just now that all the noise should have
awakened him.

I glance at him lying in the tub, just as I had left him. His chest rises and falls beneath the blanket as he sleeps.

I hear people talking, and I return to the door. I try to hear what they're saying. Then there's the sound of footsteps clomping up the stairs. I don't know what to do. I'm trapped. I turn to the window that overlooks our backyard. No way can we jump out the window onto the bricks below and keep from breaking something.

There's a knock on the door and then the sound of a voice. "Jason? It's Dr. Gomez. Are you okay?"

I don't say anything.

"Jason, it's all right. We've just come over to take a look around and have a talk."

I hear other people besides Gomez moving on the other side of the door.

FBG WITH A MUSTACHE: *Stay calm. Be cool.*

"Go away, please," I say.

There are a few seconds of silence, and then Dr. Gomez says, "You've been having a tough time of it, haven't you, Jason?"

"Go away, please. We're doing just fine. Just go away, now. Just go away."

I hear someone walking around, moving in and out of the rooms. "Please get out of my house." I make fists with both of my hands and try to keep my voice under control even though I feel hysteria rising in my chest.

AUNT BEE: *You're doing just fine. Good boy. You're a good son.*

"Jason, is your father in there with you? May I speak to him?"

"He's asleep. Go away, now."

"Where is he asleep?" asks a deep voice, a strange man's voice.

I turn away from the door and take a long breath.

CRAZY GLUE: *Who the hell is he?*

"Who the hell is that?" I say, returning to the door. "Go away! Why won't you just leave?"

I move from the door and sit on the edge of the tub, as though by doing so I can protect my dad somehow. I glance back at him and wonder how he can sleep through all of this.

AUNT BEE: *The sleep of the innocent is always peaceful.*

"Listen, Jason? I'm Sam Waldron. I'm from the Department of Family Services."

I slam my good hand down on the edge of the tub.

CRAZY GLUE: *Shit!*

"You're not taking my father away from me," I shout.

SEXY LADY: *Don't cry. I'm here to soothe you. Don't cry, Jase.*

I wipe the tears off my face and sniff. I hate that they can hear me crying on the other side.

"No, Jason, we have no plans to take anyone today," Sam says. "We just would like to talk with your father. Could you tell us where he is?"

FBG WITH A MUSTACHE: *Ah! Nobody knows he's here in the bathroom.*

"He's not here," I say. "He's sleeping at a friend's house, at—at his friend's house."

"And he left you here?"

What's that supposed to mean? "I'm almost fifteen years old. I think I can stay by myself all right—jeez!"

I hear them whispering. I hear Shelby's voice, but I can't tell what she said. Then I hear Pete say, "Shelby, why don't you just stay out of it."

And then Dr. Gomez says, "I think it might be best if you three left us alone. I appreciate your help. Really. Thank you."

"See you soon, Jason," Pete calls. "Hang in there, okay?"

"Yeah," Haze says. "See ya soon."

"Jason, don't be mad at me, okay? I just . . ."

Shelby doesn't finish and a good thing, too, because right now I want to kill her. I feel so totally betrayed by her.

SEXY LADY: *I warned you. She puts on a good show, but she's the dangerous one.*

I grit my teeth and grip the edge of the tub, an old claw-foot tub with a narrow curved edge that's getting way too uncomfortable to sit on.

FBG WITH A MUSTACHE: *Stay calm, son. You don't want to lose it in front of Dr. Gomez and this Sam guy.*

I hear footsteps retreating down the stairs, and then Dr. Gomez says, "Jason, I came here with Sam because I'm concerned about you and your father. We

162

don't want to separate you. We're just here to figure out the best way to help you. You believe me, don't you?"

CRAZY GLUE: *Oh sure. Sure we do.*

"If you want to help me, go away. Just leave. We're fine. We're doing fine. So just leave already."

"Jason," Sam says, "it would be good if we could all just sit down and talk together and figure out what would be best for you and your father. We have lots of different services available. The last thing we want to do is separate you two if we can help it. I have no court order for that with me. I can't remove you from your home today."

Does he think I'm stupid?

CRAZY GLUE: *Uh—yeah.*

Maybe he doesn't have a court order today, but if he ever talked with my dad, he'd soon have one and that would be the end. They'd haul him away and send me who knows where.

I don't say anything. There's nothing more to say. I let them talk to me through the door, trying to coax me out. They want to know where Dad is. They explain again that they're just here to help, but I don't say anything.

SEXY LADY: *Just pretend you're not here. You're invisible. Let their voices wash over you like so much white noise. That's all it is— white noise.*

Finally Sam says, "Jason, we're going to leave now, but you've given me no alternative. I'll be back, and I'll

163

have a court order for removal. Not that I'll necessarily use it, but your behavior today and the condition of this house have raised some red flags. We need to talk to you and your father. It would be better if we could do that today."

I keep silent. I hold my breath and wait for them to give up and leave.

"All right, goodbye then," Dr. Gomez says. "Just remember, if you need me, I'm always available. I'm going to slip one of my cards under the door. It's got my cell phone number on it. You call me if you want me here, okay?"

I watch the card slide under the door, but I don't move. Then I hear their footsteps retreating and, at last, the sound of the front door opening and closing.

I shut my eyes and let out my breath, but I don't get up and unlock the door, just in case they didn't really leave, just in case they're hiding out somewhere downstairs.

CHAPTER NINETEEN

I SIT ON THE EDGE of the bathtub for several minutes, listening both to the silence on the other side of the door and to my dad's breathing behind me. I'm trying to listen for some sound, some whisper down below. Something isn't right.

CRAZY GLUE: *It's your dad, goob. Why doesn't he wake up?*

I whip around to check on him. He's buried beneath so much wool, but still I can hear that his breathing sounds funny—fast and shallow. His face looks flushed. I lean over and feel his forehead. He's got a fever—great.

I slide to the floor and rest my head against the tub, my good arm hanging over the rim above my dad's body. What am I going to do now?

CRAZY GLUE: *Scram! You need to blow this joint before Sam comes back with his court order.*

FBG WITH A MUSTACHE: *Be serious. Where would he go? He can't just wander the streets. And he has his dad to consider. Living in a cave is not an option. You don't even know where a cave is around these parts. This isn't Greece, and it's twenty degrees out.*

LAUGH TRACK: *Isn't this a shame.*

I look out the window and see the snow coming down. I shake my head and turn my attention back to Dad. I need to get him out of his wet underwear, get him dry, and get his fever down. These things have to come first.

I get up on my knees, lean over the tub, and shake him. "Dad? Wake up. Come on, wake up, now. Hey, you missed all the excitement." I shake him and shake him, and at last he groans and opens his eyes.

"Dad, you need to get out of the tub. We have to get some dry clothes on you. Are you cold? You've got a fever. Is it your tooth again?"

"The boy will find my violin."

"No." I get to my feet and pull on his arm so he'll sit up. "The boy doesn't have your violin. The boy is going to get you out of this tub and get you dressed."

"The boy will find my violin," my dad repeats. He nods to himself and lets me pull him to a sitting position.

"Stand up, now," I say. "You have to help me here, okay? Are you all right?"

He places his hands on either side of the tub and struggles to stand. I can see his arms shaking. The wool blankets slide off his lap and fall in a heap at his feet. "My violin," he says, turning his head and glancing out the window.

"Yeah, Dad, it's snowing out. It's raw and gray and wet outside. What do you think? Feel like going out in that and sleeping under a bridge somewhere? See, 'cause that's what we've come to now."

FBG WITH A MUSTACHE: *Buck up, son.*

"I'm cold," Dad says, shivering and grabbing his arms. His teeth chatter.

I reach for his hand and pull on him so he'll climb out of the tub. "We're in a fine mess now, aren't we? You've got a fever."

"Fever pitch," Dad says, climbing out of the tub, his body still shivering. "Fever pitch. The Furies have lit a fire in the brain to paralyze reason—a fire in the brain."

I grab one of the blankets and wrap it around his shoulders as best as I can using my good arm and with no help from him. Then I creep over to the door, unlock it with a quiet click, and ease it open. I pause and listen.

"Okay, I give up," I call down the hallway, thinking that if Dr. Gomez and Sam are still in the house, my surrender will draw them out of hiding and I can dart back into the bathroom. The house is silent. I turn and grab Dad by the arm and walk him to his bedroom, where I help him get into warm clean clothes. He's shivering, and he keeps trying to climb into his bed before he's got all his clothes on.

"Tell the boy about the fire in the brain. Tell the boy," he says, climbing again onto his bed.

"I'll tell the boy just as soon as you get this sweater on."

CRAZY GLUE: *The boy! Now you're just the boy. He's totally whacked.*

AUNT BEE: *Maybe you should call Dr. Gomez.*

No way. He's just got a fever. Just a little fever. It's okay.

I finish getting him dressed and tuck him into bed. I grab some aspirin and, after twenty minutes of convincing him it's not poisoned, give Dad two pills with water. He burps, rolls over, and curls up into a shivering ball. I cover him with every blanket we have in the house, then start to leave to go fix him some soup, when he calls me back.

"Jason," he says.

I turn around.

"Will the pain never end?" He stares up at me, his eyes burning with fever.

I pat his shoulder. "The aspirin will start to work soon."

"No!" Dad lifts his head. "Not that pain; the pain of us. Every time I look at you, I see the pain of us."

His words startle me. What does he see in my face? Does he know what he's saying, or is this just some kind of feverish rambling? What does he mean by "the pain of us"? I think to ask him, but then I realize I don't want to know the answer. I don't want to think about "our" pain. I lean over and give him a quick hug, then hurry off to fix him his soup.

While I prepare his meal I turn on the television, which gets like two snowy channels, and I see the Stradivarius violin in the right-hand corner of the screen. I turn up the volume.

"... at the altar this morning. Father O'Connor said they were just happy to be able to return the valuable Strad to its rightful owner."

Father O'Connor appears on the screen. He's wearing his priest get-up and he's standing in front of the National Cathedral downtown. He speaks into the microphone held in front of his face. "It's a mystery," he says, "but I'm pleased that whoever took the violin felt his conscience pricked and brought it safely here. It restores my faith in humanity."

CRAZY GLUE: *Ah, humanity. Aren't they the ones trying to dump your dad in the loony bin?*

They then cut to the beaming violinist posing with his Stradivarius, and I turn off the television.

AUNT BEE: *Let's be grateful for small miracles. At least one thing went right today.*

CRAZY GLUE: *Let's not. We're still knee-deep in donkey crap.*

I pour the hot vegetable beef soup into a bowl. I wonder about the violin turning up at the National Cathedral. I figure the mailman must have been sweating it out the past week while wondering what to do with it. If he said he found it in his truck, then he could get fired for having left his truck unlocked; if

169

he said he just found it, maybe someone would think he stole it, just like we worried would happen to us.

FBG WITH A MUSTACHE: *What a great idea to leave it with a priest. Why didn't we think of that?*

I chuckle to myself, forgetting my troubles for a moment. I think about having a good laugh with Pete and Haze the next time they come over.

CRAZY GLUE: *Uh, maybe not. Remember, they're not your friends anymore. You ain't never gonna get to celebrate that close call with them.*

SEXY LADY: *Or have a good laugh over the memory of that wild ride through Haze's neighborhood.*

LAUGH TRACK: *Isn't it a shame?*

FBG WITH A MUSTACHE: *Let's focus on the positive. At least one good thing happened today. You should celebrate.*

Yeah, I should celebrate. I look around me. I grab myself a couple of pieces of bread and instead of spreading the thinnest layer of peanut butter and jelly on them the way I usually do, I slather them with the stuff. Then I put the two slices together and take a big bite, letting the sides ooze with the extravagance.

CRAZY GLUE: *There you go. Eat drink and be merry, for tomorrow we die.*

CHAPTER TWENTY

I DON'T HAVE ANY TIME to think about a plan for what my next move will be. I don't know how we're going to get away from Sam and his court order. I don't let myself go there. I spend the night taking care of Dad. He barfs; I clean it up. He barfs again, and I clean it up. I set a bucket beside his bed. He doesn't even try to aim, and for someone who never seemed to eat, he sure has a lot of food exploding out of him, and from both ends.

CRAZY GLUE: *Yeah, yeah, okay, we get the picture.*

He's sicker than I've ever seen him. I figure he must have the stomach flu or some other kind of virus.

Whenever he pukes, I pull him out of the bed and put him into mine while I clean up. Then I put him back in his own bed. Then I pull him out again a short while later and haul him down to the bathroom, where I wait while he sits on the toilet and gets sick that way. Then I clean him up and drag him back to his bed and wait a bit until it's time to do the whole routine over again—and again.

Now it's morning and I'm wiped out. Dad still has a fever. He refuses to drink anything and he waves his arms wildly whenever I come close to him with a glass of water or mug of soup in my hands. "The strings are busted. Tell the boy!" he says.

I think of setting out with Dad and heading to the clinic, but he seems too sick to make the long trip on the bus and sit half the day in the crowded waiting room. The last time I took him to the toilet, he passed out. What if he passed out on the bus?

FBG WITH A MUSTACHE: *Face it, son—you just don't have the energy.*

I spend the morning washing sheets and clothes with the last of our laundry detergent. I clean the floor several times where my dad almost made it to the bucket by his bed.

In the afternoon I eat the last of our oatmeal, then try to get Dad to drink some warm tea. An hour after eating my oatmeal I throw it up.

CRAZY GLUE: *It's just exhaustion. You're fine. Don't worry about it.*

AUNT BEE: *But he has chills. I think he has a fever.*

SEXY LADY: *I think you're hot when you're hot.*

LAUGH TRACK: *Ha-ha.*

I sit in a chair, wrapped in one of the blankets from Dad's bed, and shiver while I keep watch for that Sam guy from the bedroom window. I've decided we don't need to run anywhere; we just won't open the door. Dad's too out of it to make much noise, so I figure we'll hide out upstairs; hopefully Sam and Dr. Gomez will think we've run away and they'll give up.

CRAZY GLUE: *Oh sure. Sure they will. Please tell me I'm not hanging out with a moron.*

Got any other bright ideas? Yeah, didn't think so.

Now it's late afternoon and I'm sure I've got it, too—the creeping crud. I set up a pallet in the bathroom and lie down on the floor by the toilet. I figure it'll be easier to clean myself up if I miss this way.

CRAZY GLUE: *And it smells so good, too. Mmm, what is that, eau de puke?*

I go to sleep, but then I wake up again when I hear the sound of the doorbell and several rapid knocks. I lift my head and, with my ears pricked, wait. I pray Dad will just lie still and keep quiet. A few minutes later, I hear the doorbell and the knocking again. "Please, please, please, go away," I whisper.

AUNT BEE: *Lie back down, Jason. I'll take care of you.*

SEXY LADY: *Let me soothe you. Here we are. See us? Here we are. We'll look after you. Yes, that's right, we're all here for you.*

I sleep and dream about Aunt Bee and the Sexy Lady and Fat Bald Guy and Crazy Glue, and You. You're there, too. I *am* dreaming, aren't I?

I wake again and it's nighttime. I know I need to check on my dad, so I force myself to get up. My lower back muscles kill, they're so sore. I drag down the hallway to Dad's bedroom. I see by the light from the street that the glass of water I had set on his bedside table earlier hasn't been touched. I stumble over to his bed and feel his forehead, but with my own body so feverish, it's hard to tell how hot he is. I shake him. "Dad, how you doin'? You okay?" I kneel on the floor and lean my head against the bed. I'm too dizzy to stay standing. I raise my good arm and pat his shoulder.

"I have been in a beautiful place," Dad says, his voice sounding hoarse and dry.

"Yeah? You wanna take me there, Dad? Take me someplace beautiful and happy with lots of green and yellow."

"The boy will take you."

I lift my head. "Who is the boy? Where will I find the boy? Huh? Huh, Dad?"

"They got him, I think," he whispers.

"Who did? Who got him? The Furies? They didn't get him. I'm right here."

"They got Mother and Dad and Lara and the music and the boy, and they're coming after me. Tonight they're coming after me. Do you hear them? Do you hear the drum section?" He places his hands over his chest. *"Patta-pum patta-pum de dum dum,"* he sings.

I sit up straight and my head throbs. "No. No, Dad. I don't hear anything. Just you. It's just your voice. No Furies."

"Listen."

"Nobody's coming," I say. "Nobody's going to get you. I'll keep you safe. I always have, haven't I?" I squeeze his shoulder.

"Listen. Do you hear them?"

"No. Who?" I'm feeling sick. My stomach is cramping. I need to go to the bathroom.

"The drums. They're coming." He lifts his arm and stares at it. "The moonlight shines right through me now. It sees clear through me."

I struggle to my feet, using the bed for support. "No! No drums. No Furies. Nobody's coming. No moonlight. No one will ever take you away. Do you hear me? You're safe." I push his arm and it flops onto his chest.

"It's all right," Dad whispers. "They say I need to go."

I lean over him, holding on to the bedpost with my right hand, and gaze down at him in the darkness. His face, fuzzy in the dim light, looks peaceful, and it frightens me. I'm used to his fear. His fear is normal. This peace doesn't feel right. Is he talking about dying?

FBG WITH A MUSTACHE: *I think so.*

LAUGH TRACK: *Isn't it a shame.*

"I feel a beautiful place of moon music. They tell me it's beautiful, *patta-pum pum*. No Furies. So I must go."

I don't know if it's panic or my food rising. I search around for the bucket and grab it just in time. I retch into the bucket and wipe my mouth on a damp washcloth I had set out for Dad to use. My mind is racing. Is he dying? Have I let him die? Am I killing him? Is that what I've been doing? Not protecting him at all, just slowly killing him? Mom! Why did you leave me? How could you?

FBG WITH A MUSTACHE: *Shh!*

What does he mean when he says he must go? What beautiful place does he see? I look at him lying in the bed, so thin and pale. He smells awful. He smells like the stuff the girls at school use to remove nail polish—like acetone. I look at the room, my parents' bedroom once, but now the room—the house—has become our prison. How has this happened?

CRAZY GLUE: (Singing) *Take the keys and lock them up, lock them up, lock them up.*

I let this happen. It's all my fault, this prison we're in.

CRAZY GLUE: (Singing) *Lock them up, lock them up.*

"A rope in my throat," Dad says. "Pull out the rope so I can breathe. I can't breathe." He gasps and raises his head and tries to get out of the bed, but then he flops back, too weak or maybe too dizzy to rise. "Time to go," he whispers. "Just let me go. Pull out the rope."

SEXY LADY: *Do something, Jason!*

CRAZY GLUE: (Singing) *Lock them up, lock them up.*

FBG WITH A MUSTACHE: *Don't just stand there. Hurry. Get help. Not a moment to lose.*

I glance at the clock on the chest of drawers. It's just after eight. Dr. Gomez will still be awake.

LAUGH TRACK: *Call her!*

"Dad, I'm going to go get help, okay? We need help.

I'm letting go, but not for good. You're not dying. You're not going to die on me. Okay?" I pull my left arm out of my sling and grab the glass of water on the side table. I lean over and lift his head with my good hand. "Here, drink this. Drink this! Drink this! Please, Dad, drink this."

Dad flails, his mouth clamped shut. I set the glass back down on the table and hurry to the bathroom where I'd left Dr. Gomez's card.

"Oh please, oh please, oh please." I crawl around on the floor among the bedding, looking for the card. Finally I find it. I jump up, grab the box of baking soda we use for toothpaste off the sink, and put some in my mouth. Then I take a slurp of water and hurry downstairs, swishing the water and baking soda around, hoping it will mask my own stink. I open the front door and spit the pasty stuff out onto the street, gagging at the leftover glob clinging to the roof of my mouth. I run to my neighbors. "Please, oh please, oh please let him be okay!" I run on wobbly legs past the house next door because there aren't any lights on. I move on to the next house and see the blue flashing light of the television. I ring the doorbell, and a man in a tight white T-shirt with a big belly answers the door.

"Please, can I use your phone? My father's sick— and I'm sick. I need to get help." I wave Dr. Gomez's card in the man's face. "Can I use your phone?"

He steps back, allowing me to enter. "Sure, come

on. It's in the kitchen. I'll show you." I follow him, wishing he'd move faster. My head's swimming, my legs feel weak, and my stomach is cramping, but I don't care if I vomit all over this man's house; I've got to use his phone.

He stops in the kitchen doorway and points to a red phone hanging on the wall.

CRAZY GLUE: *A hotline! Perfect.*

I dash to the phone and call Dr. Gomez's number. She answers right away. "Hi, it's me, it's Jason—Jason Papadopoulos. Help. Help me. I need your help. Could you come—could you come, now? My dad is really sick. I'm scared. Please, could you come right now?"

CHAPTER TWENTY-ONE

I SIT IN MY DAD'S BEDROOM and wait for Dr. Gomez to arrive. Dad's asleep, but his breathing doesn't sound good. I decide not to wake him until it's time to leave. I stare out the window and watch the shimmer and shadows of the river, and listen to the wind and the clicking of bare branches hitting against one another.

I hear sirens in the distance and I wonder what other disaster is happening in the city right now.

I keep listening. The sirens get closer, and closer.

CRAZY GLUE: *They're for you, goob.*

I jump to my feet and stare out the window. A few seconds later an ambulance and police car, both with lights flashing, pull up outside the house. I don't know what to do. We have no health insurance. We can't pay for this. We can't pay for a hospital stay. "Jeez!"

I hurry downstairs.

AUNT BEE: *Just explain to everybody—false alarm.*

CRAZY GLUE: *Yeah, right. The city will love that.*

Why had Dr. Gomez called them?

I open the door and see two men holding a stretcher

between them aiming straight for the house. The front man asks me where to go. I try to tell them that we can't pay, but I can't get anything to come out of my mouth.

FBG WITH A MUSTACHE: *You know your father needs a hospital.*

I point toward the staircase.

The two men tromp up to my dad's bedroom. I wait in the hallway. I'm shivering even with a blanket wrapped around me. I don't know what I should do. The doorbell rings; I open the door again and it's Dr. Gomez. She grabs me right away and holds me tight. I want to collapse. She feels so good. It's been so long since I've been hugged. I didn't know how hungry I was for it, but I push away. I need to make her understand.

"We have no insurance. We can't pay. We can't pay." I say this over and over.

Dr. Gomez hugs me again. "It's going to be all right. You're all right, now."

It would be so nice to believe her, but now that she's here and my dad's coming down on a stretcher on his way to the hospital and out of my life, I don't see how anything will be all right, ever again. Is he going to die? I can't lose him; I just can't. And if he gets better, then what? Where will the doctors put him to heal his mind? Will it ever heal? And where will I go? Now that I've called Dr. Gomez, I have no control over anything anymore; yet all I keep saying is that we have no money. We can't pay.

The two men carrying my dad reach the bottom steps and Dr. Gomez lets go of me and opens the door for them. She tells them to take him to the Virginia Hospital Center in Arlington, and then she looks at me. "You'd better go, too. You feel quite feverish and you look exhausted."

I shake my head. I try to protest again, but she grabs my arm. "Jason, let go. It's going to be all right. They take people at the center without insurance. It's okay now. It's all going to be okay."

A policeman calls to me from the sidewalk. "Son, do you need help getting into the ambulance?"

I want to ride with Dad, so I agree to go and let a doctor look at me. I grab the keys to the house and glance about me before I leave. Already the living room looks abandoned and even strange, like it's no longer a part of me. Its cold silence warns me that the next time I see this house, everything will have changed. My life and my dad's life will be totally different. When I close this door, this chapter of my life will be over.

Thank goodness I have my friends, Crazy Glue and Sexy Lady and Fat Bald Guy and Aunt Bee. Thank goodness I have You—or I'd truly be all alone.

CHAPTER TWENTY-TWO

THEY DRUGGED ME LAST NIGHT. What right did they have to do that?

AUNT BEE: *You were a wild man. You kept kicking the nurse and trying to get off the gurney. They had to do something.*

Well, he wouldn't let me stay with Dad.

AUNT BEE: *You shouldn't have kicked him. Your father needed better care than you. He has a heart arrhythmia. That can be serious.*

They shouldn't have drugged me. Anyway, they said it was just dehydration causing the arrhythmia. He's going to be fine. It's just a stomach flu.

FBG WITH A MUSTACHE: *And you're both malnourished and seriously exhausted. Most nights you barely sleep.*

Whose side are you on here? I wouldn't have brought you along if I'd known you all were going to attack me.

AUNT BEE: *Nobody's attacking you, Jason. Calm down. Your anger is way out of proportion. We're all on your side. We're just trying to make you see reason.*

Are you saying I'm not reasonable? Are you saying I can't reason? Do you think *I'm* crazy? Huh? Well I might just drop the lot of you. Forget you, Aunt Bee! Forget all of you. Who needs you? I don't. I don't need anybody.

CRAZY GLUE: *You're acting like a baby.*

I don't care.

CRAZY GLUE: *Whaa-whaa-whaa! Now we're going to pout.*

Back off!

I look across the room at the clock. It's one o'clock. I've slept past lunch. I see a tray of brown mushy food on a table to my left and on my right is a light blue curtain. Maybe Dad's on the other side. "Hello? Dad?"

I struggle to a sitting position. "Dad, is that you?"

"Uh, are you talking to me? I'm Marshall," a kid's voice says.

"Oh, sorry." I rub my head. I swallow. My mouth feels dry. I'm lightheaded, too. When I turn my head from right to left, the room kind of floats around me. I test this a few times, turning my head to the two large windows on my left and then to the curtain, then to the windows, and back to the curtain. I feel nauseated.

CRAZY GLUE: *So stop doing that, dumb-dumb.*

Well who cares if I'm dizzy? I'm not gonna sit in this bed all day waiting for a doctor. I'm going to go find my dad.

I start to get up and I hear a knock on the door. I wait for Marshall to say something.

"Can I come in?" It's a man's voice.

I figure it's one of Marshall's relatives. The kid doesn't say anything, though, so I shrug and say, "Sure, come on in. I think he's asleep, though."

A man, youngish, maybe in his late twenties or early thirties and looking like he lifts weights, with his thick neck and stocky build, comes from around the curtain, strides over to my bed, and shoots out his hand to shake mine. "Hi there, Jason. I'm Sam Waldron."

LAUGH TRACK: *Uh-oh!*

"Oh. Yeah. Hi."

Okay, I figured I'd have to face this man sometime; I just didn't expect it to be so soon. I sit up straighter. I want to bolt and I guess the thought shows on my face, because Sam sets his big solid hand on my shoulder and says, "I'm just here to help you, Jason, that's all. Family Services' goal is to fix it so that eventually you and your father are living together on your own without any interference from us. That's what we're after. Believe me, the fewer people who need our help, the better for everybody. Okay?"

Sam doesn't wait for an answer from me. He looks around for a chair, finds one across the room, and brings it over beside my bed. He sits on the edge of the chair and leans forward. He looks straight at me. His eyes are gray, like my dad's. "Here's the plan, Jason. The hospital wants to release you tonight, which means you need a place to stay."

I cross my arms, wincing a little. They've removed my improvised sling and haven't yet replaced it. "I'm staying with my dad," I say.

Sam nods. "I understand you would like to stay with him, but just listen a minute. Your father's not likely to be going anywhere for the next couple of days. Then—"

"Then I'm staying here, with him."

Sam raises his hand. "Then," he repeats, this time with more emphasis, "your father will be evaluated, both physically and mentally, at which time a decision will be made as to the best care for him."

"And what about me? What happens to me in your big plans?" I point at the file he's holding. It's a thin file, so I assume it's ours—mine and Dad's—two new people entered into the system.

"We'll place you, temporarily, in the home of another family member, or friend, or—"

I interrupt again. "Do you think we'd even be in this situation if we had family somewhere? I don't have any family. They all died off, or they live in Greece."

"Or," he says, again with emphasis, "we'll find you a temporary foster home."

I feel dizzy, so I slouch down in my bed more so that I can rest my head on a pillow. "I don't know why I can't stay with my dad. What's so wrong with me staying with him, here?"

Sam looks me in the eyes again. He does it like he's practiced this—this deep stare. I don't like it. I look away.

"Jason, what kind of care do you feel your father needs?"

I shrug and study my hands. I notice my fingernails look really dirty in this bright, clean hospital room. "I don't know," I say. "I just want things to be the way they were—the way they used to be."

"And what way was that?" Sam asks, setting his elbows on his knees.

I look out the windows at some distant church steeple and ask myself honestly what Dad needs, and my answer is my mom. Everything would be okay if Mom were here. She was the one who could always make Dad better again. She was the one who could draw him out of his study and get him to join us on trips to the zoo or picnics in the dead of winter along the C&O canal. She was the one who could get Dad to laugh, and even though Dad was the writer, she was the one with all the stories, the memories— about how they met, about their first years of marriage, about me.

AUNT BEE: *There you go. You're remembering your mother. That wasn't so hard, was it?*

I feel a sudden burning in my chest. I swallow, thinking I can get rid of the feeling that way, but it only intensifies. I press the heel of my hand against my chest and take a deep breath. Then I turn back to Sam. "I think my dad just needs to see my mom again."

"Okay," Sam says, nodding. "But that's not very realistic, is it? Don't you think you and your father deserve to build a good life without her?"

"What is this?" I explode. "Everybody's ganging up on me! I'm not realistic? You think I'm not realistic? Like I'm crazy, too? Is that what you think? I *know* my mom's dead. Okay? I *know* she's not ever coming back. I know that! Don't you think I know that?"

Sam has jumped out of his chair. "Okay, calm down. It's all right. It's all right. Nobody thinks you're crazy." He puts his thick arm around my shoulder and does this sideways hug thing so my head is mashed against his rib cage.

CRAZY GLUE: *Yeah, goob. Calm down already. You're freaking me out, man.*

I pull away from Sam. "I'm okay. I'm calm. You can sit down now. I'm not going to do anything."

"Of course you're not," he says, but he doesn't sit. Instead he takes the file he left in the chair and tucks it under his arm.

CRAZY GLUE: *That file's gotta reek!*

"Listen, Jason—I'm going to come back around dinnertime to pick you up. By then we'll have your living arrangements all figured out. I promise, everything will work out fine. You'll see. Now, are you willing to go with me?"

"Do I have a choice?" I cross my arms again and look out the windows. I see a gaggle of geese flying past the steeple.

CRAZY GLUE: *Freedom.*

"Yes, you do. You can go with me willingly, with the intention of making the best of a difficult situation, or you can go unwillingly and make yourself and everyone around you miserable."

CRAZY GLUE: *Where'd they find this bozo?*

I don't say anything, and after a moment Sam pats my shoulder, tells me he'll see me later, and leaves.

I'm down in my dad's hospital room. The doctor came to see me for all of five seconds after Sam left, and then a nurse came and put my arm in an official sling. She said it should heal in a couple of weeks.

Dad's asleep. He's got tubes and baggies and stuff hooked up to him, and the monitor by the bed beeps and burps now and then, letting me know he's still alive. They've shaved his beard off and he looks better—cleaner—but he's so thin, he barely makes a lump in the bed. I shake his shoulder. "Dad?" He stirs and smacks his chapped lips a few times.

I imagine him opening his eyes, recognizing me, and saying something wonderful, something that makes sense.

"Dad?"

He opens his eyes; it takes him a moment to focus

and see me. "This is bad news. I got static in the attic. Tell the boy." He closes his eyes. "The Furies . . ." He goes back to sleep.

I use my good arm to pull the covers to his chin. I feel his forehead; the fever is gone.

AUNT BEE: *If only his mind were as easy to fix as his body.*

I'm just glad he's alive. Really. At least he's alive. Right? That's the important thing. That's what we've all got to remember.

I notice his wrists are tied to the bed. My chest burns again. I feel like a complete failure. Why couldn't I fix him? What did I do wrong?

CRAZY GLUE: *Maybe it's too much like the blind leading the blind.*

Shut up! What does that mean? What do you all keep implying? Why don't you leave me alone? You're all turning against me. Where's Sexy Lady? Has she turned against me, too?

SEXY LADY: *You're just so angry. Anger's not hot. Calm down, Jason. That's all we're saying.*

I'm not angry. Why does everybody keep saying to calm down! I'm calm! I'm calm! Jeez! I'm calm already!

A nurse comes into the room, holding a set of sheets. She looks like someone's grandmother, a comfortable-looking kind of person, like Aunt Bee.

AUNT BEE: *Oh dear, I think I look better than she does, don't you? Am I really that overweight?*

"Well now, you'll be happy to know we'll be moving your father out of ICU later tonight if he behaves himself and his heart rate remains stable. It converted on its own, so that's good news." She shakes her head. "He's a fighter, he is, just like his son, from what I hear." She smiles at me and I turn back to my dad. He looks so frail and vulnerable just lying with his mouth hanging open and his arms and legs tied down. Jeez, I hate this!

The nurse sets her sheets on the chair on the other side of the bed. "I'll take good care of your father; don't you worry."

She pushes on something with her foot and raises the bed.

I take Dad's hand in mine. It feels warm, a good kind of warm. "He doesn't know where he is. He's—he's . . ."

"Oh, I know all about it." The nurse nods. She grabs my dad's water pitcher and lifts the lid to peer inside. "We've got it all under control." She goes over to the sink and dumps out the water.

FBG WITH A MUSTACHE: *See. It's all under control.*

Yeah, and I'm calm and I'm not worried, and anyway, I wish everyone would stop telling me how to feel!

CRAZY GLUE: *Aye-aye, sir!*

Oh, shut up!

Dad sleeps all afternoon, so I sit by his bed and watch the TV. I don't want to think about anything. The

TV's good for that. Around five the nurse comes in and pulls out my IV thing that's still stuck in my hand, gives me my bag of clothes, and tells me I can get dressed. I do as I'm told. When I'm done, I sit back down beside my dad. I rest my arm on his shoulder and wait for Sam. The longer I wait, the sharper the pain in my chest gets. Maybe I'll have a heart attack and die. That would solve all my problems.

AUNT BEE: *Maybe all your problems are over. Your father's being taken care of; you're being taken care of . . .*

Why won't you all leave me alone! I don't want to think about it.

FBG WITH A MUSTACHE: *Maybe you're ashamed because you feel a little relieved.*

CRAZY GLUE: *Or a lot relieved.*

Relieved to lose my dad? To be going who knows where? No way! You all are the crazy ones.

FBG WITH A MUSTACHE: *Hmm. Just remember, you said it, not us.*

I hear a knock and look up. It's Sam.

"Where are you taking me?" I ask without even saying hello. I'm pissed. I just feel pissed.

Sam gives me this quick, businesslike smile, the kind of smile that means he has some kind of unpleasant news that he's going to pass off as good news. "We're in luck, Jason. I found a nice couple who have room for you in their home. They live near enough that you'll be able to attend your same school. Pretty good, huh?" He flashes another smile at me. "So, ready to go?"

191

"I guess," I say. I look at Dad and notice his hand twitch beneath his restraint. I try to stand up, but I can't. I shake my head. I can't do it. How can I leave him? It's too hard. I feel so—so—my chest hurts. He needs me. We need to stick together. I can't let go of him. I look at Sam. "Why can't I just stay here? Really, I need to be here with him. I need to." I keep my voice level, no panic, no wild guy, but inside, my chest is on fire, my bird heart is in flames.

"Hey, buddy, it's going to be all right. You can call me anytime to ask about your father's progress, and you'll get to visit with him every two weeks."

"Every two weeks! Are you kidding me? That's not often enough. I have to see him every day. It has to be every day. Every day or I won't leave." I lean back in my chair and cross my good arm over the sling.

"Jason, do you just want what you want, or what's best for your father? Let him get well, okay? Can you do that?"

CRAZY GLUE: *Ouch! The guy sure knows just where to plant his words.*

I shrug, and he says, "I know it's asking a lot of you, but you have to be an adult about this. Let him get well."

I look at my dad lying on his back with his mouth hanging open. The skin on his face is pale yellow. His hands are so long and thin, and veined like an old man's hands. He's just in his forties, too young to look so old.

I know Dad has no idea I'm even here. I think of jumping on top of him and beating him sane, or doing something, anything, to bring him back, now, right away, so that I don't have to leave him. I shake my head and feel the sting of tears welling up. I can't leave. No, I can't leave. I can't stand up and walk out of this room. I'll fall apart. My arm will break off or my heart will cave in, or all my bones will crumble into a million pieces; something terrible like that will happen. I'm sure of it.

Sam comes over to me and sets his hand on my good shoulder. "Time to go now. Here we go." He puts his big Popeye arm around my back and pushes me, and I stand. He keeps his arm around my shoulder and leads me out of the room, talking the whole time. "That's the way. Here we go now. I thought we'd stop off at the Lost Dog Café on the way. Ever been there? Super sandwiches and great pizzas. You up for pizza? They've got one there that's my favorite. It's a white pizza, no tomato sauce and lots of garlic. Lots and lots of garlic."

CHAPTER TWENTY-THREE

MAYBE I STILL have a bit of the stomach flu, because I couldn't eat anything at the restaurant. I sat across from Sam, who stuffed piece after piece of pizza down his throat, all the while talking to me about nothing, just yammering with his mouth full, exposing his half-chewed garlic pizza every once in a while, which made the thought of eating even less appealing.

I guess I'm grateful to Sam for talking, though. The music, the people, the food, the bustling of the waitresses and waiters, and Sam's voice, helped me get through that first hour spent separated from my dad.

Now we're in the car, which reeks of garlic and warm car-heater air, and we're on our way to the foster home.

I stare out at the night, watching all the lights from the cars and streetlamps and shops with neon signs that advertise beer and places that are open, while Sam tells me about the foster family.

"Their name is Lynch," he says. "Margaret and Captain Tony Lynch, naval officer."

CRAZY GLUE: *Cap'n? Did he say Cap'n?*

LAUGH TRACK: *(Laughter).*

"They have two other children living with them, a four-year-old African American girl named Gwendolyn and a seventeen-year-old Caucasian boy named Reed."

"Uh-huh." Do I care who they are or what their names are?

CRAZY GLUE: *Is that a rhetorical question?*

Sam turns onto Gelb Road and heads in the direction of Haze's neighborhood and, for a moment, before I block them out, thoughts of him and Pete and Shelby flood my mind, and then a surge of anger roils in my gut. Okay, I know they did the right thing reporting me. I'm sure that's just what Mouse would have told them to do, but I still can't forgive them, and I hate myself for that as well as everything else.

CRAZY GLUE: *Life just sucks!*

Sam turns off Gelb, still heading toward Haze's neighborhood, and I wonder for one sick moment if maybe Haze's family has agreed to take me in. Maybe Sam is going to surprise me.

He turns again and we ride down a street lined with split-level homes, brick on the bottom and clapboard on the top. They all pretty much look alike except for one that has strings of white Christmas lights outlining the whole house and more lights buried in the lawn that spotlight a bunch of weird metal sculptures. We slow down and Sam signals to turn into the driveway of that house.

CRAZY GLUE: *Figures.*

LAUGH TRACK: *(Nervous laughter).*

We ride past one sculpture that looks like a dragon with metal strips cut like flames coming out of its mouth, and then another that's a snake shaped like a loosely formed lowercase *m*, with some thick coil for its center and a metal mouse with giant whiskers captured inside.

Sam pulls into the driveway and drives up to the garage. "Mrs. Lynch is the artist," he says, turning off the engine.

I don't say anything, but already I don't like the place. I don't like metal. I like rocks and wood— natural stuff.

We get out of the car and walk up to the porch and find a life-size metal dog sculpture. It has a bell in its left paw and the sign around its chest says RING ME.

Sam reaches for the bell and rings it, like this is normal.

CRAZY GLUE: *What kind of asylum has he brought you to, goob?*

The door opens and a boy, tall and fat with a face that looks kind of like a girl's, all smooth and pink, stands in front of us. "Yeah?" he says. Then he opens the door wider and sees Sam with me. "Oh, hi ya, Sam. Come on in. Mom's in the hut-hut out back."

CRAZY GLUE: *Hut-hut? Not good.*

"Thanks, Reed." Sam steps inside and wipes his

196

feet on a mat. "This is Jason Papadopoulos. He's going to be staying with you all awhile."

I stay standing on the narrow porch while Reed glances at me a second, then says, sounding bored, "Yeah, so you told me on the phone." He turns away from the door and heads for a set of stairs.

Sam smiles at me. "Come on." He leads me through the hallway and down the same few steps Reed took. The steps are covered in a shaggy green rug that feels super cushioned underneath, and for a second, before I can block out the thought, I remember my fall down the staircase and then my dad. I don't—I can't think about him.

I follow Sam into a large room at the bottom of the steps with a huge television that covers most of one wall, and lots of oversize chairs. Reed flops down into a plastic-covered recliner and it makes a loud farting noise. He hoots, then grabs a package of Oreos and pops one in his mouth.

"What are you watching there?" Sam asks, even though it's hard to miss Homer Simpson's big mug on that television.

"*Simpsons*," Reed says. "Great religious satire, don't you think?" He pops another Oreo in his mouth. "Mom's out the back there." He points his thumb in the direction of the sliding glass doors without taking his eyes off the television.

Sam slides open the glass door, and we step back outside and go over to a miniature version of the house we just left. Sam raps on the door and a woman wearing a canvas apron and a set of large safety glasses opens the door. "You're here already? Great!" she says, pushing her glasses onto her head. She looks me over and steps back into the building to let us in. "Welcome to my hut-hut."

I step inside behind Sam and squint in the brightly lighted room. A little girl in red overalls and with waves of black hair decorated with a red ribbon toddles over and throws her arms around the woman's leg. She stares up at us.

The woman bends down and scoops the girl into her arms. "This is Gwen," she says. "And I'm Margaret Lynch, but you can call me Mom if you want, or Mrs. Lynch, and you have to be Jason." She laughs and holds out her hand for me to shake—and I freeze.

CRAZY GLUE: *Whoa! Uncanny likeness to your mom's laugh.*

AUNT BEE: *But she looks nothing like her. She's so small, with short salt-and-pepper hair and lots of lines around her eyes. Your mother was tall and graceful with auburn hair and . . .*

I know what my mother looked like. Quiet!

CRAZY GLUE: *But dude, why did she ask you to call her Mom?*

I stand with my mouth gaping open, too stunned to move.

Sam gives me a little shove from behind. "Jason?"

I see Mrs. Lynch's hand still extended and I

squeeze it, and the little girl in her arms slaps my head. "Hi ya there."

"Yeah, hi," I say to her. I let go of Mrs. Lynch's hand.

Then Mrs. Lynch says in this excited voice, "Well, this is where I create my sculptures. I suppose you saw my creatures on the lawn?" She opens a dog gate that sections off part of the room and steps inside, then nods for me to join her. "People love to stop by and see what kind of creature I have out on the lawn. It changes every time I sell a piece. They're strangely popular." She laughs. "I'm not sure why, are you?" She spreads out her free arm to indicate the workshop. "So, what do you think?"

I look around the room at all the machinery, round saws and straight saws and blowtorches and all kinds of nuts and bolts and junk, and beyond the gate on the opposite side of the room, there's an orange rug with a child's table-and-chair set, wooden puzzles, crayons and paper, and several dolls, dressed and half dressed.

I shrug. "Yeah, it's cool."

"I try to keep it tidy," Mrs. Lynch says, "but I don't always succeed. But you don't want to see all this. You want to see your bedroom, I bet. Did you bring a suitcase and your things?"

I look at Sam. All I have is what I'm wearing—jeans too short, a flannel shirt too Dad-like, and my pea coat with the newspaper lining.

Sam says, "We'll go by tomorrow and pick up some of Jason's things." He winks at me like we are great buddies now that I've watched him swallow slices of pizza whole.

Mrs. Lynch sets Gwen down. "I'm sorry you'll have to share a room with Reed, but it's a good-size room. He and Carlin, the last child, managed to get along just fine." She takes Gwen's hand and leads us back outside and into the house where Reed is still watching television and eating Oreos. The bag is almost empty.

"Reed, would you mind showing Jason the room you'll be sharing? He looks rather beat." She turns to me and puts her arm around my shoulder and kind of jostles me. "A good night's sleep will do you some good."

CRAZY GLUE: *Well, she's cheerful, anyway.*

Reed gets out of the chair with a lot of grunting and groaning from both him and the chair and says, "Follow me."

I follow, creeping up the steps behind him, while he climbs each step with his feet spread apart, shifting side to side and breathing heavily as we near the top of the second set of steps. We go down a narrow hall, also covered in green shag, to the last room on the left.

"Bathroom's there," he says, nodding at the dark room just before our room. Then he switches on the bedroom light and steps inside. I walk in behind him. The room has a thick red line painted down the center of the wooden floor. On the left side of the room is a

200

twin-size bed covered in a plain navy spread, a desk and chair, and along one wall, shelves with several model airplanes set up on them.

"Wow, lots of planes, there," I say. I remove my coat and set it on the desk over on what I figure is my side of the room. The house feels too hot—much warmer than I'm used to.

Reed shuffles over to the shelves and picks up one of the planes. "All military," he says. "This is the Japanese Zero Pearl Harbor model." He spins the propeller, then sets the plane back down on the shelf and turns to me. "See all this?" He spreads his arms, taking in the CD player, the computer, his model planes, a few books. "This is all mine. This is my side of the room. You step over that red line there . . ." He pauses, reaches into his pocket, and pulls out a switchblade.

LAUGH TRACK: *Uh-oh.*

He moves closer to me, near the red line, his eyes gleaming. "You step over that red line and I'll slit your throat in your sleep."

I look at Reed standing with his switchblade aimed at me.

CRAZY GLUE: *Buddy, you picked the wrong guy on the wrong day.*

Yeah, what do I have to lose? Nothing, absolutely nothing. I step up to the red line, my toes just touching it, maybe three feet away from Reed. I spread my good arm out, indicating my side of the room. "See this? Tomorrow I'm going to go pick up my stuff and I'm

201

going to bring it here and I'm going to keep it on this side of the room. If I ever catch you crossing the red line, if you ever touch anything of mine, I won't wait until you're asleep to kill you. I'll do it right then, right there—no switchblade, no gun, just my bare hands. You got that?"

We stand looking at each other for a few seconds, sizing each other up. Then Reed lets out a yell like Tarzan, King of the Jungle, and lunges at me with his switchblade open. It enters my stomach, and I don't even feel it until I notice the blood spreading out across my shirt.

CHAPTER TWENTY-FOUR

REED'S YELL alerts Sam, and he shows up in the doorway in a matter of seconds. Mrs. Lynch isn't far behind him. I'm on the floor, crouching down and holding my hand against my stomach as though this is going to keep the blood from pouring out of me.

CRAZY GLUE: *Out of the fat and into the fire. We got us another loony-tooney, here.*

Reed keeps whining, "I didn't do it! I didn't do it!" He falls to his knees, the bloody switchblade still in his hands and tears running down his face. "I swear to God, I didn't do it!"

Sam orders Reed to set the knife down on the desk, but Reed just keeps whining, "I didn't do it!"

"Reed, put the knife on the desk. Do it now!" Sam barks. "Now, Reed!"

"But I didn't do it. You gotta believe me."

SEXY LADY: *Oh, he's good.*

Looking at his wide-eyed, pink blubbering face, even I almost believe him.

AUNT BEE: *Oh dear, they're going to blame you for this. He looks so innocent.*

Nobody moves. Sam raises his voice and shouts again, "Put the knife down on the desk. Do it now! Now, Reed! Now!"

Finally Reed puts the knife on his desk and collapses on his bed as if he's fainted.

Sam runs in and grabs the knife, and Mrs. Lynch runs to me. She helps me to my feet. Then she sees all the blood and she lets out an "Oh!" and then, "We need to go to the hospital, Sam."

CRAZY GLUE: *Didn't we already do the ambulance scene?*

LAUGH TRACK: *Isn't it a shame?*

All I can think of as I lie on a slab with my gut cut open is that I might get to see my dad again. But I don't. There isn't time and everybody's tired, blah, blah, blah.

Three hours later, I'm back in Sam's car on the way back to the Lynches' house with a bottle of pills in my hands, to prevent infection, the doctor said, and an aching stomach. I didn't understand half of what the emergency room doctor said to me except that the wound looks worse than it is, and there's no penetration of the peritoneal cavity, which he said is a good thing. All I know is, hell, I've been stabbed!

I'm sulking because I didn't get to see Dad, and I don't want to talk, but Sam has questions.

"Jason, you've got to tell me what happened. Where did the knife come from?"

"I don't know! Reed's pocket."

FBG WITH A MUSTACHE: *Keep your cool, son.*

"So it's Reed's knife?"

I shrug and stare out at the cars rushing past us. I know Sam's driving slowly on purpose. He wants to grill me before we reach the Lynches' house so he can file his report in the morning.

"I guess it's his," I say. "It sure isn't mine."

"Did you provoke him?"

I look at Sam. "Are you going to try to make this my fault? Did you actually believe that act of his?"

CRAZY GLUE: *Uh . . . yup.*

"So you didn't provoke him?" Sam's looking straight ahead.

I stare out my window and say, giving in a little, "Yeah, I provoked him. He told me if I stepped over the line, he would slit my throat in my sleep. I thought he was bluffing. He looks so innocent."

"Those are the ones you've got to look out for," Sam says, "the innocent-looking ones."

"Now you tell me." I run my hand across my stomach and feel the thick bandage the doctor had put over this skin adhesive that's supposed to act like stitches. We'll see.

"So what did you say when you thought Reed was bluffing?"

CRAZY GLUE: *Whoops.*

"Okay, well, I told him that if he stepped over the red line and touched *my* stuff, I wouldn't wait until he went to sleep; I'd kill him right then."

"You were bluffing?"

I look at Sam. "Yeah, I was bluffing! I don't go around killing people for getting into my stuff, jeez!"

Sam glances at me, car lights reflecting in his eyes. "Well, let me give you a warning, okay? Some kids will kill you for a lot less than that, so no more bluffing. If you have a problem with someone, call me or tell the Lynches. Don't try to handle it yourself."

CRAZY GLUE: *Now, there's some crappy bit of advice.*

FBG WITH A MUSTACHE: *You asked Dr. Gomez for help and look where it got you.*

CRAZY GLUE: *Yeah, riding with Garlic Head Sam and stabbed in the stomach.*

As painful as the stabbing was, though, I feel that standing up to Reed, saying what I said, has kind of set me free. I feel different—looser. I feel like I can take on the world. Maybe I don't have to be afraid of swirlies anymore.

CRAZY GLUE: *Oh yeah? Does that go for all the Dear Mouse hate mail you get, too?*

I don't know, but maybe that's why I'm acting so pissed off with Sam. It just feels really good to know that I can stand up to Reed, to anyone, and survive it.

FBG WITH A MUSTACHE: *You're pissed off. That's what feels good.*

206

After a few moments of silence I ask, "So how am I supposed to keep this Reed guy from slitting my throat in the middle of the night? Do I wear a suit of armor to bed or what?"

"Oh, you won't have to worry about him. He's been removed from the house."

CRAZY GLUE: *What? Been removed? By who? The pod people?*

A weird science-fictionlike scene runs through my mind where men wearing white suits and white head covers come charging into the house and grab Reed, who's still hollering, "I didn't do it!" Then they stun him with their stun guns, suck him up into this human vacuum, and scuttle away.

CRAZY GLUE: *Sounds like a good movie. I wanna see that one!*

Back at the Lynches' house, I go into my bedroom, and my little scenario doesn't seem quite so far fetched. The room's been wiped clean of Reed's existence. Even his bed's been stripped and his desktop has been cleared off. All the shelves are empty—not a single military plane left. I don't like it. It's creepy how they could just get rid of him. Like he's, like we're all, just so disposable. Is that what they'll do to my dad? Suck him up and dump him somewhere where I can't find him, where nobody can, until nobody even remembers that he exists? You're here one minute and gone the next? I don't like it.

SEXY LADY: *Don't worry yourself. You're tired. Go to bed now.
You'll feel better in the morning.*

I just wonder where they put homeless boys who
stab other semi-homeless boys, that's all.

CRAZY GLUE: *Well, then ask, goob.*

FBG WITH A MUSTACHE: *Maybe you don't really want to know.*

CHAPTER TWENTY-FIVE

I FALL INTO BED, exhausted and feverish, and sleep for days, waking only to pee or drink some juice with my pills. I keep seeing the other side of the room, one minute full of Reed and his planes and the next minute empty, everything gone. I dream I see him tossed into a cement mixer with his planes, and they swirl and fart until they disappear into the cement. Then he's set on fire by a giant blowtorch, and all the nuts and bolts that held him together explode. Then in another dream, he's with my mom and dad, and he's their son, and I'm screaming for him to get away from them, but they can't hear me because their ears have been stuffed with Oreos.

Reed turns up everywhere in my dreams. He's in school with Pete and Haze and Shelby. He's in Dr. Gomez's office discussing my "terrible situation" with Dr. Gomez. He's in my house playing the violin, using his switchblade for a bow and sawing off all the strings. He's also in my suffocating dream, only instead of suffocating beneath the ocean floor, I'm buried under him. I can't breathe through all the blubber. I wet the bed. I know that I've wet the bed, but I can't rouse myself to do anything about it. I feel myself lifted and carried, but I just keep dreaming, and my wetting the bed just becomes part of one more dream.

While I sleep I shiver, then sweat, then shiver again. I hear voices all around me. I listen for my dad's voice among them, but his is never there.

Finally, after days and nights of dreams and voices, I wake up and it's morning. The sun is shining through the windows and I can hear birds singing. I see that the bed across the room from mine lies empty and someone is speaking; I think it's my mom, but it's only Mrs. Lynch.

She leans over me. "There you are. How are you feeling today? Any better?"

I look at her and I hear music. I hear "Puff the Magic Dragon," and I wonder for a second if it's coming from her somehow, but then I lift my head and look behind Mrs. Lynch and I see the little girl, little Gwen, holding a Talking Elmo CD player. I lie back, relieved.

From the doorway I hear, "Well now, he's alive after all," and a man comes into the room. I know it has to be either Mr. Lynch or Mrs. Lynch's brother, because the man looks so much like her, only taller and broader. He has salt-and-pepper hair, a thin, kind of turned-up nose, and lots of laugh lines around his eyes.

He holds out his hand for me to shake. "Hi, Jason,

I'm Tony Lynch. You can call me Dad or Tony or Captain, whatever makes you feel most comfortable."

CRAZY GLUE: *How about Cap'n? Think he'd like that?*

FBG WITH A MUSTACHE: *Or just Cap. Call him Cap.*

I shake his hand and his grip is firm. I can't look him in the eye. How can he think I would ever want to call him Dad? I *have* a father. And Tony's too personal. I'll call him Cap. Tough if he doesn't like it.

I look around the room and see my computer and backpack sitting on the desk. They've been to the house, my house. I don't know if I like this.

"How long have I been sleeping?" I ask.

"Four days," Mrs. Lynch says. "I think you were more exhausted than sick, but you did run a fever the first couple of days. How do you feel now?"

FBG WITH A MUSTACHE: *That's four days down and ten to go until you see your dad.*

I sit up and lean against the headboard. "I feel okay," I say, eyeing my laptop again and remembering the Dear Mouse letters. I need to mail those off.

"Good to hear it," Cap says. He steps over the line to Reed's side of the room and grabs the desk chair. He carries it back across the red line and sets it down beside my bed, and again I think about how disturbing it is to see no traces of Reed anywhere in the room. How could he just disappear so completely and so fast? I can't get the thought out of my head.

CRAZY GLUE: *They're all looking at you like you're some bug specimen.*

I look at the three of them smiling at me. I look away and notice one of the photos from my wall at home leaning against the side of the desk. It makes me mad. I feel invaded. How dare they take that down and bring it here. Do they think I'm going to put my photographs on these walls? I'm not sticking around that long.

CRAZY GLUE: *Don't let them get their claws into you.*

Cap clears his throat and I glance at him, then study my lap.

"So, if you feel well enough after breakfast, how about you and I going for a walk? I'll show you around the place, let you get your bearings. Then later we'll go to the post office and transfer your mail to our address. Sound good?"

No way! Jeez! I'm grateful they took care of me while I was sick or whatever, but I'm not making this permanent. No way!

CRAZY GLUE: *Yeah, back off, Cap'n!*

I shrug and don't say anything.

FBG WITH A MUSTACHE: *You need a game plan, son.*

CRAZY GLUE: *You gotta scram. You don't wanna stay here. They're not your parents.*

AUNT BEE: *They are nice, though, and something smells pretty good in the kitchen. A good meal wouldn't hurt.*

CRAZY GLUE: *They know you wet the bed.*

After a few more minutes of small talk . . .

CRAZY GLUE: *Very small.*

They leave me to shower and dress. Then I go to the kitchen, which is all cheery and warm with the walls covered in strawberries wallpaper. I eat a huge breakfast of French toast and scrambled eggs while Gwen talks a blue streak. She prattles on about Homer, who, it turns out, is a doll, and then about the snowman that she and Cap made and that she fears is going to melt. She names all the Cheerios left in the bottom of her bowl, then says she can't eat them because now they have names. I've never heard anyone talk so much, but I decide I'm glad she's here. She takes the heat off me.

I don't feel like talking and I guess the Lynches sense this, because they leave me alone pretty much. They tell me before I head back to my room that since it's Thursday, I can wait until after the weekend to go to school. That will give me a chance to rest up and prepare myself.

Whatever. FBG is right. I need a game plan. I don't feel like going back to school yet, but I don't want to sit around here, either. I want to see my dad. I wonder what's happened to him. I picture him dumped on some ash heap with Reed—the rejects. It gives me chills. I can't get it out of my mind.

Cap isn't ready for our walk yet, so I sit at the desk by my bed and open my laptop. It's nice to have an Internet connection again.

AUNT BEE: *And a full stomach and a warm home.*

Okay, okay, I know. I'm grateful, but I'm not staying here.

I send off my Mouse letters and read the new ones that have come in.

Dear Mouse:

I'm kind of a big mouth and a know-it-all, and I know I get on people's nerves, so I don't have a lot of friends. The other day I ratted somebody out, one of my friends. It was the right thing to do as far as right and wrong go, I guess, but now I think I lost my friend. I don't know how I can get that friend back. Maybe I shouldn't have told, but then my friend would have been really hurting. Did I do the right thing? How can I get my friend back? I'd do just about anything to make it up to this person.

Tattletale

Dear Tattletale:

If your friend were really your friend, then . . .

CRAZY GLUE: *Goob, this is Shelby.*

No. Is it? She wouldn't write a letter, would she? She would talk to Dr. Gomez.

AUNT BEE: *It sure sounds like her.*

CRAZY GLUE: *She knows you're Mouse! She wrote it because she knows you're Mouse.*

No. She couldn't. No, it's a coincidence.

FBG WITH A MUSTACHE: *She spent the night in your room. If she* snooped, she might have found something, like the letter to the editor you printed.

Oh man.

CRAZY GLUE: *And she's got a big mouth, like she says. By the time you get back to school, a whole mob could be after you. Still feel like you could stand up to anyone?*

I stare at the letter a long time. It makes me feel tired. Now I don't know how to answer the letter. After a while I write:

Dear Tattletale:

Did you do the right thing? Not likely since your friend isn't your friend anymore. What makes you think you're always right about everything, anyway? And now you can't undo what you've done, so you and your friend have to live with that. How can you get your friend back? It's not up to you. Why do you think you should control this person and this person's fate? You're only half the friendship. Your friend either forgives you or not. Who are you to decide everything, anyway?

I stop. I shouldn't be doing this—writing these letters. I'm asking Shelby who does she think she is; well, who do I think I am? I can't give people advice. I'm not always right, either. Nobody should listen to me. Hell, I talk to voices in my head!

CRAZY GLUE: *Maybe we're real.*

AUNT BEE: *Maybe we aren't just voices.*

SEXY LADY: *Come on over to our side, Jason.*

FBG WITH A MUSTACHE: *Life is easier over here. Don't you know that?*

Shut up! Why are you guys turning against me?

SEXY LADY: *We're for you, not against you. Don't I always remind you how hot you are?*

Not lately. Anyway, I don't like this. I'm the one who's supposed to be in control. I'm in charge here.

CRAZY GLUE: *Hey goob, don't you know anything? Characters always get out of control of their creators, just like real friends do.*

I slam my laptop shut and jump up from my chair.

"Ready to go?"

I whip around and find Cap standing in my doorway. I'm so relieved to see a real live person.

"Yeah, yeah, sure. Let's go!"

I follow him out of the room, resisting the urge to grab hold of his hand.

CHAPTER TWENTY-SIX

I START TO PUT ON MY COAT, but Cap says, "Wait a minute—I think I have something that may be a bit warmer. It just might fit you."

I imagine another pea coat, but the real thing since Cap is retired from the navy and he has one on, but he reaches into the hall closet and pulls out a jacket with red and black squares on it. It looks like a woodsman's jacket.

"It's lined with Thinsulate, so it's thin but plenty warm," he says, offering me the coat.

I put it on as best as I can, what with my left arm still in a sling. The right side fits exactly, and I wonder which foster kid left it behind. It can't be Reed's; it's for somebody long and narrow, like me.

Cap helps me get the coat buttoned; then we step outside into the sunshine. I squint and look out across the lawn. It feels strange not to see the river in front of me, its color always changing to shades of gray and blue and green and brown. Instead, I see the snow-covered lawn and a puny snowman leaning drunkenly in its center. The brick walkway that divides the lawn in two is shoveled off, and as we walk toward the street, I hear the sound of our shoes crunching on the bits of salt scattered here and there. We step out into the road where the snow is melted. There are puddles I don't see until it's too late, and ice water seeps in through the crack in the sole of my shoe, soaking my sock.

"The Army-Navy Country Club is nearby. We'll walk there," Cap says.

I nod and stick my hand in the pocket of my new coat. I feel around for something left behind by the previous owner, but I don't find anything.

I take long strides to keep up with Cap, and five minutes later we come to a large parking lot. We head toward a brick building at the far end and pass by a row of snow-covered tennis courts.

"We've got swimming here, golf, tennis," Cap says. "While you're living with us, you can use these facilities. We'll sign you up for classes or lessons, if you'd like."

"Thank you," I say. "I think I'm just going to take it easy for now, though."

CRAZY GLUE: *He's trying to bribe you.*

Cap nods and we keep walking beyond the building, where the view opens up to parts of the golf course and a big, wide-open sky. Its vastness makes my chest expand and my back straighten. I feel I need to walk taller just to try to fill all this space. It makes me wonder if there really is such a place as heaven, and that makes me think about my mom.

Cap breaks into my thoughts. "I heard about your mother," he says, like he's just read my mind. "I'm really saddened by your loss, and I'm sorry about your father, too. It's a tough break. But you know, I've learned there's really no use dwelling on what has happened in the past. Remember your mother with love, do the best you can for your father, and get on with your life. There's really nothing else you can do."

CRAZY GLUE: *Except live it up with him at the club. What a weasel. Trying to make your dad look bad.*

We keep walking, and the sun reflects off the fields of snow and shines in our faces. We both have to squint our eyes up really tight to see where we're going. As we walk, I listen to the squeak of Cap's leather shoes and the solid sound of his rugged soles striking the pavement. I squish along beside him.

A hawk takes wing from the top of a distant pine tree and Cap shades his eyes to watch. "You get back into school and get busy with your work and your friends, and you'll see, everything will fall into place again."

I don't say anything. I watch the hawk soar above us. I wish it would swoop down, grab me in its talons, and take me away—far away.

Cap stops walking, so I do, too. He takes a pair of eyeglasses out of his pocket. He puts them on, their wire frames making him look more like a professor than a naval officer, and points to the sky, squinting.

"Look at that hawk, would you. Look at her soar. Now, that's beauty in motion." His face has this look of proud admiration—the same look I've seen on my mom, and I know that like me, like my mom and dad, too, he's a bird lover. I can tell just by his expression and the way that his hand, shading his eyes, looks almost like a salute.

We watch the hawk soar in ever-widening circles above the golf course. Then Cap notices my shivering, so he removes his glasses and we set off walking again. "Better keep moving," he says. "Not much wind, but when you stand still, it starts to feel chilly. You're not too tired, are you?"

"No, I'm fine, I guess."

"Good. Then I think we should discuss the matter of your bed-wetting. Have you always had this problem?"

CRAZY GLUE: *We told you. He knows. Soon he'll put two and two together and come up with* crazy. *Just like dear old dad.*

I want to bolt, but I just stop and stand with my hand jammed into my coat pocket, my other hand in a fist.

Cap stops, too, and puts his arm on my shoulder. "Don't worry. You're not the only foster child we've had who wet the bed."

AUNT BEE: *Foster child? Is that what you are?*

SEXY LADY: *I thought foster children were little kids. Doesn't he know you're a hot, sexy dude?*

220

CRAZY GLUE: *You're nobody's foster kid. Tell him that. You're no-body's foster kid.*

I twist away from him. "I—I'm not your, I'm not a foster child. I'm just here for like a week, and I'm sorry about your bed. If I wrecked your mattress, then . . ."

Cap raises his hand and squints at me. "Nonsense, son. We're not upset with you. I just thought maybe I could help. This is a problem that needs to be nipped in the bud. You don't want to grow into an adult and still have this issue."

"I only wet the bed when I have this one bad dream," I say through clenched teeth.

Cap puts his arm on my shoulder again and kind of pushes me along so that we're walking. "Care to tell me about the dream?" he says.

"It's nothing." I shrug. "I mean, I'm just under the ocean floor, like under all this sand, and there's all this pressure—all the weight of the ocean—and, well, that's all. I pee in the bed and wake up."

I look at Cap and he's nodding. The sun makes the silver streaks in his hair shine like mica.

CRAZY GLUE: *Oh no, here comes the fatherly advice.*
LAUGH TRACK: *Uh-oh.*

"Sounds upsetting. Any idea why you keep having that dream?"

CRAZY GLUE: *He's clever. Wants you to fink on your dad and tell him about getting buried alive. Tell the dude to stuff it. Go on, tell him.*

I stop walking again. "Look, I don't know, okay?" I say, squinting into his eyes. "It's just a dream. Are you some kind of dream expert? Is that what they taught you in the navy?" I shake my head. "I don't want to walk anymore. I want to go home—uh, I mean back to the house. I'm tired. And don't worry. I always clean up my mess and I don't have that dream too often. Hardly ever."

I start to walk off and I feel this hand grab my shoulder and pull me back. I stumble, and Cap has to catch me so I don't fall. I look up and Cap looks mad. His lips are clenched like an asshole . . .

CRAZY GLUE: *We're talking a real sphincter here.*

And his nostrils are flared.

"Jason, I understand that you're upset. You're in a tough spot. I get that. But I didn't cause your problems. Get mad at the situation, not at me. I'm trying to help you. I'm on your side. And you'll find if you can talk something out, often the problem you thought was so big just shrinks or disappears altogether. You need to talk about your dream to someone."

CRAZY GLUE: *Who asked him?*

I cross my good arm over my bad. "Look, I'm fine on my own. I don't need your help. I'm not even a real foster kid, so you don't have to treat me like one. Like I said, I'm only going to be here for a few days or a couple of weeks at the most. That's all. And I already have

222

a father. He's great. He's *really* great. So I don't need another one."

I sound like a kid. I know I do, but I can't help it.

Cap tilts his head. "How about a concerned friend, then? Can you stand to have me just be your friend?" he says, his voice softer, his mouth relaxing.

FBG WITH A MUSTACHE: *You've got to hand it to him—he's stubborn.*

I bite the inside corner of my mouth and glance sideways to keep from having to look at him. "Yeah, I guess so," I say.

He tousles my hair. "Good deal," he says.

I look at him. "As long as you don't do that to my hair again," I add.

He laughs and slaps me on the back, and we head back toward the house.

CHAPTER TWENTY-SEVEN

MRS. LYNCH DROPS me off early at school on Monday so she can get Gwendolyn to her preschool and then get to her job at some crafts boutique where she works part-time. Cap, it turns out, works part-time at the country club doing some kind of office work now that he's retired. He had already left by the time I got up.

We pull up to the school, and the grounds are empty except for a couple of guys I see running up the steps and entering the front of the building.

I take a deep breath and open the car door. It feels like I've been gone forever. The weekend felt like a whole month, maybe 'cause I spent most of it alone in my room thinking too much about Dad and Reed. I hate how I keep lumping them together in my mind as if they were alike somehow, even though they're not. Dad would never stab anyone.

Anyway, I'm afraid to ask about Reed, where he is, because I'm afraid I can't handle the answer. The way people come and go in your life, where they're present and alive one minute, and missing or dead the next, is an idea that's too big for me to grasp. Life just seems way too fragile all of a sudden, and everybody seems to take it so lightly, as if they think we're all made like army tanks, big and strong and able to roll over anything in our way. And it's not just our bodies that are fragile; our minds are even more so. I don't know what fine membrane separates sanity from insanity, but after watching my dad slip-sliding around on the border between the two all my life, I know how easy it is to cross, and this scares me. This scares me to death. I've just been wondering, what if I had had the switchblade in my hand? What if Reed had dared me and I was the one with the switch-blade? Maybe I would have used it. Then I'd be the one missing. It could have been me. I could have been Reed. Reed is me and I am Reed is Dad is Reed is me.

CRAZY GLUE: *Got that?*

    It's too easy to slip up, to slip off, and flip out. That's what I was thinking about all weekend—trying so hard to hold on to me—to—to sanity.

FBG WITH A MUSTACHE: *That's what you've been doing since your mother died. You're holding on too tight. You're like your dad's violin, and all the strings are going to bust one of these days.*

    It's all I know how to do—just hold on.

FBG WITH A MUSTACHE: *Maybe Cap is right; you should tell some-one what that dream is all about.*

CRAZY GLUE: *You wet the bed twice last night. You're getting worse, goob.*

    I get out of the car and Mrs. Lynch asks me, "Are you going to be all right? Don't forget your lunch, and here"—she grabs a couple of dollars stashed in a cup holder beside her and hands them to me—"in case you need a snack. I'll pick you up at three, okay?"

"Yeah, sure," I say, but see—how is it one day I'm struggling to scrape together a few pennies to keep me and my dad going and the next day someone shoves two dollars at me just like that? That doesn't make any sense to me. How can life be like that? How can someone be alive one second and dead the next, or sane one minute and crazy the next? Is all this supposed to make sense? Does everybody get it except me?

SEXY LADY: *You're still hot, Jason. Dim, but hot.*

LAUGH TRACK: *(Laughter).*

I'm wracking my brain trying to make sense of it. A few days ago I was wearing high-water jeans and Dad's old boat shoes. Now I'm wearing jeans that fit, a new T-shirt, a pair of new running shoes, and the hunting jacket, all appearing out of that hall closet in the Lynches' house like some magic-hat trick, and I have a large sack full of food, and money to buy even more food if I need it. It's insane.

I think about my dad. I called Sam several times this weekend, and he said Dad was doing fine. He said he's been transferred to St. Mary's Hospital. I wonder if he, too, is getting lots to eat. I wonder if he gets a new set of clothes.

CRAZY GLUE: *Oh sure he does. The kind with the extra-long sleeves that cross and tie around the back. He wasn't transferred; he* was committed. Let's get real here. Isn't that what you're doing now? Getting real?

Hey, don't get mad at me. You're still here, aren't you? I haven't gotten rid of you, have I?

SEXY LADY: *You need us. Just remember that. We're here for a reason.*

I watch Mrs. Lynch and Gwen until they ride out of sight, and then I just stand on the sidewalk, frozen. I don't want to go inside the school, but I don't know where to run to if I don't go. I can't move. I just can't move.

CRAZY GLUE: *You're coming unglued, goob.*

Someone tell me what to do. Come on—one of you tell me what to do. Should I run? Tell me. Come on, Crazy Glue. You're such a big mouth. Tell me. FBG with a mustache, you always have good advice. What should I do? Where should I go? Aunt Bee? Sexy Lady? Hey You—do you know?

"Whoa, Pope-a-Dopester! You're back, man. Why didn't you call and let us know?"

I whip around and there's Haze loping toward me, coming from the parking lot where his ratty old van is shivering and shaking and coughing.

I'm confused because I'm so relieved to see him; yet I'm still pissed at him for what he and the others did to me. But since I don't know what else to do, and none of you are giving me any help, I say, "Hey! Looks like your car is sick over there."

Haze grins. "Yeah, what is that? I swear it's gonna explode on me someday."

He catches up to me and throws his arm around my shoulder and just like that we walk together toward the school.

CRAZY GLUE: *It was that easy all along, goob.*

"So, how's that wing of yours, Popester?"

I lift the arm still in its sling. "Good. It's better every day. I got stabbed with a switchblade, though," I say. I smile 'cause I know this will get a rise out of Haze, and I want it to for some reason.

Haze takes his arm off my shoulder and steps away from me. "Are you shittin' me?"

CRAZY GLUE: *Bingo!*

Haze looks so stunned.

"This kid in the foster home I'm staying in stabbed me in the stomach." I shrug, like it's no big deal, like it's just part of the foster home experience, but then I think of Reed, and the words "there one minute and gone the next" pop into my head, and I stop smiling.

CRAZY GLUE: *You don't fool us. You're so proud of your war wound.*

Haze puts his arm back over my shoulder. "Dude, you gotta be one messed-up hombre, huh? Even my parents and their shit can't compete with all *your* shit, man!" He jostles me and lets go.

Am I messed up? What's the difference between being crazy and messed up, anyway? Is there a difference?

CRAZY GLUE: *It's a matter of degree.*

FBG WITH A MUSTACHE: *Just exactly how real do you think we are?*

We reach the steps of the school, and Haze turns and looks straight at me. "Hey, sorry about what happened about your dad, okay? I mean, man, I'm really sorry. I hope he gets better really fast, and if there's anything I can do—I mean, I guess you think I've done too much already."

CRAZY GLUE: *He could have pushed him under a train. That would have been worse.*

AUNT BEE: *Oh, he's all right. Give him a break.*

"Yeah, well, thanks, Haze. Thanks for the apology." I nod and press my tongue to the roof of my mouth.

Haze frowns. "So, is he okay? Is he liking his new digs and all, or is that a dumb question?"

I'm about to answer, but then I notice he's shaved off his beard and he doesn't have any makeup on.

"Hey, what's with your face? Where are the tears?"

I expect Haze to make a joke, but instead he shakes his head and looks at the ground. "For your dad, man," he says. "For both your parents."

I blink. "What?"

He shrugs and gives me this lopsided smile. "Okay, it wasn't a tattoo, just makeup, but teardrop tattoos, real ones, they're like some gang symbol for how many people you murdered. I couldn't go around wearing that. Not now, not anymore." He heads up the steps and I follow. "I got rid of the tears and shaved the beard out of respect for your parents."

I'm not sure what to say. I'm too stunned.

CRAZY GLUE: *How about "Whoa, man!"*

"Thanks," I say.

CRAZY GLUE: *Lame!*

Haze reaches for the door and opens it, then pauses. "Maybe you don't want to hear this, okay, but after what happened that afternoon with you and your dad—I mean, the way you protected him and locked yourself in the bathroom and all, and seeing how important he is to you, it kinda woke me up. I mean, I only wore the tears and the beard in the first place to get back at my parents for all the hell they've been putting me and my sister through the past couple of years, but, hey, they don't deserve all the crap I've been giving them. My mom doesn't deserve it, you know? I need to start showing her some respect, too. Right?" Haze nods, more to himself than at me, and answers his own question. "Right."

CHAPTER TWENTY-EIGHT

IT DOESN'T take me long before I'm feeling over-whelmed in my classes. Every teacher hands me a paper listing all the work I've missed since being out. I'll be playing catch-up for the rest of the year and probably into the summer.

I'm worried about seeing Shelby in Biology, but she's not in class. I guess I'm glad. I don't think I'm ready to face her, yet. I think about the Dear Mouse letter I e-mailed and I wonder if she's Tattletale.

In History, Mrs. Trudell hands me back the essay exam I took just before I stopped coming to school and says in front of the class, "Jason, would you care to ex-plain this—this disaster to me? You've got no punctua-tion, no spacing, and all your words are written in lowercase. I didn't even bother to read this mess. I gave you a zero." She stands in front of my desk, holding out the paper. I look at my tiny scrawl. The words all run together, no beginning and no end. That's what I tell her. I say, "I don't like beginnings and I don't like end-ings, so I just wrote middles." I take the paper from her.

The whole class laughs. Someone nudges me from behind and I hear his laughter.

CRAZY GLUE: *You're even funny when you're serious, goob. Or is this just crazy?*

LAUGH TRACK: *(Exaggerated laughter).*

The laugh track's laughing, so I'm going with funny.

The morning drags on, and then at lunchtime Haze catches up with me again. "Today's Gomez day, remember?" he says.

I had forgotten, but I nod and follow him to Dr. Gomez's office, glad not to have to get a tray of food from the cafeteria first. I have my own sack lunch now.

The first thing I notice when we enter the office is Shelby's mural. She's painted over her rainbow and has created a darker, more surreal painting. There's black water with foamy waves and a threatening sky, purple mountains and an iceberg and a single black tree, and a single sexless person standing on the iceberg, arms raised to the sky. All of this swirls here and arches there and forms ragged peaks everywhere. It has a frenzied and desperate feel to it, somehow. It makes my heart race. I don't like it. I turn to Haze. "When did Shelby do this?"

Haze flops onto one of the floor pillows. "Over the past couple of weeks. She must have finished it this weekend, though. That iceberg wasn't there last Thursday." He reaches into his bag and pulls out a can of Mountain Dew, then pops it open and takes a gulp.

I move to join him, but then Pete enters the room. When he sees me, his eyes water and he hugs me without saying anything. He just holds me in this fierce grip. It makes my bad arm throb.

"Yeah, okay, thanks, Pete," I say, squirming. He lets go of me.

He smiles at me and rubs his head. "I didn't know you were back. So, how you doin'? We tried to visit you in the hospital, but you had already left. We didn't know where you had gone. They wouldn't tell us anything."

"Yeah, me either, hardly," I say, smiling. I'm surprised that I'm so happy to see him. He looks the same as always, bald, dressed in his white T-shirt and jeans, and carrying some handmade African cloth thing for a backpack—same old Pete. I like that not everything changed while I was gone.

I tell Pete about living with the Lynches; Haze tells him about my getting stabbed; I tell them both about how it happened. I feel I need to tell this story, for some reason.

Then Dr. Gomez bustles in with her arms loaded down with books and papers, and a mug of coffee in one hand and her lunch in another.

She sees me and says, "Oh! Oh!" She rushes over to her desk to drop her load; then she rushes back over to give me a hug. She smothers me in heavy perfume and color—the yellow, orange, green, and purple of her flowing blouse—but I don't mind. It makes me think of Sexy Lady.

SEXY LADY: *But I'm still prettier, right?*

All this hugging feels good. I've missed hugs. My mom used to hug me a lot.

CRAZY GLUE: *You were always embarrassed by it.*

AUNT BEE: *Shh! He's having a rare memory of his mother.*

She releases me and I push my tongue up against the roof of my mouth. It doesn't help. I know my face is burning.

"I only just got in," Dr. Gomez says. "I didn't know you were back. It's so good to see you. How are you? How's your dad?"

"Okay, I guess. They moved him to another hospital."

"Good, he'll get the help he needs. You look good—taller."

CRAZY GLUE: *The hem of your jeans actually comes all the way down to your shoes for a change, that's why.*

"So, sit down and tell us how you're doing," Dr. Gomez says. She grabs her coffee off her desk and sits on the pillow next to the one I choose.

She looks around and asks, "Where's Shelby?" Then she twists all the way around to look at the mural. "I see she finished the new mural. It looks wonderful."

We have a quick discussion about Shelby. Nobody has seen her and we all hope her mother is doing all right. This gets everybody, especially Dr. Gomez, onto the topic of our mothers. After naming something we're each grateful for (I choose lunch sacks), Haze talks about why he shaved his beard and got rid of the makeup and says he has a newfound respect for both his parents because of me.

LAUGH TRACK: *Aw, isn't that sweet.*

"That must make you feel pretty good," Dr. Gomez says to me. "Look at the effect you've had. Already something good has come out of a tough situation. We should remember that. There's always something good."

CRAZY GLUE: *Right. Sure. Great tradeoff, Haze's beard and mustache for Jason's dad.*

I don't want to remember that day locked in the bathroom, so I don't say anything. I'm hoping Gomez will move off the subject.

CRAZY GLUE: *Doubt it.*

"Jason, why don't you tell us something about your mother. What was she like? Were you two similar, or are you more like your father?"

AUNT BEE: *Oh dear. What does she mean by that? Does she think you're crazy?*

FBG WITH A MUSTACHE: *Careful. What does she want you to confess? Look at the way she's looking at you. Eyes like drill bits boring into you.*

"Oh, uh, no thanks. I don't want to talk about her."

Pete grabs my foot and shakes it. "It's safe in here, Jason. You'll see."

I try to smile or something, but I've got my tongue pressed against the roof of my mouth and I'm feeling all squirmy, so I know I'm looking weird.

"Do you have any special memories of her that you can share with us?" Dr. Gomez says, smiling and tilting her head to one side, waiting for me to answer.

"Not really. No."

FBG WITH A MUSTACHE: *Atta boy. Don't tell.*

AUNT BEE: *Let it out. Tell the truth.*

What truth? Let what out?

CRAZY GLUE: *What you're holding on to so freakin' tight, goob. Let go.*

I'm breathing funny. Haze and Pete and Dr. Gomez are looking at me, waiting for me to say something.

"I don't know what you're trying to get me to say. I mean, she was nice. She was a great mother. The end."

"My mom loves to hear herself yell," Haze says. He sticks his tongue in a container of chocolate pudding and licks it. "You should see the veins standing out on her neck—whoa! What a screamer."

"My mom didn't yell. She was—she was real quiet. She liked to hike and stuff, like me, and we both liked taking pictures—I mean that's what she did for a living. She was a photographer." I look up. Is that enough? Can we move on now?

I look at the three of them still watching me like I should have more to say. "Well, that's it." I adjust my sling and knock my hard-boiled egg against the metal file cabinet to crack the shell. I peel the egg and don't look up. I don't know why the hell they keep staring at me. Why doesn't somebody say something?

Dr. Gomez touches my leg. "Can you name some of her favorite foods, or her favorite color and how she used this color?"

Crap!

CRAZY GLUE: *Poor little bird heart, it keeps flapping like crazy, but it can't get any air.*

"I don't know—uh, red. She liked red, so our kitchen is painted red and she painted her nails red."

FBG WITH A MUSTACHE: *Don't go there.*

"Look, she was really great, okay? I don't know what you want me to say." I stare hard at my new Adidas, hoping to block their staring eyes. "She was really smart and nice. Real nice. She—she used to make me these treasure maps. They were maps of sections of Rock Creek Park. She'd take her red nail polish and mark a big X where she buried the treasure. Then we'd go there, and I'd have to follow the map to find the treasure."

"That's *soooo* cool!" Haze says, and Pete and Dr. Gomez agree.

I rub my eyes. "Yeah, it was always some kind of neat rock or a feather in a box or a book or something."

Okay, I've said enough. That should be enough. I can feel sweat beading up under the hair on my scalp.

Any minute it's going to start trickling down my face and they'll know this is getting to me. But why is it? Big deal. Nail polish, photography, hiking, buried treasure—so what?

FBG WITH A MUSTACHE: *You don't like exposing yourself.*

SEXY LADY: *I could say something here, but I won't.*

CRAZY GLUE: *Hey, that's my line.*

Why are they looking at me like they're waiting for me to say something I'm not saying? Why don't *they* say something—move on already.

CRAZY GLUE: *Because watching you sweat is so entertaining.*

Finally, at last, finally, Dr. Gomez says, "That was very nice, Jason, a very nice memory. Thank you." She smiles a big smile at me and her eyes crinkle at the sides like she's just so proud of me. Then she looks at all of us and claps her hands together. "I was thinking that today we would play If You Really Knew Me."

Haze groans and falls against Pete. "I hate this game! Ugh!"

Pete shoves him away. "You love it, admit it. If we really knew you, we'd know that you love this game."

"Yeah, and if we really knew you, we'd know that your mama . . ."

"All right!" Dr. Gomez holds up her hands. "Let's just play the game. Let's be serious now."

CRAZY GLUE: *This can't be good.*

Dr. Gomez explains that we start a sentence with "If you really knew me," and then we finish the sentence and tell something true about ourselves. I think I'm going to be sick. I mean literally. I listen to Haze tell how if we really knew him, we'd know that his feelings get really hurt when girls make fun of how thin he is. Tears roll down his face. "And guys laugh at me because I'm so uncoordinated. I'm always getting slammed in the face with a ball in Phys Ed or I'm falling over it." He sniffs and wipes his hand over his face. "If I had one wish in life, it would be that I was good, I mean really good, at sports—especially football."

Dr. Gomez gets him to talk about what he's good at, and we find out he's good at arguing and history and he's thinking of becoming a lawyer some day. "Even if my dad sucks as a dad, he's a good lawyer. He helps people. I'd like to do that," he says.

Then it's Pete's turn, which means my turn is next. I'm sweating like crazy, my heart is insane, and my thoughts are circling around the things I said about my mom. I don't want to be here. I'm scared.

Pete rubs his head and I see sweat on his forehead. Maybe this is getting to him, too. "If you really knew me," he says, then pauses. "You'd know that I once bought a gun off the black market and I was going to kill my dad's dealer. I came so close."

"Whoa!" Haze says. "What happened?"

"Zen. I found this Zen book in my parents' library—I read it and it changed my mind. Peace feels better." He looks around at us and tucks his lips in his mouth as if trying to keep from saying anything else, or maybe to keep from crying.

Haze shakes his head. "Dude! Get out of here! I can't see it. Pete the killer."

AUNT BEE: *Your turn to tell the truth.*

I don't have anything to tell.

Dr. Gomez makes her comments to Pete, which I don't hear 'cause I know my turn is next and my heart is making too much noise.

"Jason?" Dr. Gomez says.

I look at them. They're all wearing these encouraging expressions, but it doesn't help. I feel set up. My muscles are so tense from trying to hold my irritation in. Yeah, I'm mad. I don't know why, but I'm mad at this game we're playing. It sucks. Sweat trickles down the left side of my face.

CRAZY GLUE: *Stop trying so hard. What are you holding in, anyway?*

SEXY LADY: *Tell them something.*

AUNT BEE: *Tell them about yourself.*

FBG WITH A MUSTACHE: *Just tell the truth.*

LAUGH TRACK: *If you really knew me . . .*

What truth?

SEXY LADY: *(Whispers) Tell them what you're hiding.*

What am I hiding?

LAUGH TRACK: *If you really knew me . . .*

ALL: *If you really knew me . . .*

CHAPTER TWENTY-NINE

I'VE GOT TO GET out of here. I feel like my head might explode if I don't leave. I need to get out now!

CRAZY GLUE: *If you really knew me . . .*

Everybody's waiting, watching. It's my turn—my turn to tell the truth.

FBG WITH A MUSTACHE: *If you really knew me . . .*

No! I jump to my feet and rush to the door, but the phone rings. Pete says, "I bet it's Shelby," and I freeze.

Dr. Gomez answers the phone.

Pete's right. It's Shelby.

We know right away why she's calling.

I stand with my hand on the doorknob and listen. I'm panting as if I've just run a race.

"Oh, Shelby, I'm so, so sorry," Dr. Gomez says, leaning against the desk for support. "I'm so sorry. Of course you did everything you could. When . . . It's all right. It's natural to cry. Of course you're upset. You're heartbroken. It's understandable."

We can hear Shelby crying through the phone and it's making my head buzz. I don't want to hear her, and yet I'm straining to hear what she's saying. She sounds so totally torn up, so desperate. I feel like something is splitting inside me. I want to get out of here but I don't move. I can't move. I want Dr. Gomez to make her stop crying. Why doesn't she stop her? Dr. Gomez has tears in her eyes. "Let it out. Just let it all out. It's all right. You'll be all right."

Why does Gomez tell her to let it out? Now we can really hear her through the phone. It's as if she were here in the room. It's horrible. She's screaming for her mother.

I can't breathe.

CRAZY GLUE (AS JASON): *"Mommy! Where are you? Why did you leave me?"*

I can't take it. Shelby is screaming into the phone.

CRAZY GLUE: *Scream! Jason, scream!*

She needs to stop! Everybody needs to stop screaming—to shut up, Shelby, Dr. Gomez, me. Yes, I need to shut up. I'm shouting. I can hear myself. I don't know when I started shouting, but I am. I yell at Dr. Gomez to hang up the phone. "Hang up the phone! Hang up the phone! Shut up. You hear me? Shut up, both of you! Just stop it! Stop it! Hang up the phone!"

I feel hysterical. Dr. Gomez is standing with the phone in her hands looking at me, stunned, and this riles me even more. I can still hear Shelby screaming. I have to shut her up. I grab the receiver out of Dr. Gomez's hand and slam it down, missing the phone and hitting the desk. Then I hit the desk some more, slamming the receiver against it over and over again. "I hate her! I hate her! How could she? How could she leave me? Why did she do it? She left me all alone with him when she knows. She knows! I hate her! I hate her so much!"

Dr. Gomez and Pete and Haze all try to grab me and stop me, but I jump out of their way with another yell—like a roar, as if some wild bird-beast is inside me—and I stomp on my lunch, the second ham sandwich and the chips and cookies still inside bursting from the bag. I mash them into the rug, killing them before they scream out in pain. Then I lunge past Pete and Haze, who both try to grab my arm, and I reach for the stack of books and papers on Dr. Gomez's desk. With another roar I shove them off the top, and papers and books fly everywhere. Then, feeling the urge to pick the whole desk up and topple it over on its back, I move around to the front of it, kicking at the chair with another roar, and reach for the desk, jerking my bad arm out of its sling, willing to rip it out of its socket if I have to, to get the desk flipped. "I hate her!"

"Okay, now, that's enough!" Dr. Gomez shouts. She gets on the other side of the desk and sets her hands down on it, leaning her weight on it as if her body can hold back my rage.

I lower myself, preparing to lift the desk. My throat feels ripped out of me. My chest hurts; even the skin on my face hurts as though it's splitting, ripping wide open. I lift the desk and out of the corner of my eye I see Pete lunge forward; then the room goes dark. All of us are in total darkness. I choke on my last yell so that I burst out in a coughing fit, shredding what's left of my throat with each cough. I let the desk drop and I bend over to cough. Dr. Gomez and Pete both ask if I'm okay, and Haze says, "Whoa, this is intense, man."

I feel a hand clamp down on the back of my neck and I know it's Pete's. Then I feel Pete grab me around my chest and lift me off the floor as his fist goes into my stomach. I feel a thrust of air burst from my chest, and then he sets me down.

I turn around, even though I can't see him. "The Heimlich maneuver?" I say. "You give me the Heimlich maneuver to get me to shut up?" My voice is hoarse, and it hurts to swallow.

The light comes on and I look around. The room is a mess with my food mush everywhere, books and papers scattered, the desk off center, the chair against the wall, and the pillows scattered from when Haze tripped over them in his attempt to stop my rampage. Haze is by the door now, his hand in midair making him look like he's playing freeze tag, and Dr. Gomez is frozen, too. She watches me, like she's waiting for my next move.

Pete stands beside me, looking surprised by his own actions. "It seemed like the right thing to do at the moment," he says to me, shrugging.

We hear a knock on the door. Dr. Gomez leaps over the pillows and calls out in an overly cheerful voice, "Come in!"

Dr. Woods, the principal, sticks his head in the room. "I just wanted to make sure everything is all right. Some students said they heard a commotion in here."

"Everything's fine," we all say, each of us wearing some kind of ridiculous grin on our face.

Dr. Woods nods, glances at the four of us, and then at the disaster around us. "I'll leave you to it, then." He withdraws his head from the room and closes the door. We look at one another and burst out laughing.

CHAPTER THIRTY

I STAY BEYOND the lunch hour to clean up the mess I made in the office. I don't want to go to my next class, anyway. Before I exploded, I wanted like anything to get out, but now I don't want to leave. It feels safe here. It feels like the only safe place on the planet, so I take my time cleaning up. It's weird. My body hurts as if I threw myself against a wall over and over. All my muscles feel sore and so does my throat. I know I made a total ass of myself, but for some reason I feel okay about that.

CRAZY GLUE: *At least nobody called you crazy.*

But maybe that's 'cause they don't know everything.

AUNT BEE: *They don't know about us.*

I'm on my knees cleaning up my lunch mess and Dr. Gomez is picking up the stuff I swiped off her desk. She keeps reassuring me that my outburst, as she calls it, was a normal reaction. "Good for you," she keeps saying. "Good for you, Jason. It's perfectly natural to be angry with your mother for dying. Everybody who loses someone special goes through that. It's just part of the grieving process." She's got all the papers I knocked off her desk in her arms and she sets them on the desk, adjusting them until they're back in a neat little stack.

I think about what she just said. I feel so guilty for saying I hated my mom. I didn't even know I was so angry with her. I didn't realize this was hiding inside me. I want Dr. Gomez to know that I love her, too. I tell her this. "I loved my mom," I say. "I love her, but I'm just so angry." The pieces of mashed bread I had scraped off the rug I toss into the wastebasket.

"Of course you are. And maybe she's not the only one you're angry with."

I pause with a bunch of cookie crumbs in my hands. Jeez! "Who else?"

She stoops down beside me. "Any number of people, I'm sure. But who comes to mind?"

I drop the crumbs in the wastebasket and think about this.

Then I go ahead and blurt out my story about the fifth grade, and being betrayed by my best friend, and the swirlie. I don't know why I reach all the way back to that old story, but as I'm telling it, I feel a strange peacefulness inside.

"That's abominable what they did to you," Dr. Gomez says when I finish. "I'm sorry, Jason—so, so sorry. But you know, you're going to have to find a way to keep the torments from your past from scarring the rest of your life."

"Yeah." I pitch a paper towel full of gunk into the wastebasket. "I kind of just realized that. I mean, I feel like I could have died the day they flushed my head in the toilet. I passed out and everything." I run my hand over the bandage covering my stomach. "And then when Reed stabbed me, I could have died then, too, but I've been thinking that maybe it's worth the risk of almost dying to speak out and just be myself, because inside I've been dying most of my life, anyway. It's like this slow death trying all the time to hide who I really am."

"And that's what you've been doing." Dr. Gomez stands up and leans against her desk.

"Yeah, only I think lately bits and pieces of me are starting to leak out. It's—it's crazy." I laugh.

Gomez tilts her head. "What do you mean?"

CRAZY GLUE: *Don't tell her about us.*

FBG WITH A MUSTACHE: *Or Dear Mouse.*

"Oh, well, like I've always tried to just be invisible in school, partly 'cause of my dad and then because of what happened with the swirlie. I figured who needs friends if all they're going to do is turn against you. I thought it was safer and easier to be on my own. But I don't think I want to be invisible anymore because— because it's lonely, and I don't want to be lonely. I don't want to be alone."

CRAZY GLUE: *You mean you're scared shitless of being alone.*

SEXY LADY: *That's why you have us. You're never alone with us, Jase.*

I scrub real hard at this spot on the rug so I don't

248

have to look at her. "Like writing the wrong dates on my papers and not punctuating my sentences and stupid stuff like that. I think I just wanted to get attention, get noticed, just to kind of see if I could." I laugh again. "I think I was starting to really believe I was invisible—practically."

"And what do you believe now?"

I look at her. She's leaning against the desk, waiting, her arms crossed. "That my teachers think I'm a pain in the ass, but I think I can be funny, too."

Gomez stirs. She picks up some pencils and puts them back in her pencil holder. "Just what this school needs, another class clown."

"Yeah, okay, maybe not like that, exactly."

Dr. Gomez smiles at me and pushes up the sleeves of her puffy shirt. "I'm proud of you. I think you've made an important discovery about yourself."

I've finished cleaning the mess, so I set the wastebasket back over by the side of her desk. I feel better about stuff, I guess, but something nags at me. I don't know what it is and I don't feel like digging around in my head anymore to figure it out.

Dr. Gomez hands me a pass for my next class and then, just as I'm leaving, she says to me, "Forgive yourself, Jason."

I stop. "Huh?"

"Think about it," she says, then smiles this Mona Lisa–type smile that I can't read at all. She lets the door close on me, and after just standing in the hall for a minute or so, stunned, 'cause what the hell did she mean by that, I make my way to class.

For the rest of the school day, I keep going over and over my explosion in Dr. Gomez's office and our conversation afterward. These thoughts make me restless all over again. I can't sit still. I need to do something, get up, run, pace, something. During the last period of the day, I get so restless, I can't stand it anymore. I walk out of the classroom, leaving behind my books. I wait for my teacher to stop me, but she doesn't. She lets me go because my mom's dead or she knows my dad's crazy, or she thinks I'm crazy, I don't know, but she doesn't stop me. I hurry through the hall, past the lockers and classrooms. "Forgive yourself," she said. I start to jog, and two students standing by the lockers look up at me. I feel their eyes on my back as I jog past them, and then I go into a full-out run and hit the exit doors, bursting through to the outside.

The first few gulps of cold air sting my still-sore throat, but it feels good, too. The sky is real gray and the wind is high, its sound competing with the noise of the highway traffic. I keep running, feeling the chill of the air passing through my jacket and shirt and jeans, and it feels like freedom to me—the wind and the sound of the rushing traffic. I race across the playing fields to a tunnel that runs under the highway where students who walk to and from school pass to get to the quieter, safer streets. Shelby must use this path. I remember that she walks to school. I remember she told me once that she lived nearby, on Vinton. I run through the tunnel and think about Shelby walking to school in winter, in shorts and no socks. I take a set of stairs on the other side of the tunnel, climbing up to a wide road with a good sidewalk. I keep running away from the highway and the school. I don't know where I'm going—I'm just going—but then I find myself near Shelby's house, and I realize I was headed here all along. It's a crazy thing to do. Her mother's just died, but I need to see her. I need to be in her presence. I don't know why, but as I run down the street I feel desperate to get there, to see Shelby, to see her face, to touch her, to just be with her.

By the time I reach Vinton, I'm out of breath. I lean against a stop sign on the corner and bend over, resting my right hand on my knee, and watch puff after puff of cold vapor escape through my mouth. For the first time I feel just how cold it is outside. I stand up, still breathing hard. A gust of wind hits me full in the face and chest, and I feel its bite on my nose and ears. I shiver and look down the street at the row of houses on either side, all of them white and stark-looking against the gloom. I know right away which house is Shelby's by the line of cars pulled up outside the house. I start jogging again, and then when I get there, when I find myself standing on the short walkway leading up to the front door, I can't move. How can I just barge into her house? Maybe this isn't even her place after all. I check the mailbox and see the name Majors—it's hers. I rub my bad arm, feeling the cold, and pace up and down the walkway, trying to decide what to do.

CRAZY GLUE: *Go on, goob. Go see your girlfriend.*

She's not my girlfriend. I don't even know why I'm here.

AUNT BEE: *Go on, Jason. Ring the bell. Take a chance.*

SEXY LADY: *Why do you want to see that big mouth? Come on, Jase. I'm the one who thinks you're hot. What does she think of you?*

Good question. What does anybody think of me?

LAUGH TRACK: *Forgive yourself.*

Yeah, and what does that mean? For what?

FBG WITH A MUSTACHE: *You know.*

AUNT BEE: *He was only six years old. He was going to be buried alive.*

"Jason? What are you doing here?"

I jump, I'm so surprised to hear Shelby's voice. I can't answer her question because I don't know. I look at her blotchy-red face, with her eyes, her cheeks, even her mouth, looking swollen, and I know it's a mistake for me to be here.

I back away from her. "Sorry, I—I don't know what I'm . . ." I turn to run but get no farther than the mailbox when she calls to me.

"Jason, what are you doing? Come on inside—it's freezing out here. Come on."

I turn around and she waves me toward her. I head back down the walk, climb the two brick steps to her house, and follow her inside.

I'm hit with the warmth of the house as soon as I enter, and I feel my fingers and toes, cheeks, nose, and ears start to tingle, then itch as they thaw. I'm in the living room, a large room with green walls and a deeper green carpet. The room seems dark, and then I notice that all the curtains are drawn. I wonder if Shelby's family drew them because of death or do they always live this way, in the dark.

I follow Shelby to her kitchen and notice the house smells funny, like cough syrup, or maybe it's embalming fluid.

CRAZY GLUE: *This place feels creepy.*

Everything in the house seems to speak of death, the dark rooms, the smell, the people in the kitchen talking in somber tones, their heavy, dark clothes. What am I doing here?

I wait in the doorway of the kitchen while Shelby enters the circle of people. "Dad," she says, "that's Jason. We're going to go up to my room, okay?"

Her father, a heavyset man with the thickest eyebrows I've ever seen, nods. "Just leave your bedroom door open, sweetheart."

Shelby makes no reply to this and as soon as we enter her room, she closes the door behind us and I'm suddenly in a jungle. She's painted the walls of her room in a wild jungle theme with all kinds of trees and ferns and grasses everywhere. There are animals, too—monkeys, zebras, lions, tigers, and elephants—all peering at me from various places on the walls. There's even a snake wound around the trunk of a tree, giving me the eye, and a couple of colorful parrots staring out at me as if they're considering attacking my head. The whole effect of the dark jungle scene is disorienting, and I'm still lost in the mural when Shelby bursts into tears and dives onto her bed. I wonder again why I'm here.

I watch the way she folds into herself and cries in a way I've never seen anyone cry before. It's so loud, so close to screaming, and her whole body shakes, even the bed shakes. As I stand watching her, it finally occurs to me why I've come. I need to see this. Shelby is acting out everything I've felt inside about the loss of my own mother. I can see her pain. I can hear it. I walk over to the bed and reach out for her hand, and it's hot. It's her pain. For the second time today I'm flooded with my own grief over my mom's death and my dad's illness. I grab Shelby. I pull her off the bed and draw her to me and I hold her tight.

We stand for several minutes, or maybe it's hours, just like this, holding on to each other and crying— both of us crying. I feel out of control with my grief, first in Dr. Gomez's office and now here, with Shelby, and I don't like it. I can't stop myself and I don't know what I might do next, and this scares me.

CHAPTER THIRTY-ONE

I HAVE THIS sudden urge to kiss Shelby. One second I feel all out of control with my emotions and then this. I want to kiss her. We stand holding on to each other, crying into each other's shoulders, and I don't even know whose sound is whose; we just meld into each other. With my thoughts already so wild, feeling Shelby's hot body up against me, her hair smelling like perfumed peaches tickling my nose, her arms holding me as tightly as I'm holding her, I feel I just have to kiss her.

CRAZY GLUE: *Goob, you've never kissed a girl in your life. You'll do it all wrong.*

No. I don't care. I don't care about anything except kissing her. That's all. That's all there is in the world right now—Shelby, with her sweet, freckled, tear-stained face.

She notices how still I've become, how silent. She looks into my eyes and I lean in to kiss her, but she draws back and says, "How 'bout a haircut, Jason?"

I stare at her, uncomprehending. "What?"

2 5 5

"A haircut. I want to cut your hair. It's too long. You really need a haircut."

"What?" Why is she talking about a haircut? Weren't we about to kiss? Haven't we both just been crying our heads off? Where is this coming from?

Shelby pulls away from me. She moves over to the mirror hanging from her closet door and looks back at me. "Come on—look at yourself. What do you see?"

I don't know what to do, so I do as she asks and join her in front of the mirror and stare at myself. What do I see?

CRAZY GLUE: *Yup! Bad idea. It's that broken mirror. The one you smashed. You don't like mirrors, goob. You'd better close your eyes or you might see crazy.*

I squint at the mirror. At first all I see are these jungle animals, tigers and elephants and zebras, peering at me from behind my back. It takes me a second to even find myself, but when I do, I see a squinty-eyed, red-nosed, blushing skinny guy with hair down to his shoulders. I look away.

"You've got really nice hair, all wavy and soft," Shelby says. She grabs some of it in her hands, runs it through her fingers, and drops it. "You could donate it to Locks of Love. You know, the people who make hairpieces for people with cancer?"

I look at Shelby. "What are you talking about? Locks of Love?"

"Yeah, you know them." Shelby doesn't look at me.

She moves over to her desk, reaches into a drawer, and pulls out a pair of scissors, a comb, and a plastic squirt bottle as if she's been waiting for me to drop by just so she can cut my hair. She turns around and holds up the implements. "So let me cut your hair." She drags the chair out from her desk and pats it and, stupidly, I go sit down.

She pulls my hair back from my face and peers around to look at me. "That's better. You've got that Mediterranean kind of nose, you know, with the high bridge and kind of longish—in a nice way, I mean, but it's too big to wear long hair. There's all this hair and then this nose poking out from it."

Shelby combs my hair while she talks, and I sit staring at the two of us in the mirror.

"Gee, thanks."

"My mother once told me the nose and feet grow first, so that's why teens look awkward for a while. So your nose has grown. Eventually the rest of your face will match, but right now . . ."

CRAZY GLUE: *Goob, what's her problem? Why is she blathering on about your nose?*

SEXY LADY: *Long noses are hot, anyway.*

"Hey, enough about my nose, already. Okay?" I jump up and pull my hair away from her with my good hand. "I know my hair's too long. I've been cutting it myself for a while, but okay, things have been a little crazy lately and I haven't, but jeez, what the hell? Why do you suddenly want to cut my hair? I mean, we were just—just . . ." I can't finish my sentence. I don't know what we were just doing, but it had nothing to do with hair and my freakin' long nose.

Shelby blushes and sets the comb and scissors on her desk. Her eyes fill with tears again. "I don't know why I want to cut it. I used to cut my mom's hair all the time." A tear rolls down her face. "It always made us feel better, so I just—I just thought that maybe you'd feel better, too, and there's the Locks of Love, so . . ." She shrugs again, looking totally helpless. I can't stand to see her like this, so I plop myself in the chair.

"You're right—cut it off!"

"Really?"

I hear the hope in her voice and I nod. "Sure, cut it all off." I wave my hand and look at her through the mirror, and she smiles. Then I correct myself and say, "I mean, not like Pete's. No bald head for me, okay. I want *some* hair. I have a big nose, after all."

Shelby nudges me. "It's not *that* big. And anyway, I like it. It's distinguished-looking."

I feel my nose. It feels like it grew overnight. I hadn't even noticed, but it's bigger, and the high bridge is more noticeable. I look at it in the mirror.

CRAZY GLUE: *Looks like you've sprouted an exact copy of your dad's nose.*

I'm not ready to think about my dad just yet . . .

AUNT BEE: *Forgive yourself.*

I say out of the blue, "Did you know I got stabbed by this kid in the foster home I'm staying at?" Why do I keep bringing this up?

"What?" Shelby leans forward and bugs her eyes out. "Are you kidding?"

"No, I'm not kidding. I got stabbed. Right here." I lift my shirt and Shelby leans over farther to take a look at my bandaged wound.

CRAZY GLUE: *You didn't show everyone else your bandage, hot stuff.*

"Gross." She straightens up and looks at me in the mirror across the room. "That's all you needed, huh?" She combs out the tangles in my hair.

"Yeah, and the guy who stabbed me? It was weird 'cause he was in my room—I mean, we shared a room—and he had all this stuff, model airplanes and his computer and stuff. Then after he stabbed me, I went to the hospital and when I got back, he and his stuff had completely disappeared. It—it was kind of, I don't know, surreal the way he was just gone like that. It was like he never even existed in the first place." I pause and stare down at my hands, noticing that I not only have my dad's nose but his hands, too—palms like spatulas with long fingers, very straight. I think about my dad—gone.

I look up at Shelby, who's stopped combing my hair and is just standing, listening, her head tilted to one side.

"I keep wondering what happened to him," I say.

"I even dream about him. He's one of us, in a way. I mean, he's had bad shit happen to him, too, you know? So I wonder where . . ."

Shelby shakes her head and laughs. "That's easy. He's in juvie, where else?"

"Juvie?"

"Sure, that's where they put kids who stab people."

"Oh yeah," I say, feeling stupid. I imagine Reed in one of those orange jumpsuits they make prisoners wear, looking something like a pumpkin with legs. I imagine him sitting in the juvie cafeteria plowing through a bag of Oreos. Just like my dad, he's locked away, separated from society—invisible to the world. He has no parents to remember him or to worry about him, and my dad, all he has is me. I'm the only one to remember him and to care, and to carry on his genes.

FBG WITH A MUSTACHE: *Ah, but what genes did you inherit? There are the visible and invisible.*

"Jason, will you sit still? What's wrong with you? You want me to cut your ear off?" Shelby puts her hands on either side of my head to hold it still. "Now come on—let me cut your hair."

A few seconds later the door opens and in walks a girl who looks a lot like Shelby, only taller and thinner and more sophisticated-looking with her sleek, pulled-back hair and dark suit of clothes.

"Mind if I join you?" the girl asks. "I need a break."

She sits on Shelby's bed, then flops back onto her pillow with a grunt.

"That's my sister," Shelby says, "in case that isn't obvious. Nora, this is Jason. Jason, Nora."

I raise my hand and say, "Hi," but Shelby's got my bangs combed in front of my face so I can't see her anymore.

"Yeah, hi," Nora says. Shelby hands me a pillowcase. "Here, put that around your shoulders like a towel so you won't get hair down your back."

"Why don't you just get him a towel, Shelb?" Nora says. "Why use something *like* a towel when you can just use a towel?"

I've never had a brother or sister, but the way Nora says this seems to me that she's laying down some kind of challenge for Shelby, or maybe setting a trap, but Shelby doesn't fall into it. She just says in her matter-of-fact way, "The pillowcase is handy." Then she squirts something on my hair, and I jump in my seat and I pull my hair back. I look at Shelby. "What was that? I don't want hair spray on my hair. I'm not some Ken doll you're playing dress-up with, okay?"

Shelby and Nora laugh, and Shelby shoves my head with the tips of her fingers. "It's just water, silly. I need to wet your hair before I can cut it. It's too wavy." She shows me the plain plastic bottle and squirts me right in the eyes.

"Hey! Cut it out!"

"That's just what I'm trying to do." Shelby laughs again and combs my hair back in front of my face.

We're all silent for a couple of minutes, and then Nora says, "Shelby, how can you sleep in this room with all these creatures staring at you? Aren't you a little old for a zoo in your room?"

"It's a jungle, and I hope I never get too old for it."

"I guess you're still planning on being like that Jane Goodall and going to live among the monkeys."

"Gorillas," Shelby says. "I want to study gorillas, if that's all right with you. And anyway, Jane Goodall studied chimpanzees."

"Whatever, it's your funeral."

Shelby stops cutting. "Great choice of words, there, Nor."

"Okay, so, while we're on the subject, tell me about it. What happened? Were you with Mom when she died?"

I stiffen, bracing myself for another outburst of tears from Shelby or a story I don't want to hear—not today. I'm glad my face is hidden beneath all my hair.

"No," Shelby says. She cuts my hair, moving across the front of my face right at the bridge of my nose, and I shiver as the cold steel edge of the scissors touches my skin.

"No, I was asleep. We were both asleep—Dad

and I. When I went in to check on her, I just—I just found her."

"Well, she's at peace, at any rate," Shelby's sister says. "She's finally at peace."

"Yeah," Shelby agrees, even though I notice a certain tension in her voice. "She's at peace, all right."

We go silent again after this, and then I hear Nora moving on the bed. She gets up and walks over to the door. I notice her red painted toenails as she brushes past me, because, like Shelby, she's barefoot. Her feet look sexy somehow with the polish on them. I glance down at Shelby's feet and wonder what hers would look like with polish.

CRAZY GLUE: *She's not the type.*

"Well, I'm going to go take a nap in my room. I'm exhausted. Call me if you need me," Nora says at the door.

"Right, sure," Shelby says, again with that tension in her voice.

Nora leaves, and Shelby follows behind her and elbows the door shut.

I peer between my much-shorter bangs and ask, "What was that all about?"

"Call me if I need her," Shelby says. "Right! When did that ever work? Her college is just two hours away, and yet ever since she left, she just couldn't be bothered to come home and check on Mom, even in the summer."

Shelby pulls my hair in a ponytail and yanks and cuts and yanks some more. It feels like she's fighting a war with my hair and my hair is winning.

"You wanna watch it with those scissors?" I lean away from her.

"Sorry. It's just she gets me so mad." She pulls me back and snips and yanks one last time, then holds my ponytail up to me. "For Locks of Love." She sets the hair on her desk, then starts back on my hair again.

"So you were asleep when your mother died, then," I say, kind of changing the subject but not really. The edge in her voice when Shelby told her sister this makes me wonder. I remember the time we had the conversation in Dr. Gomez's office when she said her mother wanted Shelby to let her die and not try to resuscitate her. Is that what happened? Did Shelby sit there and watch her mother die? Could she have saved her?

CRAZY GLUE: *Could you have saved her?*

AUNT BEE: *Forgive yourself.*

What? We're talking about Shelby's mother, not mine.

FBG WITH A MUSTACHE: *Are we?*

I notice Shelby isn't cutting my hair anymore, and I look across the room at the mirror and see her face. Beneath all her freckles she's blushing, and her mouth is turned down. It looks like she might burst out crying again. I want to kick myself for bringing up her mother's death. I'm doing just what Gomez did to me. I think to apologize, but Shelby says, "No, I was awake. I was with her when she died, but I didn't want to tell Nora that." She sniffs and starts cutting again, tiny snips this time. "What happened between my mother and me is special. It will always be special—our own private time no one can ever take away from us."

"So it was peaceful, then?" I ask.

"In the end, yeah." She keeps snipping away at the back of my neck, taking my hair shorter and shorter.

"But what about your father?" I ask. "Where was he? Doesn't he sleep with your mother?"

CRAZY GLUE: *What's with all the questions, Gomez?*

I can't help it.

Shelby laughs a bitter sort of laugh, abrupt and sharp. "My father wasn't even home last night. I don't know where he goes and I don't care anymore. He's just like my sister. He hides his head in the sand and waits till everything's over, and now he pokes his head up and plays the part of the long-suffering husband with all our relatives gathered around him." Shelby cuts around my left ear, and I lean away from her and her scissors when the steel grazes my ear.

"Hold still!" Shelby says. "You want me to cut your ear off?"

"That's exactly what I'm afraid of."

Shelby swats my shoulder and I straighten up, and she continues cutting and talking as though I hadn't interrupted her.

"Both my father and my sister were so scared of my mom's illness, they couldn't even stand to be around her, like maybe it was catching."

"Yeah, I know what that's like." I nod.

"Hold still," Shelby says, clamping her hand down on my head to steady it. Then she shifts to my right and cuts on that side of my head.

"I was the one who took care of her, so it's right that I was the one to be with her in the end," Shelby says. "Really, I can't stand cowards. They're cowards— my sister and Dad. They think that by hiding they can keep it all from hurting them, but they can't. At least I had those last moments with my mom. I've got nothing haunting me, but those two, if they've got any conscience at all, they'll have their own guilt for company for the rest of their lives." Shelby smiles. "And that's okay by me. They deserve it."

Her words sting me. Am I a coward?

CRAZY GLUE: *Is the pope Catholic?*

What am I hiding from?

FBG WITH A MUSTACHE: *You tell us.*

Shelby sounds so angry and bitter. I turn my head and look straight at Shelby. She stops cutting and holds her scissors and her comb above my head, waiting.

"Maybe they were just doing the best they knew how," I say. "I mean, everyone's not like you."

"Yeah, maybe, but what if I weren't here for my mom? Or what if I had been just like Nora and Dad? Who would have taken care of her then?"

I shrug and turn back around. "But you were here, Shelby, and your father and sister knew that. They knew they could count on you. Maybe if you weren't here to help out they would have done more; you never know."

"I doubt it," she says, yanking on my hair again.

"Do you really want them to feel guilty the rest of their lives?" I ask, reaching out for her hand to stop her from pulling my hair out.

"Oh, sorry." She snips some more around my ear. "Maybe—yeah. At least—at least I want them to feel *something*. It's as if they don't even care."

"Yeah, but maybe that's their way of grieving—to hide, and to hide their feelings, too," I say, these thoughts just occurring to me as I speak. "And anyway, maybe you won't have the guilt over your mother like them, but you sure seem angry. So maybe you're just going to be this bitter person the rest of your life because you can't forgive them for not being like you." I twist around and look at Shelby. "Maybe you need to forgive them—you know, for your own sake."

Shelby and I look at each other and I hold my

breath, waiting for her to speak. I want her to forgive her father and sister, because somehow I feel that by doing so she will be forgiving me, too. Dr. Gomez told me I needed to forgive myself. I don't know how she knew this, but she's right. I blame myself for my dad. I even blame myself for my mom's stroke. I was up there on that mountain. I saw her go down. I should have done more. I should have run and gotten help instead of staying with her, but I couldn't move. I couldn't leave her. It's just that I feel everything bad that's happened in my family is my fault, and I don't know how I'm supposed to forgive myself. So it's like I need to see that something horrible, like the way Shelby's sister and father treated her mother, could be forgiven, and then maybe I can step back and look at my own situation and find a way to forgive myself.

I hold my breath and wait for Shelby's verdict, my heart in my throat.

Shelby shakes her head. "I hadn't thought about that," she says, blinking several times. "You're right. They're not me. I know they loved my mom." She pauses and tears roll down her face. "My mom knew it, too. I just wish they could have been here, you know? Mom needed them and"—more tears—"I needed them, too. It was so hard." She sniffs and wipes her nose with her wrist. "I needed them, too."

CHAPTER THIRTY-TWO

I FEEL LIGHTER all over by the time I leave Shelby's house, with my hair cut short and my mind more at ease. I sit in the back seat of Shelby's sister's car on my way to the Lynches' home, while Shelby and her sister sit up front and argue about the fastest way to get across town. I stay out of it. I think about my day, first at school and how great Haze and Pete were to me. They didn't laugh or look at me as if I were some monster when I went berserk. It surprised me that Haze shaved off his beard and took off his makeup out of respect for my parents. I guess I feel really good about that.

I think about my explosion in Dr. Gomez's office and my tears with Shelby and how I've been afraid to lose control like that because I thought I would end up spilling all my secrets, which I kind of did, or that I might go crazy, like Dad, which I kind of did, too. But I'm thinking that talking to Gomez about how I hated my mom for dying and how I've been invisible for so long and that telling her about the swirlie have freed me, the same way standing up to Reed did. I don't know, but maybe I can lose control a little and still be sane. Maybe there's still hope for me.

CRAZY GLUE: *Aren't you forgetting about us?*

You're a figment of my imagination.

CRAZY GLUE: *Yeah, yeah. Keep telling yourself that, goob.*

Just leave me alone.

I feel pretty good. I feel more like myself, my real self, not the scared-of-my-shadow self, than I have in a long, long time. Yeah, I'm calmer now, and I'm not so afraid of what's going to happen next. I even feel—surprise, surprise—less guilty and less angry at my mom. I know she didn't have a stroke on purpose. I know that. And I like remembering her. I just miss her. I need her so much. If only . . .

Nora turns onto the street where the Lynches live and I see a row of cars, a lot like the row out in front of Shelby's house, but here they're in front of the Lynches' house.

"What's going on up there?" Nora says. She slows down and we creep along the street.

As we draw closer to the house, I see a police car, and all my old feelings of dread and anxiety spring back to life. What's going on? I sit forward in my seat. "You can let me out here. Just let me out, okay? I need to get out of the car."

"Jason, what's going on?" Shelby turns around to look at me.

"I don't know. All the lights are on in the house. Just stop the car. I need to get out."

Nora stops and I jump out.

Shelby pokes her head out the window. "Should we wait?"

"No, go on. Thanks for the ride. I gotta go."

I recognize Sam's car parked in front of the patrol car and I think of Dad. Has something happened to him? I run across the lawn, my feet crunching in old crusted snow. I leap onto the stoop and open the front door. "Hello," I call out. "Where is everybody? What's going on?"

A rush of people come out of the kitchen into the hallway—Mrs. Lynch first, then two police officers, then some man I don't know, and Captain Lynch and Sam, and then two other women, one carrying Gwen in her arms.

"Jason, thank goodness! Where have you been?" Mrs. Lynch says.

"Why? What's happened? What's going on? Is my dad all right?" I look at Sam and then at the police officers.

"What's happened, Jason, is that you've been missing for the past three hours," Captain Lynch says, breaking through the small group to get to the front and face me.

"What? I haven't been missing. I didn't run away,

if that's what you're thinking." I glance at Mrs. Lynch's angry face and then at Cap's. He looks like he wants to knock my head off.

"Where have you been, son?" one of the police officers asks me.

"Jeez. I was just at a friend's house."

"What friend? We called the friends on the list the school gave us," Mrs. Lynch says, pulling a folded piece of paper out of her pocket.

"Shelby Majors. I was with Shelby Majors."

"We called there and spoke to Mr. Majors. He said you weren't there," Mrs. Lynch says.

"What? Jeez, what is this?" Why are they making such a federal case out of the fact that I went over to a friend's house? What do they think I was doing over there?

SEXY LADY: *Oh, I can think of a few things.*

"I was there," I say. "Her sister just drove me home." I pull my hair. "Shelby gave me this haircut."

"Mr. Majors said you weren't there," Cap says in a tone indicating the matter's closed.

"Well then," I say, getting irritated, "he was wrong. Look, his wife just died today, okay? Shelby's mom died today. So I went over there to see her."

"In the middle of class? Without calling us first?" Mrs. Lynch says.

"What? What is this?" I flap my arms, slapping them against my thighs. "I'm almost fifteen years old.

I've been in charge of my own life for a long time and now suddenly I'm what? I'm supposed to ask permission from perfect strangers if I want to go somewhere?"

The same police officer who spoke last time interrupts us. "Well, looks like he's safe, so I think we'll leave him to you, now. Good night, Captain Lynch, Mrs. Lynch."

Then everybody leaves, including Sam, who gives me the eye and says on his way out, his voice stern, "We'll be in touch, Jason."

The three strangers are Gwen's birth parents and her caseworker. They leave with Gwen to go out to dinner. Then Cap closes the door, and I'm alone with him and Mrs. Lynch.

"Jason," he says, "we'll finish our conversation in the living room." He gestures toward the room. I follow behind Mrs. Lynch and sit down in a chair across from the sofa where the two of them sit.

LAUGH TRACK: *Uh-oh!*

The walls of the room have been decorated with African masks, Peruvian rugs, and a set of ancient-looking pistols, stuff I figure Cap collected during his naval travels. The masks, with their turned-down mouths and their creepy, missing eyeballs, stare at me from behind the Lynches, so I've got several faces watching me with disapproving expressions.

"So you think you should be able to go wherever you please whenever you please, is that right?" Cap says.

CRAZY GLUE: *Yup!*

I shrug. "Pretty much, yeah. You're not my parents. You're never going to be my parents, if that's what you think, so—"

Mrs. Lynch interrupts me. "So if you were expecting to come home tonight and we were gone, gone for three hours after we had told you we would be here, you would think what? How would you feel?"

CRAZY GLUE: *Ooh, good one.*

I look down at my lap. "Worried, I guess," I say.

"Is that okay if we make you worry? Is it okay if we take off on vacation, say, and leave for a few days without telling you? After all, you're not our *real* son, so why should we tell you where we're going, right?" Mrs. Lynch says, totally irritated.

CRAZY GLUE: *Zing!*

"I don't know. I hadn't thought of it that way. I mean, today"—I look up—"I wasn't really thinking of anything. I didn't *not* tell you where I was on purpose. I just didn't think about it. I was kind of upset."

"Even upset, Jason, you have a responsibility to those who care about you," Cap says. "And like it or not, we not only care about you, but we're in charge of caring for you, and that means that you never on any condition make us worry like that. Do you hear me?"

I stare at the two of them sitting on the couch and picture my own parents sitting there giving me this lecture. I know my mom would have said the same thing they just said to me, and Dad would have, too, in his right mind. I nod. "Yeah, uh—yes, sir, I hear you. I guess I'm not used to thinking about people worrying about me. Lately, I've always been the one doing the worrying."

"It's no fun, is it?" Mrs. Lynch says.

I shake my head and feel myself getting choked up like I might start crying any second as I think of the times Dad disappeared. I had been so scared. Anything could have happened to him. No, it's no fun worrying about where people are when they're supposed to be right there with you, no fun at all. I stare at my lap, sucking in my cheeks to keep from crying, and just sit.

"Well then, all right," Mrs. Lynch says after a long silence. "Why don't we all go have some dinner? I don't know about you two, but I'm starving."

The two of them stand up, so I do, too, and I follow them into the kitchen, where we put together a mess of chicken salad sandwiches and heat up some soup. Then, while I set the table, putting the fork on the left and the knife and spoon on the right, with the glass as an exclamation point over the knife, just the way Mrs. Lynch tells me to do, I decide that all this feels okay, the anger, the lecture, and now setting the table according to Mrs. Lynch's instructions. Yeah, it feels normal, sane. A guy could get used to this.

CHAPTER THIRTY-THREE

Dear Mouse:

A couple of nights ago on the way home from practice, I ran over some kind of animal. All I could see was the flash of white just as it ran under my wheels. I couldn't stop. I know I hit it. I killed a live creature! I can't get over this. I know some people think it's no big deal—so you killed a squirrel or whatever—but to me it is a big deal. How do I get over this? How do I deal with my guilt? Please don't say I'm being silly. This matters to me.

Deadly Driver

Dear D.D.:

I like animals, too, so I think I would feel like you if this happened to me. But you didn't mean to do it. If you could have prevented it from happening, you would have, right? I mean, you didn't do it on purpose. And you can't fix the past. It happened. So now I guess all you can do is be careful driving and maybe do something good for some other animal. What's the use of feeling guilty? It won't bring the animal back to life, so feel sad and then

276

do something for the animals in the world that are still
alive and need our help. So like, forgive yourself.

    Mouse

Okay, I know, I stole a little bit from Dr. Gomez, but I've been thinking about what she said. Maybe there was something I could have done for my mom when she had her stroke, but I don't think so, really. I think I've just been carrying around a useless sack of guilt over it and even more guilt over my dad having to go into the hospital. All that stuff's in the past. All I can do is fix the present. So I'm trying to let go of feeling guilty, and, funny thing, I feel less and less angry at my mom the more I let go of feeling guilty about her dying. And I think it's weird how I didn't even know I was angry with her. I didn't know how guilty I felt until the other day in Dr. Gomez's office when I went berserk. So I think I forgive myself. I think I'm feeling better now—sort of.

The rest of my first week back at school is the best week I've had in a long time. I feel like an honest-to-goodness normal person.

CRAZY GLUE: *Let's not get carried away, goob. We're still here, aren't we?*

SEXY LADY: *He needs us.*

AUNT BEE: *It's all right. He knows we're just a figment of his imagination.*

That's right. That's what I keep telling you.

So I go to school each day wearing decent clothes

and a decent haircut. I've got friends—real friends—and they're happy to see me, and the teachers are helpful about my getting caught up with my schoolwork.

After school each day I go home, eat a snack, and do my homework. After dinner I go to the club with Cap, and we shoot baskets or swim for an hour or so. Then I come home and read or something and go to bed.

CRAZY GLUE: *Aren't you leaving something out?*

AUNT BEE: *Some things should be private.*

CRAZY GLUE: *He's the one who's opened his life to the whole world here.*

All right, yeah, I cry myself to sleep every night. But it's a good cry. I cry over my mom. I think about her. I remember our hikes together and her teaching me stuff about photography, and junk like that, and it's just, I miss her. I really miss her. And my dad. I'm all he has.

Anyway, as sad as I feel every night going to sleep, somehow every morning I wake up feeling great, as if I've washed away a little more of my grief and guilt every time I cry.

The hardest part of the week is Thursday morning at Shelby's mother's funeral, but even that turns out all right. At first I didn't want to go. I thought the funeral would be way too painful for me. I didn't tell Shelby this, but she must have noticed the way I was dragging my feet about going, because she took my hands and squeezed them, and told me she needed me there. "I need my friends by my side," she said.

"Then I'll be there," I said to her.

CRAZY GLUE: *Aw, she needs you.*

I borrow a suit from Haze, who surprised me because I never would have expected him to own even one suit, and he owns two. We look so different all suited up, Haze, Pete, and I, like waiters at a fancy restaurant. It makes us act different, too, more formal, more dignified, that is until the actual funeral service where I cry like crazy . . . and I didn't even know Shelby's mother.

We didn't have a funeral for my mom. She was cremated. We have her ashes in an urn in Dad's study. I've decided I want to scatter them on top of Mount Washington some day 'cause I've realized that my mom had her stroke doing what she loved to do. She was on her favorite mountain, looking out at her favorite view.

Shelby seems different during the funeral, too. She seems older, more mature. For one thing, she's wearing a dress, a form-fitting dress, and I can't help noticing her form. She's hot!

SEXY LADY: *I get the feeling I'm being replaced.*

She looks really beautiful with her hair pulled back in this kind of knot thing, and she wears these tiny dangling earrings. Yeah, she looks beautiful, and still a bit fragile in her grief, and it makes me feel protective of her. I think Haze and Pete feel the same way, because the three of us stay really close to Shelby. We hold her hand, put our arms around her, hug her a lot, make sure she eats something at the reception. We stand beside her like bodyguards while people offer her their condolences (man, I hate that word), and we make sure no one talks her ear off. But Shelby holds her own, acting like the hostess. She's gracious to everyone, the teachers and other students who have come, her parents' friends, and her relatives, and even her sister and father, who both talk like they're the ones who stayed by Mrs. Majors's side throughout her illness.

By lunchtime, we're all back in school sitting in Dr. Gomez's office for our usual Thursday session. Even Shelby surprises us and returns to school, leaving her father and sister to deal with the relatives and friends still at the house.

We sit on the floor of Dr. Gomez's office, eating from a plate of brownies and cookies Shelby brought with her from the reception, and we talk about the funeral. All of us feel kind of giddy for some reason, so instead of sounding sad and mournful, we crack jokes and make fun of one another.

"Jason, you were such a crybaby," Shelby says, jabbing her elbow in my side. "I couldn't look at you at all during the service or I would have totally lost it."

"Oh, like you were Miss Composure there," I say. I'm blushing, but for once I don't care, and I don't even try to stop it. "How many boxes of tissue did you go through, anyway?"

"Yeah, well she was *my* mother—what was your excuse?"

"He was crying 'cause that lady with the hat and the green hair turned him down when he asked her for a date," Haze says. He stuffs a whole brownie in his mouth while he's talking and he chokes on it and coughs most of it back out.

"You are the grossest eater!" Shelby says, leaning away from him. Haze just laughs and tries to gather up the spray of brownie around him.

"Who was that lady with the hat, anyway?" Pete asks.

"Shelby's aunt, and Shelby's going to grow up to look just like her," I say.

"Shut up!" Shelby says, falling against me and laughing.

Finally, after we've downed most of the brownies and cookies, we fall into a mild sugar coma and calm down enough so Dr. Gomez can talk to us.

She asks Shelby how she's feeling, and Shelby says she's okay because she knows her mother is at peace.

"I get what people mean when they say that now," she says. "And I feel like her peace is my peace. I really feel that. I know I did a good job taking care of her, so I'm okay." She nods, looking satisfied, and relaxed, even. She's got her dress shoes kicked off, and she's sitting on a pillow between Haze and me and leaning half her body against her mural and half against me. I like that she's chosen me to lean against, and I notice that we're all sitting closer than we usually do.

Dr. Gomez asks me how I felt attending the funeral, and I tell the truth. I say it was hard but that I'm doing okay.

She reaches out and pats my hand.

Then Pete, who's been quieter and less obnoxious than the rest of us, says that his mother has a boyfriend.

"This is going to kill my dad," he says, rubbing his hand over his scalp. "He gets out of rehab in another week. Where's he supposed to go then? What's he supposed to do? He went through rehab for us, for my mom, and now what happens? This could send him right back out on the streets, using again." Pete looks at us with fear in his eyes.

"Listen, Pete," Dr. Gomez says. "If your father's only reason for getting clean was to please you and your family, then it's not likely to stick. He needs to do it for himself. You know that." She puts her arm around his shoulder and pulls him to her so he falls sideways, unfolding out of his cross-legged position on the floor. She gives him a squeeze. "He's a grown man, Pete. He'll work this out. He's been an addict for a long time. He probably knew there was a possibility that your mother would find someone else."

"Yeah, maybe," Pete says, regaining his balance after Dr. Gomez lets go of him. "But what bad timing. It really sucks."

"Yeah, you're right. It really does suck," Dr. Gomez says, surprising us all.

CHAPTER THIRTY-FOUR

SOMETHING HAPPENED at Shelby's mother's funeral that none of us talk about because it's hard to put into words, but I know we all feel it. Through our grief, and our understanding, and our caring for one another, and by standing up together as one at the funeral, Shelby, Haze, Pete, and I have gotten even closer to one another, and it's left us feeling good, proud even, because we know we belong to one another in a way that no one can ever break apart. We—we're like a family.

AUNT BEE: *I think I'm going to cry.*
SEXY LADY: *Pass me a hankie.*
CRAZY GLUE: *You two are too much!*
LAUGH TRACK: *(Sniff).*

During school on Friday, when we're not in classes, we hang out together and we have this new kind of energy buzzing around us and between us, a confident, happy kind of energy, like we're just so excited to be together and to have found one another. We make plans to meet on Saturday right after I get back from my first visit with my dad in the hospital, and I just can't wait for Saturday to come. I'm flying so high, so strong, with all these new feelings of family and belonging. It's like nothing can ever shake me again.

Saturday morning I sit down in the Lynches' kitchen to a plate of waffles with strawberries and whipped cream.

"We need to fatten you up; you're still too skinny," Mrs. Lynch says, smiling at me from across the kitchen table. Gwen sits in her lap, sucking on a spoon. Mrs. Lynch looks bright and fresh, as if she's been up awhile.

"Yeah, but fatten me up for what?" I only half joke, thinking about Reed.

Mrs. Lynch glances at Cap, who's sitting next to me and is wolfing down his plate of waffles. I see him catch her glance and pause a second, his fork hovering just above the plate and his mouth open, waiting for the food, and then he shoves the bite in and smiles at me and gives me a slap on the back—*ho, ho, ho,* like everything's fine and dandy.

I set my fork down. "Okay, what's going on? Did something happen to my dad?" I look from one to the other. "I'm still going to see him, aren't I?"

"Well, I think so," Mrs. Lynch says. "Although it *is* snowing pretty hard out."

"Then what? What is it?"

Cap tousles my hair. "Finish your breakfast; everything's fine."

CRAZY GLUE: *He's forgotten you hate that. Something's up.*
LAUGH TRACK: *Uh-oh!*

I give him a look that shows I don't trust him.

"Don't worry. Your father is fine. Now eat up." He shovels another load of waffles and strawberries into his mouth and smiles.

I notice Cap's face looks like he's been up awhile, too. I've seen them both in the early morning before, and they usually still have on their "sleep faces," making them look older and puffy around the eyes. Their fresh faces and their glances at each other make me worry enough so that I can't eat.

I tell them I'll wait in my room for Sam, who's picking me up to take me to see Dad.

A few minutes after nine I hear the doorbell ring and I think Sam's arrived early, but it's Gwendolyn's social worker. She's come to take Gwen out for the morning.

A half hour later the doorbell rings again and it's Sam.

"Hey, look at you," he says when he sees me. He shakes the snow off his coat and hangs it on a peg on the wall. "You've got your sling off."

I lift my arm. "Yeah, I took it off last night. It feels good." I nod.

"And your stomach?" he asks.

"All fine," I say, feeling uneasy, like he's stalling for some reason.

CRAZY GLUE: *Notice he took his coat off. He's totally stalling.*

"I'm ready to go," I say. I grab my own jacket off its peg, and I see Sam glance at the Lynches.

I jam my jacket back on the peg. "What the hell is going on? What's with all the looks? Are we going to see my dad or aren't we? Stop bullshitting me and tell me the truth!"

"Hey, calm down," Sam says, while Cap sets his hand on my shoulder.

"Well, just tell me what's going on and I'll calm down."

Sam rubs his hand over the top of his head where his dark hair is cut short and bristly. It reminds me of the way Pete rubs his head whenever he's stressed.

"We just need to have a little talk, okay?" Sam says.

"About what?" I feel a knot forming in my stomach.

"Why don't we all go sit in the living room," Mrs. Lynch says, turning and leading the way into the room.

Once again Cap and Mrs. Lynch sit on the couch so that I sit staring at those African masks, their tortured faces mirroring exactly how I feel. Sam sits in the chair next to mine, his large muscular body filling the chair, making it seem too fragile, like a piece of furniture from Gwen's dollhouse.

Once we're seated, Sam says, "Look, Jason, here's the deal. Your father is very ill. Mentally ill. You know that."

"Yeah."

Sam shifts uncomfortably in his chair.

CRAZY GLUE: *Jeez! Get on with it, dude.*

"Yeah, so? I know he's got mental problems. Is that what you wanted to tell me? I mean, what's happened? Is he okay?"

Mrs. Lynch slides sideways and pats the space between her and Cap. "Jason, why don't you come sit here, next to me."

"No, I'm okay here," I say, keeping my eyes on Sam.

Sam puts his hand on my foot, which I have propped up on my knee and which I only now notice is jiggling like crazy. I stop, and Sam removes his hand.

"Come on," I say. I look at Sam.

Sam licks his lips. "Well, things have gotten a little complicated, Jason. I don't have a lot of information, but what the doctors have told your father's caseworker, after a very lengthy and thorough examination and reports from all the staff who care for him, is that your father—they doubt he will ever return to his old self. He'll never be able to write another book or hold down a job. So what they're saying, Jason, is that he's likely to be in this state of mental dysfunction for the rest of his life."

I straighten up in my seat and my foot starts doing that jiggling thing again, but then so does my heart. "How do they know that? How can they say that? These doctors, what do they know? Look, he was sick before and he got well. Up until a few months ago he was fine. He was fine. He's going to be fine. I know he is. I know it. And what about medication? Won't that help?"

Sam gives me this sad smile. "Yes, medication could help. It could help a little or a lot, over time, but still it's doubtful he'll ever regain full mental function even if he were willing to take his medication regularly, which apparently is a big if. Right now they have to force the meds."

"Well, I can get him to take them. I have before. He just needs new medication, that's all. They just need to find the right combination of pills. That's happened before, so . . ."

I catch the way the three of them are looking at me. I see the pity in their eyes. I can't stand it. I don't want pity. I want my dad. I want to see my dad and see for myself how he's doing.

I stand. "I need to see my dad, now."

Sam stands, too, and starts to speak to me, placing his hand on my arm. "Jason," he says, but I cut him off.

"Now! I need to see him *now!*"

"Jason!" Sam grabs my upper arm and holds it firm. "You'll get to see him. They're releasing him today. Okay? You'll get to see him, but we need to finish talking first. You need to sit down."

LAUGH TRACK: *Phew!*

CRAZY GLUE: *He's free. You can go home!*

FBG WITH A MUSTACHE: *Let's not jump to conclusions. He's ill, remember?*

288

Cap and Mrs. Lynch get up and steer me over to the couch to sit between them, and I let them do this. I sit down and Mrs. Lynch sets her hand on my leg.

"They're releasing him? I don't get it. He's still mentally unstable and they're releasing him? That doesn't make any sense."

Sam sits and leans forward in his seat, setting his elbows on his knees. "Tell me about it," he says. "It's not about his condition; it's about insurance. You have no insurance, so they're letting him go."

"So what does this mean? Do I go back home to-day? It's over? My dad and I can live together again?"

Mrs. Lynch squeezes my leg.

CRAZY GLUE: *What's that supposed to mean?*

AUNT BEE: *Maybe she'll be sorry to see him go.*

FBG WITH A MUSTACHE: *Maybe you hurt her feelings by sounding so hopeful.*

Sam says, "No, Jason. No. Your father has a court-appointed guardian who will visit with him once a month and see to his needs. If you returned to your home, everything would be just as it was before. We can't allow that. You'll remain here with the Lynches for now. We have to look after your best interest."

"So you're saying they're going to just let my dad go and nobody will be there every day to take care of him? Are you kidding me? How can they do that? You just said he would never get better, so how could he be coming home? How's he going to live by himself?"

I stand up again. I feel all shaken inside. Cap pulls on my arm and says, "Sit down, Jason. You need to listen to Sam and understand this."

"What? I understand," I say, sitting. "My dad's always going to be sick and he's coming home, but I'm not going to be living with him, so he's probably going to go wandering off somewhere, never to be found, and die alone in the cold." I gasp, trying not to cry. "What don't you think I understand?" I look at the three of them, waiting for an answer.

Sam nods. "I hear you, Jason. I know it's scary, but it's temporary. Your father's guardian has already started the process of applying for disability so he'll have some money, and Medicaid for health insurance, and she's working to get him placed in a residential program where he'll be taken care of the rest of his life."

"You mean, like what? Like a nursing home? He'll go into a nursing home?"

Sam shifts uncomfortably. "It's a little bit like that, sure. But it will be the best thing for him. They'll see to it that he takes his medication, and make sure he doesn't wander off. They'll give him daily activities and exercise. He'll be fed and clothed, and you can visit him there once a month. It's really the best thing for him," Sam repeats.

"Once a month! What's this once-a-month bullshit? No! Uh-uh, I don't like that idea. No, I'll take care of him. If he's living at home I can see him every day, right? I can go over before school, and then after school I can go over there, too, and fix him dinner and stay there until he goes to sleep. And if he gets that disability money and the insurance, then, well, we'll have more money coming in and . . ."

"Jason." Sam shakes his head.

CRAZY GLUE: *Shake it enough and maybe it will fall off, jacko.*

Cap sets a firm hand on my leg as though he's trying to hold me still.

"I'm afraid you don't have a say in the matter. It's all out of your hands," Sam says.

"Like hell I don't. He's *my* dad." I shove away Cap's hand. "Of course I have a say. I'm his family. I'm his *only* living relative. I'm all he's got! If I don't have a say in this, then who does? Of course I have a say!"

CRAZY GLUE: *That's what happens when you're young and alone in the world, goob. Other people are gonna run your life.*

Sam leans forward and looks me in the eyes. "No," he says. "It's out of your hands."

CRAZY GLUE: *What did I just say?*

"Why? How? I don't understand. How can this happen? And what's supposed to happen to me?"

Sam looks at the Lynches and I say, "What? Why are you looking at them like that? Stop it!"

Sam sits back and takes a deep breath. "Jason, it's the way these things happen sometimes. I'm afraid your father will lose his parental rights and you'll be put up for adoption."

LAUGH TRACK: *(Gasp).*

I'm so stunned I can't even speak. I spread my hands and shrug and open my mouth, but nothing comes out. I start to feel something rumbling in the pit of my stomach. It rises up, and up, into my throat, and then with my eyes closed and my hands in fists, it finally explodes in a yell that sounds something like "Mom!" Or maybe "Dad!" But it doesn't matter, because neither one of them can hear me.

CHAPTER THIRTY-FIVE

SAM AND THE LYNCHES gather around and try to comfort me, but I won't be comforted.

"You lied to me, Sam," I say when I can speak again. I'm all choked up, and for some reason it hurts my Adam's apple to speak. "You said it was only going to be temporary and that's total bullshit!"

"I didn't realize then how serious your father's condition was," Sam says. "I made a mistake. I'm sorry. I shouldn't have said that."

"Well, I can tell you I'm not going to be put up for adoption." I look at the three of them and they just give me their pitying looks.

"You can't just decide my whole life for me. I'm not some little kid."

Nothing I say makes any difference. Dad and I are in the system now, and the system has rules and laws and procedures that must be followed, no matter what. Our desires are not part of the system.

I tell Sam and the Lynches that I need to cool off and take a walk. I need to be alone. I grab my jacket and leave the house.

It's a freakin' blizzard outside. I swear it has to be the snowiest year on record. The snow blows in my face and collects on my eyebrows and ices my cheeks so that they feel like these frozen knots on either side of my face. Snowdrifts are forming everywhere, against houses and garages and trees and mailboxes. The storm swirls around me, and the blustery cold feels good.

I stuff my hands in my pockets and head down the street, grateful that at least I have on a decent pair of shoes—hiking boots—another gift from the Lynches' closet. I imagine there's some poor naked kid stashed in there who keeps having to hand out his clothes.

AUNT BEE: *You have to admit, they're awfully good to you and life is a lot easier now.*

So what? They're not my family. I have Dad and he has me. I don't want to be adopted.

FBG WITH A MUSTACHE: *But that's not up to you anymore.*

CRAZY GLUE: *Anybody could adopt you.*

Yeah, anybody, and anything could happen to me. That's what's so scary. My life is just one big out-of-control ride, and all I can do is close my eyes and hold on while all these random acts of shit just keep flying at me. Out of the blue my mom has a stroke and dies. Out of the blue my dad goes crazy. Why? No reason. Shelby's mom gets sick and dies. What for? Pete's father gets addicted to drugs. Why Pete's father? What choice does Pete have in the matter? Or Haze and his parents' divorce battles—what kind of say does he have? All this crazy shit happens that's so totally out of our hands, and all we can do is duck and dodge all the crap as it comes flying at us.

CRAZY GLUE: *You're a bad dodger, goob, 'cause fate keeps hittin' the bull's-eye on you.*

I realize I've walked to the club and I keep walking through the almost-empty parking lot while the wind dumps snow on my head and down the back of my neck. I shiver from the cold and decide to see if the clubhouse is open.

The main entrance is open and I step inside. The lobby is warm, the dark paneled wood and the fire in the fireplace inviting. "Jason, how you doin'?" Elliot, the guy who mans the front desk, says. "Cold enough for you? You're the first person here this morning. Did you come for a swim?"

I don't know what I've come for except to get out of the cold, but then I see a phone sitting on the desk in front of Elliot. "Actually, I just came in to use your phone. Would it be all right if I used it? It's a local call."

Elliot gives me the hairy eyeball. "Phones out of order at the Lynches'?"

"No, I got some bad news and I needed to take a walk," I say, surprised by my own honesty. "I want to call my teacher and talk to her a second. Could I? I won't be long."

Elliot looks left, then right. "Well, okay, if you keep it short," he says.

I nod and pick up the receiver. "Oh, and do you have a phone book?" I set the receiver back down while Elliot reaches under the desk and pulls out the phone book. He dumps it on the desk. "Here you go."

I look up the number and call Dr. Gomez, hoping she won't mind that I'm calling her on a Saturday. I just feel I need to talk to her and get her advice. She's a psychologist. Maybe she can tell me some way to keep my dad out of the nursing home, or whatever Sam had called the place they were sending him. Maybe she can tell me I don't have to be put up for adoption. I need her to tell me that. I need her reassurance. Fortunately, she's home and answers the phone right away.

With Elliot pretending he isn't listening to everything I say, I tell Dr. Gomez what's happened. I tell her I feel like I have no control over my life at all.

"I'm sorry, Jason," she says. "That's a lot of news that's hard to hear, isn't it?"

"Yeah. Really hard." I blink my eyes, trying not to cry.

"What you have to realize, though, is that as much as you'd like to help your father and maybe you still feel some guilt about his situation, you first have an obligation to yourself, to your own well-being. Even though you weren't included in their decision, it sounds like they've made the best choice for you and your father. He'll have a place to live with all the support services available for him."

Now I'm crying and sniffing and wiping my nose on my jacket. This isn't what I wanted to hear. "So, I'm supposed to take it, then," I say. "The crap gets dumped on me . . . and I'm supposed to just smile and go along with it." I sniff. "That's just life, right?"

"Jason, you can't control the universe and everything that happens in it, but you can control your reaction to it. You can control you, and how you choose to live each day."

"No, I can't. What if I'm put up for adoption and some abusive people get me and stuff me down in a basement and feed me on chicken wings or something?" I glance at Elliot, who looks like he's trying not to laugh. What's so funny, I'd like to know.

"Come on, Jason," Dr. Gomez says. "That's not likely to happen. And even if it does, you still have a choice as to how you're going to take it, how you're going to feel about what's happening to you. Look at the prisoners of war, or Nelson Mandela—he spent thirty years in prison. He had no control over that except how he thought about his imprisonment, what he made of the situation, and that's what makes all the difference." Dr. Gomez pauses a moment, then adds, "Anyway, most likely you'll live in foster care until you're eighteen and then you'll be on your own, if you want. But you know, it's nice to have a family to come home to, a family for the holidays, people who love you no matter what. And you aren't losing your father any more than you've already lost him. You just wouldn't live with him anymore."

"I have a family already," I say, badly in need of a tissue for my runny nose. "I have that with my dad, and with the group. Pete and Haze and Shelby are my family. I don't need anybody else for the holidays."

CRAZY GLUE: *Yeah, you tell her!*

"Now see there? That's the good that's come out of your particular set of circumstances," Dr. Gomez says. "You have these special friends and they have you. Together you've created something good out of some pretty rotten things that have happened in your lives. You have to look at life that way, see the good in it, the good that can come out of a tragedy, and let go of the rest. Don't hang on to your life as a tragedy you have no control over, Jason. Don't act the victim, or you'll become one. And don't shut the Lynches, or anybody, out," Dr. Gomez says. "You never know who may come into your life."

"Yeah," I say, wiping my nose on my coat, feeling only slightly better. "That's what I'm afraid of."

CHAPTER THIRTY-SIX

I GET THIS WILD IDEA while I'm trudging back through the blizzard to the Lynches' house. I'm thinking about my dad coming home and wondering who's going to keep him from burning out the pots on the stove and who's going to make sure he eats and takes his meds and doesn't run off, or hurt himself. I'm also thinking about what Dr. Gomez said. She's right—I don't want to hang on to my life as a tragedy—but how do I get some control in my life? If all I can do is control myself and my reaction to things, well, my reaction to this plan for my dad is that it's total bullshit. All this court-appointed stuff—well, why can't I be his court-appointed son and visit him every day?

FBG WITH A MUSTACHE: *Is there such a thing?*

I stop in my tracks. The snowflakes swirl around me. Maybe there's no such thing, but why couldn't I convince a judge to give me permission to see Dad every day? These are extenuating circumstances. Any judge in his right mind can see that Dad needs care more than once a month. He needs his son. He needs me. Yes! I start walking again. I'll go to court. Why not? Gomez says don't be a victim. Okay, then, I won't be.

When I get back to the house, I find out that Sam is gone and my dad's release has been postponed until tomorrow because of the snow. Even my afternoon with Haze, Pete, and Shelby is canceled, so I spend the day learning how to play chess with Cap, and the next morning I tell Sam my great idea. We're on our way to my house to meet Dad and his guardian. I'm excited and nervous about seeing him again. I wonder if he's changed any and if it's for better or for worse. I know I'll feel better if I can just get Sam to go along with me on my plan.

He shakes his head as if what I've suggested is impossible. "You've got school and other obligations, Jason. You can't drop everything, ruin your whole life for your father. He'll be all right, you'll see."

"I don't want a life without my dad. Don't you get that? I'll go to school. I'll even live with the Lynches. All I want is to be able to visit every day and spend some time with him—and without you there watching over me. I mean, this whole system is whacked. You think my dad's going to hurt me? I'm grown up now. I don't know why I can't just go over and see him. My friends can go visit him whenever they want, but I can't. That's insane! Don't you see how insane that is?"

Sam frowns. "But it's for your protection, Jason."

"No, it's not. That's such a load of crap!" I slap my thigh. "We don't need supervision. It's not like he's an abusive parent who might beat me. This is an exception. Isn't that sometimes why people go to court? To make an exception to the rule? That's all I want to do."

Sam's face, usually set like a brick with his jaw clenched and jaw muscles bulging, softens.

"It might take a couple of weeks to get a hearing for this, Jason. In that time you'll probably see that your father is doing just fine."

"But this is an emergency," I say, seeing my chance. "Can't you push this? I looked it up on the Internet. You could push this if you wanted. It's just until they find a home for him."

Sam moves his head side to side as though trying to decide which way to go with this.

CRAZY GLUE: *Come on, Sam—be a sport.*

"Please, Sam. A son should be able to care for his dad. Come on. My friends, or anybody else even, could drop by and visit him anytime, but I can't. How is that fair? Please, Sam."

"Yeah, all right." Sam grips the steering wheel tighter. "I'll see what I can do. No promises, though."

"You'll push it, then? You'll get me a hearing right away, right?"

"I'll do my best, Jason. That's all I can do," Sam says.

"Yeah," I say. "That's all I'm trying to do, too. Thanks." I smile at him; then I turn to look out my window. I notice the sun is shining. There's not a cloud in the sky.

A few minutes later we roll up outside my house, and I see my dad sitting in the car in front of us.

I jump out and rush over to the guardian's car to open the door for him.

"Hey, Dad. How you doin'? It's so good to see you."

I take his hand and help him out, and he stands on the sidewalk and looks at me.

I give him a hug, but it doesn't seem to register.

"Jason, the Furies are just infuriating today," he says. He covers his ears with his hands. "Do you know Atropos, here? She's come to determine my fate."

CRAZY GLUE: *It's like he just saw you five minutes ago instead of two weeks ago.*

An old woman with pinkish purple hair comes around to our side of the car and holds out her hand.

"Hi, I'm Clara Brown, your father's guardian. You must be the son."

I shake her hand, feeling all choked up for some reason. I look at my dad. He's staring at the house as though trying to figure out why it looks so familiar. I take his arm and lead him up the steps. I pull the key out of my pocket and unlock the door.

The inside of the house feels even colder than the

weather outside. It's dank and moldy smelling. We all enter, and Clara wanders from room to room. I try to look at the house through her eyes and I'm embarrassed. I know my mom would be ashamed at how far we've let the house go. But we had no choice. I watch Clara taking note of the paint peeling off the walls and the cracks in the ceiling, and the fallen plaster upstairs, and no furniture in some of the rooms.

"Oh my, this is a problem, now, isn't it?" she says, after she's made the tour of the house and returns to the living room. "Well, hopefully it won't be for long. Can we do something about the cold in here? Your father could catch pneumonia." She rubs her arms and shivers.

CRAZY GLUE: *Yeah, if she wants to pay for it.*

"I've kept the heat down to save money," I say. I go to the thermostat and turn it up.

"This is not a good situation here," she says.

"It's going to take quite a bit of work to fix this place up. It will probably have to be sold 'as is,' and the new owners will then fix it," Sam says.

I turn to Sam. "What? Now you're selling our house out from under us? What gives you the right to do that? My dad *owns* this house."

"I have no right, Jason, but Clara, as your father's conservator, does. We're just thinking of your future. Would you rather it continue to deteriorate so you get even less money for it?"

303

"You know," I say, fuming, "maybe you should stop thinking of my future so much, because every time you do, you just dish up another load of crap for me to swallow. We're not selling the house!"

Dad turns around and faces the two of us. "Houses are strangers to me," he says.

I go stand beside my dad. "See? How's he supposed to live here on his own? He needs food. He won't shop for himself. I need to go shopping and get him some food and . . ."

"Oh, I've got food in the car," Clara says, her voice all cheery. "I went shopping before I picked your father up at the hospital. Come on—we'll go get it."

CRAZY GLUE: *Well that solves everything.*

The four of us tramp back outside and Sam, Clara, and I head for the car. Dad heads across the street toward the river.

"See! See!" I say. "This is what's going to happen." I run after Dad and lead him back toward the others. "He's just going to wander off when I'm not here."

"It's so long," Dad says, his eyes still on the river. "And you know who lives in the water, don't you?"

"Look, Jerry," Clara says to me, "we're all doing the best we can here, all right?" She lifts her pink head above the open trunk of the car to look at me. "In an ideal world your father would be all better, your house would be warm and wonderful, and the two of you would live together, but the reality isn't quite so rosy."

She lifts a grocery sack out of her trunk and Sam lifts out another one. "We've just got to each do our part to make the best of a difficult situation. All right?"

"My name is Jason, not Jerry," I reply.

CRAZY GLUE: *Dude. You're acting like such a turd.*

AUNT BEE: *He's scared.*

FBG WITH A MUSTACHE: *Living by himself will never work. They have to see that.*

After we unload the groceries and tidy up a bit downstairs, Clara and Sam say it's time for us to leave.

"But I need to wash sheets and make the beds— or at least my dad's bed—and I need to fix him his lunch. He won't eat unless I fix it." I look at him rummaging through a stack of papers he found on top of his desk. He's wearing a fresh set of aluminum foil ear covers. "Will you, Dad? Are you going to make yourself some food? Will you take your medicine so you'll get better?"

Dad stares at the three of us standing at the front door. "Have you seen my violin?"

"Goodbye, Mr. Papadopoulos," Clara says. "We'll see you later. You take care now, won't you?"

"Jason, say goodbye to your father. We need to go, too, now," Sam says.

I look at Sam and shake my head. I can't understand how they can just turn their backs on my dad. Can't they see that he's in no shape to be left alone? Doesn't anybody care?

FBG WITH A MUSTACHE: *You do.*

I wade through the books Dad's just dumped on the floor and I grab his arm. He stops pulling the books off the shelf and blinks at me. "Dad, I've got to go now. But I'll be back. Turn on the radio so you won't have to listen to the Furies, okay? Please eat something, and take good care of yourself, and I'll . . ." I stop and turn back to Sam and Clara. "You know how many pots he's burned out on the stove? He'll set this place on fire. We can't just leave him. Come on!"

Sam steps over the books and takes my arm. "Time to go, Jason. I promise. I do. I promise I'll get you in to see the judge, but now it's time to go."

"Hey, have you seen my violin?" Dad asks.

CHAPTER THIRTY-SEVEN

A WEEK LATER, on Friday morning at nine o'clock, I'm sitting in the courtroom with Sam, Clara, Captain Lynch, Dr. Gomez, Haze, Pete, and Shelby. All of them have agreed to come and speak for me.

Sam stunned me when he told me just before we entered the courtroom that my grades might be the deciding factor. "This judge takes education very seriously, and I've just had a look at your recent records." Sam shakes his head. "They don't look good."

CRAZY GLUE: *You had to go and write 'Cap'n' on that exam.*

The courtroom is small. There are a few benches in the room, a table where I suppose lawyers might sit with their clients, or whatever they're called, and then a raised platform in the front of the room where the judge is sitting at his table staring at notes about my case. He's got a gavel on his right. His assistant, or whoever it is I see taking notes, is sitting to the judge's left, and a man in a policeman's uniform stands by the entrance. It's just like on television, only this is for real. This is for my dad.

The judge tells us all that this is an informal hearing, no jury, no lawyers, no witness box, just us. We don't even have to stand up to speak, so we can all relax.

CRAZY GLUE: *Got that, goob? Relax!*

He leans over his notes and studies them for several minutes, ignoring us as if we aren't even here.

CRAZY GLUE: *He's looking at your grades. He's probably trying to read that history test with no beginning and no ending.*

SEXY LADY: *Just the middles.*

FBG WITH A MUSTACHE: *You don't feel so clever now, do you?*

I jiggle my knees up and down until Sam, sitting on my left, sets his hand on them to stop me. I can't help it. I'm so nervous and jittery. Let's get this show on the road already.

Finally the judge looks over his glasses straight at me. "So, you want to change your visitation hours, do you?"

I stand up halfway and nod. "Yes, sir." I sit back down.

He leans forward, setting his elbows on the table. "Jason, do you understand why your current visitation rights have been set at once a month?"

Again I stand up halfway to speak and Sam pulls me back down in my seat. "Yes, sir," I say, blushing. "I'm supposed to get on with my life. It's to give me a chance to lead a normal life, and to—uh—to do well in school and stuff like that."

"Good enough," the judge says. He pauses and

looks down at his notes a second before returning to me. "Tell me about your father, Jason."

CRAZY GLUE: *Careful, not everything. Not about that time when you were six.*

I scratch the side of my face. "Well, he's my dad, and he's always been there for me, and—but now he's sick and it's bad and they—the doctors—say, or think, that he won't get well enough to live on his own, so they're putting him in a residential center place—I mean—what I mean is he can't live on his own, but that's what he's doing right now." Now that I've started speaking and telling my dad's story, I feel angry at the hospital, and this gives me a surge of energy. I stand up all the way, and Sam doesn't pull me back down.

"They say he can't function on his own and that he'll never write any more books—he'll always be sick—but then they just dumped him. They released him from the hospital. He doesn't eat." I lift the papers in my hands, the notes that I took about his behavior to give to the judge. "He doesn't take his medicine—and maybe, maybe if he did, maybe he'd get better. He's got new meds now. And he's gotten better before. He just needs to take his medicine regularly and in time he could get better. Right?" I glance at Clara, who gives me a slight nod; then I return to the judge. "He could get better if he'd take his medicine. Maybe he could even be well enough so he wouldn't have to go to that residential place, but right now—I mean, he could burn out the pots the way he's done before, or wander off, which he's done, and never be found again, and—and I'm just worried about him all the time now that he's on his own. I can't sleep 'cause I'm so worried about him. So if I could just see him every day and make sure he's still there, and if I can get him to eat and take his medicine . . . that's all I'm asking."

I look at the judge, who's staring at me with his glasses pushed down to the end of his nose. He's an old guy, like in his sixties or older, with silver hair and heavy-looking jowls.

Finally the judge speaks. "It says here in my notes that you've missed a lot of school this year and your grades have steadily dropped. Is that because of your father?"

LAUGH TRACK: *Uh-oh!*

I blow out my breath. I don't want to wreck my chances, but I know I have to tell the truth. "Yes. Yes, sir—Your Honor—it is, mostly, only I got stabbed and my mother died, so I missed some school, and that added to my dropping grades some."

"Yes," the judge says. "Yes, I'm sorry about your mother. But perhaps that's all the more reason for you to get some distance here. You may have forgotten what it's like to have a more—how should we say it— predictable life."

"No, sir, I know what it's like to have a normal life. I remember, and I have that now with the Lynches—

my foster parents." I glance at Captain Lynch, and he lifts his head at me and smiles, encouraging me.

I return to the judge. "I know my grades aren't the greatest, okay? But, if I could have this time with my dad, you know, see him every day, I swear—I mean—I promise I'll pull my grades up and I'll go to summer school."

The judge leans back and scowls. He looks doubtful.

"Look, I'm not asking to be there full-time. I understand that I can't do it all on my own. That's why I've missed so much school, because before, you see, I had nobody else. It was just me and my dad, and I couldn't—I couldn't do it. But Clara, here, is his guardian—I mean, you appointed her, or somebody did, to be his guardian and to look after his money and stuff—and I have Sam, and the Lynches—my foster parents—and my friends—I have friends, Shelby, and Pete, and Haze—they're the best, and I have Dr. Gomez, she's my—the school psychologist." I turn and gesture to them, aware for the first time how much my circumstances have changed. Until now I've been resenting Sam's interfering and Clara's acting as Dad's guardian, and the Lynches' taking the place of my parents. I've been resisting it all, but now I'm looking at these people, every one of them here to help me and my dad, and I realize how much better my life has gotten because of them.

311

I look at the judge. "I have all these people now to help me, so it's different. It's all different. I'm not alone anymore. Before—before I was all alone."

I don't know what else to say, so I just stand with my arms locked straight in front of me, crossed at the wrists, and my hands in fists. I chew on the inside of my cheek and wait.

The judge doesn't look convinced.

He tells me to sit down, and then he asks for Clara's evaluation of my dad's situation.

I sit down and brace myself, expecting Clara to tell the judge that Dad is doing just fine on his own and that he doesn't need me.

She describes the condition of the house and Dad's mental instability. Then she says that she doesn't feel he's a danger to me or to himself, but that he does require extra care in terms of feeding and cleaning and other daily maintenance tasks and that I might be the only one able to get my dad to take his medication.

CRAZY GLUE: *Thank you, pink-haired lady!*

Then Dr. Gomez reports on our lunchtime meetings at school, and I'm starting to feel hopeful. The judge's face doesn't look quite so stern.

He stares out at Cap and asks him if he would be willing to supervise these extra visits with my dad if extra visitations were granted.

Before he can answer, I stand up again and interrupt. "Excuse me. But I'm almost fifteen years old. I would like to have unsupervised visits with my father. I thought that was understood."

The judge just kind of glares at me, so I sit down and Sam whispers, "Just wait."

Cap says, "I am willing, Your Honor, to see to it that Jason gets to his father's home and back safely. I am also willing to see to it that he doesn't neglect his schoolwork, and that it doesn't interfere with other activities that we might plan for him and the family. He has to keep his room neat and help out around the house. I'm willing to see to it that he attends to these things. As for accompanying him and supervising him while he's with his father, I don't feel that is necessary."

"And his adjustment in your home?" the judge asks.

Cap clears his throat. "Adjustment in a new home is always difficult," he says. "And while he's been with us such a short time, he has received some disturbing news, which, though it upset him greatly, I believe he has handled with maturity and wisdom. He's played by the rules, even when he hasn't liked them. He's good to his foster sister and respectful to me and my wife. He's a good boy, Your Honor."

Cap looks at me and winks, and I press my tongue against the roof of my mouth. I make a promise to myself to be much nicer to everybody after this.

Finally the judge asks for Sam's opinion about my visitation rights.

Sam says, "I've been put in charge of Jason's welfare, and so it is his welfare and not his father's that I am most concerned about here, as I believe we all are."

The judge nods and says, "Indeed."

CRAZY GLUE: *There goes your case down the drain, goob.*

I swallow and close my eyes, and wait for Sam to bring up my bad grades.

"And as with all my other cases, Jason's visitation has been scheduled for once a month. I think there would have to be pretty extenuating circumstances for you to order a change in this schedule. As you've stated, Jason's grades have slipped and he's missed quite a lot of school, this year in particular. I wasn't aware until this morning when I got a copy of his records exactly how dismal Jason's grades are."

I sink down in my seat. What is he doing?

CRAZY GLUE: *He's crucifying you—and your dad.*

"These grades are a real concern, of course." He glances at me. "Poor grades are a clear indication of your state of mind and how you are coping, Jason." He looks at the judge. "I think it would be good if Jason could prove to us over the next several months that he's serious about his desires to improve in school. Then we could look at changing his visitation."

I shake my head. I don't believe what I'm hearing. He's just stabbed me in the back. I lean forward and glare at Haze and Shelby and Pete, who are sitting to my right. All three of their faces have gone white.

I want to cry. I put my head in my hands. We don't have several months to test me. Dad needs me now.

AUNT BEE: *Oh dear, I'm so sorry. This is too bad.*

"Excuse me. Excuse me, Judge. I'm sorry, but I have to say something here."

I lift my head and see Shelby standing with her hands on her hips.

I sit back in my seat.

"And you are . . . ?"

"Jason's friend, Shelby Majors, and I'm probably, no, I *am* the reason everyone is here today. I caused all this. I'm the one who reported Jason's father to Dr. Gomez, so I think I should have a right to say something."

Shelby's voice is loud—louder than it needs to be, and forceful, as usual.

The judge nods for her to continue.

"You're talking here like it's separate—Jason's welfare, his father's welfare, Jason's grades. But it isn't. They're all connected—don't you see, 'cause we're all connected. You can't separate it out the way you're trying to do. We've all"—Shelby turns to indicate me and Haze and Pete—"we've all had really crappy stuff happen to us the past year or two. My mother just died. She had ALS. And you all act like that's not supposed to affect me? Like our grades shouldn't be affected? Of course it affects us! What happens to our parents happens to us, too. We feel it, too, you know? So my grades are in the toilet and so are Haze's and Jason's, and the only reason Pete's aren't is because he's some genius—sorry, Pete, I know you like to keep that quiet." She looks at Pete, and so do I, only slightly surprised by this information. Pete's face is still white. Shelby turns back to the judge. "But even he's not one hundred percent. But somehow you think all you've got to do is put Jason in a nice foster home and his grades will improve. How is that possible, when he can't even sleep because he's so worried about his father? His father isn't safe, and until he is, until Jason can assure himself every day, by visiting him, that his father is okay, his stupid grades, as if they're the be all and end all of everything, won't get better." Shelby takes a breath.

I'm sitting, like the others, with my mouth hanging open.

She continues. "Jason needs to be with his dad. I mean not all the time, but you should see him. He's patient and gentle and loving, and he gets him—he understands his crazy father in a way no one else does. And like Jason said, he's not alone in this anymore. We'll be there, too. We're there for one another. So don't make him promise to keep up his grades and keep his room neat—man, give him a break. How's he supposed to care about that when his dad is in trouble? His dad needs him *now*, not months from now after you've tested him to see if he's really serious about bringing up his grades." She takes another breath. "Okay"—she looks around at all of us—"I guess I'm done."

She sits down and I reach across Cap and squeeze her hand. "Thanks," I whisper, wishing I could say more.

The judge's face is like a mask. He clears his throat and speaks to Sam. "Did you have anything more to say, Mr. Waldron?"

Sam smiles. "Miss Majors pretty much said it all, Your Honor. If she had given me the chance, I would have gone on to say that although it would be nice, we really don't have the time to test Jason to see if he can bring up his grades, given the seriousness of his father's circumstances. I believe Jason could help his father and with all the support he now has, I believe he can manage the extra visitations on his own quite well."

"Yes!" I whisper to myself, clenching my hands in fists, while the others reach over and pat me on the back.

The judge checks his watch, then looks at us. "We'll take a twenty-minute recess," he says, "and reconvene here at a quarter past ten." He pounds his gavel.

The policeman says, "All rise."

CHAPTER THIRTY-EIGHT

During the recess, we stand out in the hallway drinking Mountain Dews and talking. I tell Sam I thought he had stabbed me in the back. "Yeah," my friends all agree. We gather around Sam and wait for him to reply.

"I had to show the judge that I knew what the objections might be. I wanted to put the objections and the possible solutions he might come up with before him first, so that then I could say why these wouldn't work under the current circumstances—that's all."

"Well, you could have told me beforehand," I say.

"And you could have told me how badly you were doing in school."

"It's not *that* bad." I take a sip of my Mountain Dew. "I'm not failing, and the semester's not over. I just have a lot of catching up to do. Do you think the judge is going to let me have the extra visitations?"

Sam shakes his head. "Hard to say with Judge Langston. He's fair, but he's not one to bend the rules, and he has a thing about grades. He uses them as a marker for everything. Sorry, Jason."

FBG WITH A MUSTACHE: *Buck up, son. Look around you.*

AUNT BEE: *All these people, here just for you.*

I look at everyone gathered around me with expressions of concern on their faces. It really is great that they're here—Dr. Gomez and Cap and Haze and Shelby and Pete and Sam and Clara. I smile. "Hey, thanks, everyone, for being here. Whatever happens, it means a lot to me that you came this morning to support me."

I get pats on the back, and everyone says how they're happy to help me.

Then Haze surprises us all by announcing that he wants to become a judge. "No kidding," he says when we all look at him like he's crazy. "I always thought I'd become a lawyer, like my old man, but this is what I want to do. Really. I'm inspired. I want to become a juvenile court judge. What do you think? Can you see it?" Haze straightens his back and walks somberly down the hallway. Shelby laughs so hard she spews her Mountain Dew on the floor, and with a minute left before we have to return to the courtroom, we all rush around grabbing paper towels from the bathroom to clean up the mess.

We're back in the courtroom a minute later and we're waiting for the judge's decision. I notice Shelby sitting with her legs crossed and jiggling her foot. Haze is rubbing his hands up and down his thighs as though trying to wipe the sweat from his hands. Dr. Gomez is tapping her fingers on the bench. Pete is sitting beside me with his eyes closed; it looks like he's praying or meditating. I hope that whatever he's doing, it works. Cap is sitting on my other side, looking very stiff and straight.

The judge lifts his head and says, "Jason Papadopoulos."

Everyone gets still and I stand. "Yes, sir—uh, Your Honor, sir."

"You have a job to do, and do you know what that job is?"

I don't know what to answer. Sam said he was big on grades and school, so I think maybe I should answer "school," but my honest answer is to take care of my dad.

CRAZY GLUE: *Well, say something, goob.*

"I—uh—I have many jobs, your sir—uh, Your Honor."

"I'm a judge; that's my job. Sam's a social worker; that's his job. You're a student; that's your job."

I bite down on my upper lip and nod.

"You've got to do the job that's set before you, and do it to the best of your ability."

"Yes, Your Honor," I say, feeling my heart sink.

"Education is the key to everything. You'd like for your father to get well, and there are doctors out there who are trying to help him get well, and pharmaceutical companies working on new medicines that may someday find a cure. These are educated people working to solve your father's problem." The judge jabs his index finger into the table over and over as he speaks. "Education is the key to becoming a productive and contributing member of our society. I do not take it lightly, nor should you."

"No, Your Honor, I don't."

"Going to school, studying, learning new material, advancing—this is your job. I cannot stress it enough." He eyes Shelby and points in her direction. "And when things are falling apart in your life, that does not give you permission to let it all go to hell." He returns to me. "If you have disaster in one part of your life, you make extra sure the rest of it is working. Otherwise you have to work twice as hard later to make up for the total mess you've put your life in. Your father's condition is, for the most part, out of your control. Your schoolwork isn't. Got it?"

I nod again, unable to speak with the lump in my throat. I blink several times and bite down harder on my lip. I refuse to cry in front of the judge.

"My concern, Jason, is that you have spent too much of your time as a caretaker for your father. This is not your job. You are the child. He is the parent."

I rub my face and stare at my feet. I let out my breath.

"I don't want to see you spending all your time with your father at the expense of your education,

3 2 1

your friendships, and your relations with your foster parents."

I look up. "No, Your Honor."

"I want your assurance that if you receive daily visitation rights, these things will not suffer."

AUNT BEE: *Hope at last.*

"Oh, no, Your Honor, no they won't. I'll show you. I can do it."

I see a hint of a smile on the judge's face. "I'm glad to see that you have this support system in place for both you and your father, and I'm hoping you will continue to rely on them—not take it all on yourself— because if I get reports back that you have, I will revoke your visitation rights. Do you understand?"

"Yes! Yes, I do. I will. Yes! Yes!"

"You will be granted two hours maximum visitation a day."

I hear cheers behind me, and I blush and break out into the biggest smile. My heart is so full of gratitude, I feel like getting down on my knees and kissing the judge's feet.

The judge raises his hand for silence. "I want you to keep a record of your visits, and if you can't catch up with your schoolwork, I want to see that you've got a tutor working with you." The judge nods in Pete's direction. "Maybe your genius friend can help."

"Yes, Your Honor, I'll catch up. I will."

"I will be receiving regular reports from Mr. Waldron. Don't let me down, Jason." The judge bangs his gavel. Dismissed.

"Thank you!" I raise my fists in the air and fall to my knees. I did it! I got daily visitation rights. I did this! Finally, I have some control of my life back. I did it. I succeeded.

LAUGH TRACK: *(Cheers and applause).*

Everyone rushes up to me, and I get up off my knees and hug Cap and Shelby and Haze and Pete and Dr. Gomez and Sam and even Clara, amending my thoughts in my mind—I succeeded with the help of my friends.

CHAPTER THIRTY-NINE

LATE SATURDAY MORNING, I arrive at my house for my first official visit with Dad. The whole house is in a shambles—books, records, pillows, dishes, everywhere, and music is blaring.

The first thing Dad says when I walk in the door is, "Have you seen my violin? The Furies have eaten it, I'm afraid."

He's found the helmet I hid under my bed and he's wearing it. He needs his pills badly—and some food. His bloodshot eyes stare out from the holes in the helmet. Pete, who had been checking in on my dad for me, told me he wasn't eating, but he didn't tell me how bad he looked. He's just so thin.

"Hey, Dad," I say, turning down the music and trying not to let my anxiety show on my face. "Let's go get something to eat. Come on."

"Coffee would be good. The Furies haven't poisoned that." He follows me to the kitchen. "Have you seen my violin?" he asks me on the way.

A few minutes later, while I'm preparing lunch, Dad wanders off. I find him in the empty bathtub with his radio resting on his stomach.

I grab the radio. "Dad, no music in the bathroom! Never! Okay?" I unplug the cord, then I march out the door with the radio and set it on the floor. "Leave the radio right here and don't move it. Don't ever move it!"

CRAZY GLUE: *Ah, just like old times.*

I turn the radio on and look at him. "You can hear the music fine from in there, can't you?"

"I can't hide in the music from there, but I can hear it."

"Well, it's going to have to do." I turn the radio up, but I leave it on the floor. Then I return to the kitchen to finish making lunch.

Crazy Glue is right. It feels like old times again with Dad in the tub and me in the kitchen, but it doesn't feel like I thought it would. It's not a comfortable or happy feeling at all. I'm nervous and edgy, just the way I used to be. I was always on the alert in case Dad should call to me or should do something crazy like set the house on fire or electrocute himself. It's only been a few weeks since we were alone together in the house, but it feels like months. So much has happened since then. I've experienced another kind of life and I like that life. I'm glad I have someplace to go to get away from the craziness.

After lunch, which doesn't go well because Dad won't eat and he won't take his meds, Haze arrives with his "bed head," and Pete, wearing some kind of Zen outfit that looks as though he's just come from karate lessons, and Shelby, wearing a brightly colored striped hat and a big grin. I'm so relieved to see them, and my relief again makes me feel guilty. What's wrong with me? I love my dad. I would do anything for him. I went to court for him. I don't want to feel relieved. I want to feel right—to feel that I'm doing the right thing.

I look again at Shelby's beaming face. "What are you so happy about?" I say, opening the door wider so they can all come in.

"I'm in celebration."

"Yeah," Pete says. "She's in celebration."

"In celebration?"

Shelby pulls off her hat. "Yep. I've been in mourning for my mother for the past three years. So, I've decided it's time to be in celebration now." She slaps my shoulder and heads for the living room.

Everyone greets Dad, who has come downstairs wearing my mom's pink flowered bathrobe over his clothes and her fuzzy pink slippers, which don't fit, so his heels hang off the back.

I love that they don't even blink when they see the helmet and Mom's clothes.

"The Argonauts and Athena!" Dad says. Then he runs back upstairs as we all parade back to the kitchen.

"So, Pope-a-Dope, how's it goin'?" Haze asks. He picks at the grapes left on Dad's lunch plate. "I bet it feels great, huh?"

"Yeah, sort of. It's great to see my dad, but I can't get him to take his pills and you see what a mess the place is."

Pete lifts the plate with Dad's uneaten sandwich on it. I wrapped it in plastic in case he wants it later.

"What do you call this?" he says.

"What?" I look at the sandwich. "That's ham and cheese. Ever heard of it?"

"On white bread with mayo, right? No wonder your father's sick, Jason. This food is garbage. You need to get him whole grains and organic foods. I brought him organic whole grains every day, not this crap. You need natural food. This is junk."

"Yeah, and he's not eating any of it, so what does it matter?"

"You ought to let me fix him up with some herbs—hops, catnip, skullcap."

"Oh yeah, that would probably go over real well with the doctors," I say, drying the pot I just washed. I hand it to Shelby, who puts it away in the cabinet below the counter.

"Many hands make light work," Shelby says, turning to face Haze and Pete. "Hint, hint, boys." She tosses them each a dishtowel.

I smile. "When I talked to Dr. Gomez on the phone last week, she said we had made something good out of all the crap we've been handed by having this group and becoming friends—helping one another out."

"Right-o," Haze says, popping another grape into his mouth.

Shelby slaps Haze's hand. "Would you leave those

grapes alone? You just ate lunch and those are for Dad." Shelby turns to me. "Go on, Jason—we're listening."

CRAZY GLUE: *Did you hear that? She called your father "Dad." You really are family.*

"Well, so I want to make something good come out of what's happened to my dad, but I don't know how. I can't cure him. I can't make him sane. He seems even worse today. It's—it's kind of discouraging. I mean, jeez, I can barely get him to eat his food. I want something good to come out of what's happened, but he's just falling apart." I hand Pete a sponge, and he wipes down the counters while Haze puts the grapes away in the fridge.

I continue talking. It feels good just to have the chance to think out loud. "My dad's all I have left, you know? And maybe it's a long time ago, but we used to have so much fun canoeing and reading *The Iliad* and *The Odyssey* together, sneaking the Oreos out of the house under our shirts so my mom wouldn't see. He's always been there. In some strange way, I've always been able to count on him. He's my constant, you know—like my true north. I want my true north back."

"Hey!" Shelby says, banging Dad's coffee mug down on the counter. "Did you ever stop to think, Jason, that it's the other way around? That maybe you're *his* constant; you're *his* true north. Sheesh, you just went to court for him and everything. Maybe *you're* the good that comes out of your family's bad situation, you know? You're the good that comes out of your mother's death and your father's illness. You're the best part. Look at what you've done. I mean, you've done everything you could to make it work for you and your dad."

"Yeah, and look how that's turned out," I say.

"Okay, but, sheesh, Jason, you sacrificed everything for him. It's not your fault he's crazy. Give yourself a break. Let him go into that home where he'll be taken care of and, like the judge said, you get your life together and be that good thing you're talking about, 'cause you already are. Just keep going."

Shelby looks at Haze and he's got his hand over his heart like he's listening to "The Star-Spangled Banner."

Shelby gives him a look of irritation. "What are you doing?"

"You just sound so noble, so honorable. Have you ever considered going into politics? Or maybe speech writing?"

"Haze, sometimes, I swear," Shelby says.

Pete and I laugh, and we, too, put our hands over our hearts and face Shelby.

"You know, you guys are impossible sometimes. We need another girl in this group. We really do."

The three of us laugh and make fun of Shelby, but I heard what she said, and it makes me nervous, as if there's something I'm missing—something I'm not getting.

SEXY LADY: (*Whispers*) *You know.*

CHAPTER FORTY

AFTER MY VISIT with Dad, I go home to try to catch up on the tons of schoolwork I've missed. I spend all afternoon and evening doing biology, but it's hard to concentrate, because something is bugging me.

SEXY LADY: *You know.*

Quit saying that. What? Yeah, I'm resentful that I have to work while Haze and Pete and Shelby are out having a good time, but it's my own fault. That's what's bugging me. I tap my pen on the edge of my dad's head of Socrates coffee mug. For some reason I had it in my hand when I came home today.

CRAZY GLUE: *That may be what's bugging you, or maybe . . .*

Quiet!

AUNT BEE: *It was so hard being with him today. You had forgotten that.*

No, I didn't. It's just that until the Lynches came along, I never knew how much better things could be, that's all. And I guess I feel guilty for thinking this way.

The words on the page in front of me blur, and I don't know if it's because I'm so tired or it's some kind of hallucination. They almost seem to dance. I slam the book shut. I jump up and stuff my schoolbooks into my backpack. I'm just tired and grumpy, that's all. I need to go to bed.

"Let go, Jason."

I turn around. No one's there.

"Who said that?"

It was a real voice. It wasn't any of the usual voices—not Crazy Glue, or FBG, none of them. It wasn't You, was it?

No. It was a real voice. I'm sure of it.

CRAZY GLUE: *Well, well, here it is. Crazy at last. You knew it would happen. Like father, like son.*

My hands are shaking. "Let go? Let go of what? Let go of school? Life? Dad? What? Who said that? What do you mean?"

FBG WITH A MUSTACHE: *You realize, don't you, that you're talking out loud to a voice no one else can hear, just the way your dad does.*

LAUGH TRACK: *Isn't it a shame.*

No! Shut up, everybody, and let me think.

AUNT BEE: *You've been waiting for this to happen since you were six years old.*

SEXY LADY: *I always said crazy was hot.*

No!

CRAZY GLUE: *Now who's going to look after you? There's nobody. You're all alone in the world. Just like Reed. You'll be locked away—forgotten.*

AUNT BEE: *That's what you've been so afraid of. You'll become invisible again—even to yourself.*

331

I pound my fist on the desk. No! I can't go crazy.

I jump up from my seat and pace. "No, this is not good. I can't start hearing voices or seeing things or any other crazy thing. No, I can't do that. I won't!"

CRAZY GLUE: (*In a singsong voice*) *You're still talking to yourself.*

LAUGH TRACK: (*In a singsong voice*) *All alone in the world. Forgotten. Invisible. Isn't it a shame?*

FBG WITH A MUSTACHE: *All alone and going crazy. Who will look after him?*

CRAZY GLUE: (*Singing*) *Take the keys and lock him up, lock him up, lock him up.*

I stop pacing. You know what? I'm over you. I'm *so* over you. I'm not listening to any of you. I refuse this. I won't go crazy.

FBG WITH A MUSTACHE: *It's not up to you, remember? Everything is out of your control.*

No, it's not! Dr. Gomez says I'm in control of myself. That's the one thing I can control.

FBG WITH A MUSTACHE: *But your dad can't control himself.*

CRAZY GLUE: *Like father, like son.*

Get out! Get out of my head.

LAUGH TRACK: *All alone. Forgotten. Invisible. Isn't it a shame?*

I pound the desk again and my dad's coffee mug accidentally falls and breaks.

FBG WITH A MUSTACHE: *Don't you know, there are no accidents.*

"Shit!" I stare down at the pieces. A dangerous thought lurks at the edge of my mind, but I can't bring it forward.

AUNT BEE: *Go on—it's time you faced it.*

Faced what?

SEXY LADY: *The truth.*

That I'm crazy? I wipe the sweat off the side of my face.

CRAZY GLUE: *You've helped to take care of him all your life.*

Who? Dad? So what? I love him. That's what you do when you love someone.

AUNT BEE: *And?*

And nothing. That's all.

FBG WITH A MUSTACHE: *Ignoring it just might be what's driving you crazy.*

What? What am I ignoring?

SEXY LADY: *You know.*

AUNT BEE: *You've always known.*

What? I love my dad. I love him!

AUNT BEE: *You've known since you were six years old.*

He couldn't help it. He didn't mean to do it.

FBG WITH A MUSTACHE: *He never meant to harm you, but . . .*

But he did. He tried to bury me alive. My eyes sting and I rub them.

AUNT BEE: *And . . .*

And—and he's still doing it, isn't he? Having to live with him the way he is. It's like being buried alive—it's suffocating. There! I've said it. And I'm so mad. I'm so mad at him!

I kick the broken glass.

LAUGH TRACK: *Aha!*

He did this to me! *He* did this. He made me afraid to have friends and afraid that I'm going crazy, and afraid to go to school because of what might happen to him while I'm gone.

I think of my dad in the tub wearing that insane helmet.

How could he? How could they? How could they have children when they knew they could pass his illness on to me? How could they do it? How could they risk it? Am I crazy, too, listening to all of you and hearing that voice?

CRAZY GLUE: *We'll never tell.*

"He almost killed me! He almost killed me!"

AUNT BEE: *But he doesn't know that.*

Yes! Yes! And I hate that he doesn't know. He doesn't even remember it. Mom would never let me speak of it. He's not sorry, because he doesn't know what he's done. And I hate how this makes me feel. I'm there in that sick house with my sick dad, and I feel so guilty because I want to run away from it. I want to stay with the Lynches and never go back. But I know I'm all he has. If I don't fight for him, how can I ever expect anyone to fight for me if I go crazy? Who is here for me?

SEXY LADY: *Just us.*

I hate that I feel this way—scared, crazy, resentful. I hate that he makes me feel this way. I hate that maybe the only reason I fought so hard to get extra visitations is because I feel guilty. Do I even love him?

334

FBG WITH A MUSTACHE: *Well now.*

I stoop down and pick up the broken glass and throw it in my wastebasket.

Socrates' broken face looks up at me from inside the can—all knowing, all wise.

I'm not alone. I'm not Reed. I've got friends now. And I've got the Lynches, Dr. Gomez, and Sam. I stand and hold out my hands and stare at them—my dad's hands. They're shaking. I go to my desk and turn on my computer.

LAUGH TRACK: *All alone. Forgotten. Invisible.*

"I'm not alone!" I type an e-mail to Haze and Pete and Shelby and send it: *What if I get sick, too? What if I get what my dad has?*

I wait, staring at the computer. Please, someone be there. Please be online. Please, please answer. It feels like a matter of life or death to me. Someone has to answer me.

I tap my fingers on the side of the computer and wait. And wait.

I have mail!

It's Pete!

Thank you, Pete.

He gives me the facts:

I looked it up. You have a ten-percent chance of becoming mentally ill as opposed to a one-percent chance if nobody in your family is sick. So that's a ninety-percent chance you won't get it. Pretty good odds, huh? Did something happen?

I pause. Do I dare tell them?

LAUGH TRACK: *All alone. Isn't it a shame?*

I'm not alone. I type: *I heard a voice.* I send it to all three of them.

THEN SHELBY WRITES: *You don't have it. Don't worry. You're just totally stressed. What did the voice say?*

"Thank you, Shelby!" I let out my breath.

PETE: *I hear voices, sometimes. I think I hear my mother calling or my sister yelling at me. It's rare, though. What did the voice say?*

HAZE: *Make hay while the sun shines, dude. We never know what life has in store for us. Did the voice ask you to kill anybody?*

I answer their e-mails. I tell them that the voice said, "Let go, Jason," and that it sounded like my mom's voice.

SHELBY: *Let go. That's good advice for you. Maybe it really was your mother. My mother has been visiting my dreams every night. The dreams feel so real and they stay with me all day. I like it.*

PETE: *Sounds like your conscience. I wouldn't worry about it.*

HAZE: *My dad just blew up the snowblower! Ten at night and he's out there blowing things up. Gotta go. TTFN.*

We write back and forth a couple of more times, and then Cap sticks his head in my room.

I wipe my face. I feel calmer now that I'm talking to my friends, but I've been crying and I know it probably shows.

"Hey, buddy, we're all down in the family room. Don't you want to join us? Georgetown's playing on

EPSN, and we've got popcorn and a card game going. It might do you some good."

I look at Cap standing in the doorway with his eyebrows raised, looking hopeful that I will join him. I hesitate for just a second. I don't want to hear any more voices, even if the advice is good, even if it doesn't mean I'm going nuts. I need to be with people. I need the Lynches. "Okay," I say. "I'll be right there. I've got to answer an e-mail first."

Cap smiles. "See you in a few, then." He leaves me and I turn back to my computer.

I reread Haze's message: *Make hay while the sun shines, dude. We never know what life has in store for us.*

His words scare me. Mom once told me that my dad's first psychotic episode happened when he was just eighteen years old. I'm going to be fifteen soon. In three years I could be sick the way my dad is, or maybe I'm already sick. I hope Shelby's right and I'm just stressed out, but maybe these are the best days of my life right now. I mean, nobody gets a guarantee in life. Maybe this is the best I'll ever get.

I write to Pete and Shelby that I have to go, and then I head downstairs to make some hay.

CHAPTER FORTY-ONE

I'M LYING IN BED, afraid to go to sleep. I feel like a wreck. The card games and basketball helped some, but now that I'm alone again, I've started thinking about that voice telling me to let go, and about my dad, and I'm so confused.

I remember what Shelby said today in the kitchen. She said I needed to be the good that comes out of my family's bad situation. I needed to get my life together and let my dad go into that residential program and be the good thing. I think that Haze and Pete and Shelby are all the best that has come out of their families' tragedies, and I believe it's a great goal to be that good thing, that is, if I can let go of my dad enough. And I don't know why that's so hard, especially since I'm still so angry. It should be easy to let him go.

LAUGH TRACK: *Forgotten. Invisible.*

Okay. I know. I'm scared of that. Maybe I'm afraid that I might forget him once he goes into that program. Maybe I want to forget him because I'm so angry with him and maybe I don't want to be around crazy anymore. It's getting too close to me.

*   *   *

I hate that I've spent my whole life scared of going crazy. I hate that I keep wetting the bed because of what my dad did to me. Why can't I stop having that dream?

FBG WITH A MUSTACHE: *Because you never see it.*

See what? Shit! I roll onto my back and stare up at the ceiling. I wish tonight I had my glow-in-the-dark stars on the ceiling. I long for the comfort of those plastic stickers.

Nobody answers my question, so I ask again. "See what?" Still there's no answer. I'm worn out, but I can't sleep. I don't know what to do about my anger now. What's the good of yelling at Dad and blaming him? He doesn't care. He's in la-la land, the same place I could be in a couple of years.

Do I have to go around yelling at the world, tipping over desks and throwing tantrums to get rid of this anger? I hate him for this—for all of it!

Finally, I fall asleep and I dream that dream. There's the ocean; it's green and foamy and deep, so deep. I go down and down and down to the sandy bottom and then below this to the pitch-black terror of the underworld. I hear screaming voices and I see that somebody is there. Somebody is struggling under the weight and pressure of all this water and sand—he's alive. He's alive. Somebody . . .

I sit up in bed, panting, trying to get air. My blankets are twisted around me. Sweat trickles down my sides. I scoot to the edge of the bed and feel for the wet spot on the sheets, but they're dry.

FBG WITH A MUSTACHE: *What did you see?*

It's dry.

FBG WITH A MUSTACHE: *In the dream. What did you see?*

I stop and think. I recall the dream—the ocean, the sand, the darkness, a chilling terror—voices screaming—Furies? I'm fighting, struggling to breathe, to break free, but there's all this weight and pressure and—wait—no, it's not me. That's not me down there. It's Dad. Dad's the one buried alive. It's not me at all. I jump out of the bed.

"It's Dad!"

I pace, then stop, pace, then stop. "It's Dad!" I stand still, my legs straddling the line down the center of the room as I feel the weight of this dawning knowledge—my dad, my brilliant, wonderful dad, buried beneath a craziness he can't break free of or control.

LAUGH TRACK: *Isn't it a shame.*

AUNT BEE: *Poor, poor Dad.*

It isn't me at all. I start to cry and I try to stop. I wipe away my tears, first with my arm, then with the front of my T-shirt. I rub and rub my face, but I can't stop. I flop onto my bed and cry some more. I feel so sad, so sorry for all that my dad has lost: my mom, his writing, his sanity, his house—everything but me. All the anger I felt last night is gone. I thought I could never get rid of it, but now I see. He's lost everything and I have so much. I can leave. I can get away from the insanity, but he can't. And I have this warm place to live with food and clothing and the Lynches looking after me, and I have my friends and, at least for now, my sanity.

I look at my watch. It's only six in the morning, but I just have to see my dad. I convince Cap to take me to the house early. We pull up outside, and I jump out of the car and run into the house. I rush down into the basement and go through the files of Mom's pictures till I find the one I want; then I rush upstairs to my dad's room.

I step into the room. He hears me and rolls over.

"Apollo! What news have you of the war?" He sits up and adjusts the aluminum foil on his ears.

"Dad." I climb onto his bed and kneel beside him, sitting back on my heels. "I had to come and tell you that—that, when you leave here, I'm letting go, but it doesn't mean that I'm giving up on you. You'll be taken care of in that residential place, and I'll be able to have a normal kind of life, but I know what's inside you, and I won't give up until we've found the right medicine or the right diet or the right doctors or whatever it takes. I know what it's like to feel buried alive, and I will never, never give up. I'll come see you and you'll always be my dad and you won't be forgotten and you won't ever become invisible. I'll bring my friends to visit you, and I'll make more friends and I'll bring them, too. You'll always be a part of my life. Do you know what I'm saying? Do you hear me?"

Dad reaches for the helmet and puts it on, then looks at me through the eyeholes. "They'll pluck your eyes out," he says.

I take his hand in mine and it's cold and bony. I squeeze it. "Dad, I know that you're still in there, somewhere." I poke him in the chest. "You're in there." I poke his head. "And you're in there. And I know you want to come out." I look in his eyes and they stare back at me blankly.

"I—I've been so mad at you, and I didn't even know. I couldn't let myself know because, as Mom used to say, you can't help the way you are. But deep down I've been so angry, and I think since I couldn't get mad at you, I took it all out on myself. But I forgive you— and I forgive me. And I forgive Mom." I take a deep breath and let it out. "What I know is that I love you, Dad. I don't think I knew that for sure until this morning. I really love you. There's no more pain, no more pain of us. Remember when you said that? Well, it's over. It's just us, okay?"

"Jason, what is all this dithering? Have you brought the Golden Fleece or haven't you?" Dad says.

I smile. "Well, maybe I have." I lift the picture I brought with me from the basement and show it to Dad. It's a picture of the three of us on top of Mount

Washington. I'm ten years old in the picture and it's my first time climbing the great mountain. Mom and Dad stand proudly on either side of me, squinting into the bright sun, and I stand pointing to the sign marking the top of the mountain.

Dad takes the picture from me and stares at it for a minute. Then he places his hand over my mom so that it's just the two of us. "That's the way it is," he says.

I look at him and I see tears in his eyes.

"I knew it. You're still in there," I say. I grab him by the head and hug him.

My dad lets go of the picture and hugs me back.

CHAPTER FORTY-TWO

Dear Mouse:

I've wanted to write this letter for a long time. I'm almost fifteen years old and I have these imaginary friends I talk to. I can't see them and I can't hear them; they're just thoughts in my head. But they're very real to me. I have a whole cast of characters in my head. The problem is, I like having them around. They give me good advice, most of the time, and they're kind of addictive. They were my only friends for so long. They've been with me since the fifth grade. So I want to get rid of them, but I don't know how to say goodbye. Any ideas? Do you think I'm crazy?

Mouse

CRAZY GLUE: *You're crazy if you send that out to anybody.*
AUNT BEE: *We'd all miss you so much if you let us go.*
SEXY LADY: *Who's going to tell you how hot you are?*
FBG WITH A MUSTACHE: *I think we're being replaced.*
LAUGH TRACK: *Uh-oh. (Nervous laughter).*

I reread my letter several times; then I send it—to Dr. Gomez, to Shelby, to Haze, and to Pete.

I stare at my computer a long time before I leave it. Then I go take a shower and eat breakfast. At the table, Gwen sticks a Daffy Duck and Bugs Bunny decal on my cheek and kisses it.

As far as little sisters go, I don't think she's half bad.

I borrow a hammer and some picture hooks from the Lynches and head back to the room to hang my photos of Crete and the new one I brought from the house this morning of me, my mom, and my dad on top of Mount Washington.

On my way down the hall the doorbell rings.

Cap answers it and I stand behind him waiting to see who it is. It's Shelby. She's wearing her biking clothes and she has her helmet tucked under her arm. Her hair is pulled back in a ponytail and she looks so fresh faced and beautiful that my heart leaps in my chest.

"I'm here to see Jason," she says.

I call out. "Let me get my coat and I'll be right there."

I put the hammer and nails on the hall table. I feel nervous. I wonder if she's read the letter. Ever since I sent it, I've been too scared to look to see if anyone has answered it.

I wonder what Shelby's going to say.

CRAZY GLUE: *She's going to tell you you're crazy, you goob. You shouldn't have sent that. It's all over now.*

Cap pats me on the back as I step outside to join Shelby. He closes the door behind us and I feel even more nervous. I stand on the stoop and kind of bounce on the balls of my feet like I'm really cold or something, but it's all nerves.

Shelby sets her helmet on the metal dog sculpture, then puts her hands on her hips and squints at me. "So you're Mouse," she says, and her voice sounds angry.

"Uh, yeah. I guess I am."

CRAZY GLUE: *Goob.*

"You give crappy advice." She turns and goes down the steps. I follow her.

"What's so crappy about it?"

She walks toward her bike parked at the curb. I'm right behind her.

"You keep telling everyone to dump their friends and dump their boyfriends and girlfriends and dump their parents. You're always dumping people." She spins around and glares at me. "Is that how you treat your friends? Ever heard of working things out and working through your problems?"

"Yeah, sure, but . . ."

"Is that what you'll do to me if things don't go your way?"

"No, of course not, I just . . ."

"'Cause I want a boyfriend who can stick it out through thick and thin—not one who's going to dump me at the first bump in the road."

"The first bump? Your road is so full of bumps, you make my teeth rattle."

346

"I know that! That's why I'm saying . . ."

CRAZY GLUE: *Take the cotton out of your head, goob. She called you her boyfriend.*

"Wait, did you just call me your boyfriend?" We're standing facing each other now. Shelby is leaning against her bike and I'm in front of her with my hands dug deep into my coat pockets.

She looks down at her feet, then off to her left. "Yeah."

"What about the letter? Do you think I'm crazy? With all my imaginary friends?"

Shelby reaches up and puts her hands on my shoulders so that we're standing really close. I lick my lips.

"Jason, I think that's probably the sanest thing you could do, given what you've been going through, don't you? I mean, they're not telling you to jump off a bridge, are they?"

I swallow. "No. They tell me to keep my cool and to shut up and, I don't know, do the right thing. They're just kind of fun characters I've invented."

"Right. They'll go away when something better comes along to take their place, don't you think?"

"I think something already has," I say. I set my hands on either side of Shelby's waist.

She tilts her face up to me and smiles. "Are you going to kiss me?"

"I will if you don't tell me I need a haircut first."

Shelby laughs.

CRAZY GLUE: *Way to go, goob.*

Sorry, you're not invited.

CRAZY GLUE: *You mean this is goodbye, after all I've done for you?*

AUNT BEE: *Say goodbye, Crazy.*

CRAZY GLUE: *Goodbye, Crazy.*

LAUGH TRACK: *Ha, ha.*

AUNT BEE: *Take care of yourself, Jason.*

FBG WITH A MUSTACHE: *Well done, son, well done.*

SEXY LADY: *There'll never be anyone hotter.*

I lean in to kiss Shelby and she stands on her tiptoes. Our lips are about to touch.

YOU:

Oh, no you don't. You had your chance to say something. You chose to stay a part of the audience. You can't change your mind now. It's too late. This isn't a peepshow, you know. I'm doing this completely on my own.

Audience, out!